When We Touch

By Tia Louise

Theresa
Never stop
believing!
xoxo

When We Touch
Copyright © TLM Productions LLC, 2017
Printed in the United States of America.

For Mr TL, always…

And to my readers — a new book boyfriend to love.

Contents

Prologue

Ember

Where we begin…

Jackson Cane tastes like red-hot cinnamon, salt water, and sin.

When he concentrates, his long fingers twist in the back of his dark hair, right at the base of his neck, and he tugs.

Tugs…

Tugs…

I like to weave my fingers between his and pull.

Then ocean-blue eyes blink up to mine, sending electricity humming in my veins. He smiles. I smile, and it isn't long before our lips touch. I straddle his lap as I open my mouth, and his delicious tongue finds mine, heating every part of my body.

Our kisses are languid and deep, chasing and tasting.

We sizzle like fireworks on a hot summer night.

Eventually, with a heavy sigh, I pull away, but hours later my mouth is still burning. I taste him everywhere I go.

Lying in my bed in the dark room, my heart aches, heavy and painful in my chest. Every breath is a burden. I blink slowly at the ceiling and slide my tongue against the backs of my teeth thinking about hot cinnamon, tangy salt, caramel and sugar, sunshine, and the best summer of my life.

The instant I hear it, I'm on my feet, tiptoeing to my open window. The low growl of an engine tells me he's there in the darkness, out on the street in the shadows just past the streetlight.

The late summer humidity hangs heavy in the air. Cicadas *scree* from the limbs of the mighty oak tree beside the house. Their damp wings make them too heavy to fly, and the sadness in my chest is replaced with breathless anticipation.

I'm panting. I've never felt this way for anyone, and I'm desperate to hold onto it. Somehow I know I'll never feel this way for anyone ever again.

Quiet as a mouse I scamper to my door and listen. The only sound is the hum of Momma's oscillating fan pushing the warm air around her room. I can't hear her breathing. I can't hear anything... except the noise of Jackson's engine on the street below, waiting.

Red-hot cinnamon.

Salt water.

Sin.

Pressure tingles around the edges of my skull, and a bead of sweat tickles down the side of my neck, dropping past my shoulder, slipping between my breasts.

I'm at the window slowly lifting the glass, and I don't care if she hears me. I dive through the space, out onto the cedar shake roof in my bare feet. I'll get a splinter if I'm not careful...

So many reasons to be careful...

I ignore them all.

8

I'm going to him like a siren's call in the ocean, like the mermaid story in reverse. I'm the hypnotized sailor. He's the promise of so many wicked pleasures.

Reaching for the tree limb, I swing my body across the narrow gap two stories high, gliding down the trunk as the skirt of my dress rises to my hips. My bike sits where I left it at the side of the house, and I carefully pull it away, holding it as I tiptoe down the gravel driveway to the street.

I can't take a chance on anyone seeing us together and telling my mother. Instead, I dash across the street between the thick beams of his headlights. He flickers them to let me know he sees me, and I plunge into the dark woods, pedaling fast.

Tires crunch on gravel, and I shoot down the pine needle path leading away from this place, through the tall, skinny trees, all the way out to the barren jetty of sand stretching under the moonlit sky filled with stars, surrounded by the clear blue waters of the ocean.

It's our place.

The place where we're the only two people on Earth.

In the summertime, the visitors to our sleepy little town use it to spend the day sunbathing and playing on the wide stretch of undeveloped sand. Now, on the edge of fall, with all the children back in school and Jackson leaving for college tomorrow, we have it to ourselves.

His engine roars on the road above, and I stand in the pedals to push harder, fueled by the burning desire twisting in my lower pelvis. I want to be with him now. I don't want to waste a moment.

I go even faster as the trail slopes downhill. A narrow wooden bridge *thump... thump... thumps* with the pressure of my tires distressing the aging slats.

The instant the trees part, I toss my bike aside and run out of the darkness onto the glowing white sand. The sizzle of waves crashing on the shore fills the night, and the black ripples are tipped with silver light.

Jackson stands in his canvas shorts, his hands in his pockets, and a thin white tee rippling across his back in the slight breeze.

I'm breathing hard when I finally reach him, and he turns. White teeth in a full-moon night, deep dimples in both cheeks, he smiles down at me, and I feel so small. A lock of too-long dark hair falls over his blue eyes, and my breath catches. He's so beautiful.

I swallow the knot in my throat as I gaze at him. What star crossed what planet in what solar system and said I could have him, even if it's only for a little while?

"You made good time tonight." His voice vibrates the warm air between us.

I force a laugh, moving to him until my hands are around his waist. My forehead rests on his chest, and I inhale deeply. He's leather and soap and a deeper, spicier scent that's pure Jackson Cane.

He feels so good in my arms.

His mouth presses against my head, and I lift my chin, reaching for his face. He leans down and claims my mouth, warm lips pushing mine open. I kiss him eagerly, curling my tongue with his, threading my fingers into the soft, dark hair falling around his cheeks, tugging.

An aching moan rises in my chest as he lifts me off my feet. Chasing his kisses, my mouth burns with cinnamon, my core tingles with need. He carries me to our place, a little shelter near the water's edge where an enormous log is slowly turning to driftwood. We lower to the sand, me on my back, him on his knees looking down at me.

My dark hair is all around us, my skirt is up around my waist. My panties are far away on my bedroom floor. A soft hiss comes from his lips, and he slides a finger down my center. My eyes flutter shut.

"Jackson..." I whisper. *I love you I love you I love you...*

He leans down to taste me, his tongue lightly tracing the line between my thighs, and my back arches off the soft sand. My body takes flight on the motion of his mouth, kissing me so deeply, tracing a pattern over my most sensitive parts.

The first time he did this to me, I didn't understand. I'd been embarrassed by how fast my body responded, the way I shook, how wet it was between my legs when the shudders subsided.

Then I was afraid of how I tasted. I was afraid it was dirty and wrong like my momma would say. *Sin...*

Then he kissed me, and my mouth filled with a delicate, clean ocean flavor, like the air after a storm. It was our first time, and when he pushed inside me, my mind came apart. My soul shifted, and I was forever changed.

I was forever his.

The flutters begin in the arches of my feet, and he kisses his way up my stomach.

"Jackson... Jackson..." I can't stop chanting his name as I thread my fingers in his soft hair.

At last his mouth covers mine. At last we're one.

"Ember..." His mouth breaks away with a groan, and I lean up to run my tongue along the ridges of his neck. *Salt water...*

I lick his Adam's apple up to his square jaw.

Rough stubble scratches my tongue.

My legs are around his waist and we're working together, chasing that glorious release. He stretches me and fills me, massages me so deeply, I feel it the moment I start to break apart.

"Oh!" My fingers tighten on his back as every muscle in my body clenches...

Tighter...

Tighter...

Then *Yes!*

Glitter gun showers of pleasure flooding my insides.

"Yes," he groans, and I feel him finish deep inside of me.

Our bodies unite, but at the same time we're flying apart as waves of ecstasy fill our veins. It's magical like the ocean, silvery water tipped in moonlight.

We kiss softly now, rich and gentle, over and over. His tongue touches my upper lip, and he pulls the bottom one between his teeth. *Red-hot cinnamon...*

We're breathing hard, and he slides a hand under my ass, turning us without ever losing contact, so I'm sitting in a straddle across his lap.

My dress is around my waist, and moonlight touches the tips of my breasts. We hold each other, skin against skin.

A hot tear spills down my cheek.

I'm not full-on crying. I'll save the ugly tears for tomorrow when he's gone. Instead, I find his blue eyes.

Dark brows quirk together, and he kisses my nose. "You're crying?"

My voice cracks with a whisper. "Aren't you sad?"

"I'm only going to college, Em. I'm not going to war."

"But we won't see each other for months."

I don't say what's truly scaring me. I don't voice the fear that I, a mere high schooler, couldn't possibly hold onto him.

He's traveling far away to where the girls are more mature, more experienced, more sophisticated.

"You're right," he nods. "It's going to suck. Especially when I want to kiss you."

He pulls me flush against his chest and groans deeply. Strong arms circle my shoulders, and I cling to him.

"But it's not something to cry about," he argues. "You're my girl, Em. That's never going to change."

My eyes squeeze shut, and I inhale his scent, doing my best to hold it in my memory, trying to absorb every part of him.

There's no way in hell I could even begin to argue. I am his, and he's... my everything. Jackson Cane is every first I've ever had. My first real kiss, my first real boyfriend, the first time I had sex... made love...

"Hey." He pulls back, blue eyes full of concern. "I'm right, aren't I?"

Blinking quickly, I try to find my bearings. "What?" I don't know why he looks so worried.

13

"You are my girl, right?"

My chin jerks forward, and I have to cover my mouth. "You have to ask?"

Warm hands cup my cheeks, and he trails his thumbs lightly along my cheekbones. "So beautiful," he murmurs. "My Ember Rose."

His eyes move around my face, along my hair, down the side of my jaw like a caress.

"I'll never forget this." I'm ashamed at how desperate my voice sounds. "I mean... I just..." I'm such a baby.

He blinks a few times, and a smile curls his lips. With a nod, he pulls me against his chest, strong arms surrounding me. We stay that way a long time, listening to the crashing of the surf, the beat of our hearts. The seagulls cry, and the moon climbs higher. It's all so perfect, but it's all at an end.

Finally, with a sigh, he lifts me, helping me stand. We hold hands as he takes me into the gentle waves to clean up. I slowly restore my dress.

I feel so stupid. College girls don't need to be cared for like babies. They don't whine and cry about being left behind. They blow kisses and wink over their sunglasses. They sway their hips and turn the tables on saying goodbye.

My best friend Tabby is already one of those girls, and she's my age.

I'll never be one of those girls.

"Don't cry, Ember Rose," he says in a low whisper. "I never want to see you cry."

I hold him a while longer, listening to the steady rhythm of his heart. His hands slide up and down my back in a soothing motion.

After a while, they slide down my forearms to lace with my fingers. He steps back and leads me the way we came, stopping at the edge of the woods where I left my bike.

"Get on home before your momma wakes up."

That sexy smile curls his lips. He shoves his hair behind his ears, and I step forward again, clutching the front of his shirt before I press my lips one last time to his.

Red-hot cinnamon.

Sparkling blue sin.

Salt rocks breaking my heart.

Chapter 1

Jack

Ten years and eleven months later...

"Last one in has to ride home naked!" Tiffany hurls her silky red dress over her head and runs through the trees headed for the lake.

The wheels on my black Audi R8 have barely stopped moving. I haven't even killed the engine. An empty wine bottle clatters against an empty tequila bottle rolling around on the floorboards, and I briefly think I should toss them in a nearby trashcan.

Propping my elbow on the steering wheel, I scrub the back of my neck with my fingers. My hair is so short now, it's the best I can do.

I haven't had a drink in almost an hour. I'd finished a bottle of scotch in my office, standing in front of my floor to ceiling glass windows looking down on the city, disbelief vibrating in my chest.

My career...

My reputation...

It's over.

All of it.

File after file, telling me my win, my multi-million dollar defense... all of it is based on lies.

"Fuck!" I shout, slamming my palm against the wheel.

The buzzing in my head is gone along with the numbness in my chest, and all the shock and pain and pure, unadulterated outrage rush back like a wall of water before a hurricane.

A hurricane that will send everything I've worked for these last ten years crashing down around me.

Pulling the handle on the door, I push it open and step out into the darkness. The ground is covered in moldering leaves, and it smells like faintly mildewed canvas, damp lichens, and dirt.

"Jackson! What are you doing?" Tiffany shrieks between splashes out in the black water of the lake.

Exactly. "What the fuck am I doing here?"

My chest is tight, and each inhale is like claws ripping my lungs from the inside.

It took an hour to drive from my Eighth Avenue high-rise corner office building to this lonely, two-lane highway leading to the lake. Somewhere along the way, I realized I didn't know what the fuck Tiffany was talking about or why she was even in my car. She followed me down the elevator, into the parking garage, laughing and pouring another shot of tequila on the way.

I've got the fucking receptionist with me.

I need to get her back to the city.

Digging in the pocket of my blazer, I pull out my phone and stare at the face. My lock screen is a photo of crystal blue waters, and for a moment, my thoughts blur. I left my home near the ocean with big dreams.

Half of them came true.

I finished undergrad at the top of my class, went to law school on a free-ride, headed straight into a Top Five firm when I graduated, and now I'm one of the highest-paid litigators handling mostly corporate corruption with the occasional car crash thrown in for variety.

My face is in every "Top Thirty under Thirty" feature in the city and online. My phone never stops ringing.

My fucking dad is so fucking proud.

I've done it all.

And I'm all alone.

"I've got to get out of here." Dropping my chin, I rub my eyes.

The *shush* of feet running through the leaves is punctuated with high giggles breaking the silence. My eyes have adjusted to the semi-darkness, and I see Tiffany coming back, completely naked, blonde hair glistening with water, tits bouncing with every step.

"What are you doing back here?" Her voice is thick, and she curves into my chest, holding my neck and trying to kiss me.

She's slippery and loose. Her kiss is easy to dodge, but not her wet body pressing against my dress shirt.

"I was just thinking the same thing," My jaw tightens, and I lift my chin away from her face.

"God, you're so hard," she giggles. My brow furrows. I'm not the least bit aroused. "Like a wall of granite."

"Look, Tiff, I'm calling you a Lyft." I'm back to tapping my phone. "What's your address?"

"What?" she whisper-shrieks. "Wait a second-"

"Never mind." I bring up the firm directory, and she's gone from my chest. It takes me a second to realize she's dropped to her knees in front of me and her hands are on my belt.

"Stop..." I tap the buttons on the app faster, using my free hand to sweep her away from my fly.

"Stop, stop..." She laughs, her voice high and teasing. "What guy doesn't want a blow job?"

"Stop!" I've managed to book her a ride, but she's got my pants open and is handling my dick.

"Fuck me," she moans. I look down, and she looks up. The whites of her eyes are visible, and her mouth is a delighted O. "The rumors are true!"

"Get up." Shoving my phone in my pocket, I grasp under her arms, pulling her to her feet.

"Oh, Jackson!" She pokes her lips out, face pouty. "Let me ride your big... huge... cock!"

"Where's your dress?"

Moving fast, I refasten my pants with one hand. I'm still holding her by the upper arm, keeping her with me as I circle, looking for where I saw red silk fly over her head.

"There it is." I take her to where the dress is laying discarded on the path.

"You're always alone," she sulks, stomping beside me as I lead her to the car and hold her against it. I brace her with one leg so she can't wiggle away, while I fumble with the fabric, searching for the neck hole.

"Are you gay?" Her voice sounds like every drunk college girl I ever turned away.

"No," I answer flatly.

"When's the last time you got laid?"

Her blonde hair catches in the fabric, and I untwist it, pulling the material down her sticky body as best as I can.

"I get laid," I growl, considering it has been a while.

I've been so focused on my work, this case... Now the last thing on my mind is fucking some drunk girl. First, her consent is dubious. Second, she's our receptionist and could yell sexual harassment or worse.

"I'm not dipping my pen in the company ink."

"I'll quit my job!" she cries, still holding onto me. "Just kiss me once."

"Where is that fucking Lyft?" I reach into my jacket again. "He's here!"

Sure enough, high beams cut through the woods, curving around the black trees. I start up the lane in the direction of the road.

"My shoes!" she shrieks, trying to run back the way she came. "They're Louboutins!"

My grip tightens on her arm, until I'm practically carrying her to the waiting car. "I'll ship them to you at the office."

"You're not coming back to work? What are you going to do?"

Hesitating a moment, I realize it's a good question. I know what I want to do—what's nudging at my brain. What I've wanted to do for so long...

I'm tired and my thoughts are twisted and cloudy, but I know what I want more than anything. "I have a meeting to attend."

"Now?"

"Right now."

The Lyft pulls away, taking Tiffany back home. I head straight to my car, pulling out my phone as I walk. My disbelief is gone, my head is clear, and I have to face this.

* * *

"Jackson." Brice Wagner's low voice is laced with condescension as he ushers me into his enormous wood-paneled study. "What brings you all the way out here at this hour?"

It took me two hours to drive to my elder partner's ocean front estate north of the city. From the smell of his breath, he's been working on his own scotch, luxuriating in the close of our case, no doubt.

Thinking how much we could have lost...

How much I saved.

How much he covered up.

"I was doing some housekeeping before I shut down tonight."

"You young bucks." He slaps my back, barking out a laugh as he rounds his desk. "After today's win, at your age, I'd be out on the town, a bottle in each hand and a blonde on each arm."

"No doubt," I say, placing a hand on the stiff leather wingback across the massive mahogany desk from my partner. "I had something like that in mind."

It's true. I'd been finishing up, pulling all the files together ahead of what I hoped would be a long weekend.

Until I opened the office intranet we shared on the case.

Until I discovered the hidden folder labeled "Disposed documents."

The folder password protected with a dead child's name.

"Well?" He pours a crystal tumbler of amber liquid and holds it out to me. "What stopped you?"

I take the crystal and tilt it side to side, studying the trail of the liquid as it moves. The room smells of antique furniture and oiled leather. It's moneyed and ancient, and knowing what I know now, it's all the rotten stench of corruption.

A strange calm filters through my chest as I say my next words. "I had in mind a long weekend, possibly a week off. We put in a lot of hours on this one."

"You're right." He rocks back in his desk chair and props a foot on the corner. I watch as he pulls out a fat cigar and clips the end. He doesn't offer me one, not that I'd take it.

Eventually, the pungent scent of cigar smoke drifts across to me as I continue. "But the settlement agreement and release need to go out. I had to be sure Lori could find what she needed to get it done…"

"Okay."

I've reached the end of my patience, so I say what I came here to say. I speak the heart of the prosecution's case. "Johnny Mauck had been driving for thirty hours straight when he lost control of his rig and skidded across that median."

Brice lowers his foot and turns slowly to face me. Anger fires red in his watery eyes, but it's nothing compared to the fucking inferno in my chest.

"Stop right there." His voice is a calm warning.

"Big Traxx paid for the amphetamines that kept him driving. You were at the scene. You knew it all along." Every breath is hot. "I found the documents, the logs, the prescription… everything that should have been provided during litigation."

"You found nothing." He speaks the words slowly, ominously, dark eyes like stone.

My eyes are flint. "I found it all."

We're silent, sizing each other up. The brass clock on the mantle above the fireplace is the only noise, ticking louder than the beating of a drum. If I had any lingering doubts, any question of what I had to do on the long drive out here, his response put the final nail in that coffin.

Finally, he leans forward. His leather chair creaks under his weight. "So you've made your decision?"

The fist in my chest still hasn't unclenched. Perhaps it never will. Either way, the answer is yes. "I'm not doing this anymore."

He has the nerve to look smug. "Where will you go?"

"Back to the beginning."

If I've lost everything, I might as well. I'll walk away. All the way to the only place I've ever known happiness.

I'll pick up the pieces and start over.

Chapter 2

Ember

It's a penis.

I stand in front of the table looking down, and there is no mistaking what it is.

Hours of online courses, too many YouTube videos to count (so many YouTube videos), correspondence courses at the community college, and this is what it comes down to...

Penis cakes for money.

Tabby rocks forward on her stool, leaning on her elbows watching me carve the corners off the beige sheet cake. Her jet-black hair is smoothed into thick curls, and a red handkerchief is wrapped around her head. Severe bangs, arched brows, and velvet-red lips. My best friend is punk rock Bettie Page.

"How can you make these and be so unaffected?"

I continue carving two round balls at the bottom of the long, almond-colored shaft. "It's cake."

"Still... you haven't been with a guy in what? Five years?"

"Don't go there."

"I'm just saying. That's one well-constructed penis."

"Again, it's cake."

"I wish Liam was black." Instantly her green eyes go round, and she leans closer, whispering,

"Is that racist?"

"Depends on what you say next. Why?"

She falls back on the stool, her eyes fluttering shut. "Because your Devil's food cake with the coconut pecan buttercream icing and dark chocolate ganache is better than sex."

"Then you're not doing it right."

"You're not doing it at all!"

Cutting my eyes at her, I set the sharp knife aside.

She sniffs. "Well, you're not."

Choosing to ignore her jab, I return to her original statement, reaching for the bowl of vanilla pastry cream. "Liam is white. His penis has to match him." Pausing in my filling, I study the bisected cake in front of me. "I was planning to use all this cream for the inside, but maybe I should save some for the tip..."

"Oh my god," Tabby snorts. "Mousey little Donna White has totally knocked my socks off. This is the tackiest order in the history of Ember Rose Cakes!"

I arch an eyebrow at her. "Donna didn't order it."

Red-velvet lips part, and Tabby's eyes sparkle with mischief. "Who did?"

"Help me."

She lifts the opposite end of the top layer, and together we slowly place it over the cream-filled bottom.

The little bell over the door rings, and I step back, crossing my arms, admiring the lifelike almond-sponge penis cake with vanilla cream filling. "She doesn't like fondant, so I'm thinking I'll cover it in beige marzipan —"

"You're working late tonight, Ember." My mother's stern voice echoes through the large, empty store (a.k.a., my future bakery-slash-home).

With a hiss, Tabby spins beside me, blocking the cake with her body. I freeze, my heart thudding frantically in my chest. *Oh, shit.*

"Uh..." Tabby walks fast to meet my mother halfway between the front door and the large table at the back wall where I do my decorating. "We got a last-minute cake order for Donna's shower."

I frantically look for anything to cover the oversized male member — as if that could possibly save us from the shit-storm about to erupt.

"That's nice." Condescension is thick in her voice. "Donna's mother has been a faithful member of the church since you were little girls. I'm sure she'll appreciate your talent..."

My mother stops, and a knot lodges in my throat. Seconds like hours tick past as she steps around my best friend, arms crossed, frowning down at the phallus. Thank God I haven't added the extra cream to the tip yet.

"What is this?" Her voice is hard, disgusted.

"Just what the doctor ordered!" Tabby calls out. "A little taste of what's to come!"

It's no use. My mother is impervious to humor.

"God gives you a talent, Emberly Rose, and this is how you thank him? By making *porn*?"

My mind drifts to a list of questions, the way it always does when her lectures start: *Would God really be angry about a cake shaped like Donna's future husband's penis? Doesn't God have bigger fish to fry? Does God even fry fish? Jesus ate fish...*

"Are you listening to me, Emberly Rose?"

27

I blink back to attention. "It seemed like an interesting challenge."

The sweetest little voice cuts through the tension in the air. "Mommy's cake! Mommy's cake!" Everything is forgotten as I dash forward, scooping my little girl into my arms.

"Coco bean!" I spin her around and kiss her velvety cheek. The entire world is suddenly brighter.

"The purple monster says *tres*!" she chants.

"*Tres*?" I pretend to be confused. "What is *tres*?"

"Three!" she cries holding up three small fingers.

"That's right!" I hug her body snug against mine.

All the shame and fear are gone when I hold Coco, but she starts to wiggle. She wants to get down.

"I want cake! Mommy cake!"

My mother is quick to interrupt. "Colette, come to Grandmother."

"Cake! Cake! Cake!" Her little eyes sparkle and two dimples punctuate her cheeks as she cheers for cake.

Happiness rises in my chest with every pump of her cute little fist over her head.

"How about this..." I go to her and kneel, putting my hands on her tiny waist. She puts her hands on the tops of my shoulders, her dark eyes suddenly serious. "I'll make you a special cupcake with a purple monster and a big three on it."

"I'm four now."

"This isn't a birthday cake." I smooth my fingers in her hair, moving a cluster of silky brunette curls behind her ear. "It's a special cake, and I'll give it to you tomorrow."

"You won't spend the night?"

My heart sinks with her question, but I can't spend another night in my mother's house. I just can't.

"I have to fix this house for us. Remember? We're going to live upstairs. And I'll be over first thing tomorrow with your cupcake."

I carry her to the door where my mother waits, disapproval lining her thin lips. "Church tomorrow. I expect you to be there."

"I will." I give Coco another hug, taking a deep inhale of her sweet little girl scent. "Go with Granny now."

"Grandmother." My mother corrects me. "Come, Colette."

"Let's go, Granny!" Coco wiggles out of my arms to the floor then hops out like a kangaroo.

Tabby snorts behind me, and my mother's eyes narrow. "We'll finish this tomorrow."

With that she strides out, and I push the door closed behind them, resting my forehead against the glass.

"I swear, if that little girl were any less stubborn, I'd be worried about her," Tabby says from behind me.

I watch them a few seconds longer—my mother trying unsuccessfully to hold Coco's hand while they walk the four blocks to her house, the old house where I grew up.

"She'll be okay a little while longer," I say, feeling like my heart is hopping away from me, batting at her grandmother's hand with every bounce.

"Old battle axe. I guess you survived living with her."

"She wasn't like this before Minnie died." My voice is quiet, repeating a memory.

"Says who." It's not a question. It's a skeptical retort from my bestie.

"Aunt Agnes. She said my mother used to know how to have fun."

"I don't believe it."

"To be honest, I've never believed it either." I don't even remember my older sister.

"You're too independent for her. She can't handle it. She almost lost her mind when you took up with Jackson Cane so young—"

Cutting my eyes, I stop that line of conversation. "We don't talk about him."

"We should." Tabby studies my face. "He's the only guy you were ever serious about."

He said he'd come back, and he never did...

Exhaling deeply, I return to my phallic creation. "Ancient history. Now let's finish this thing before it's too late."

I ditch the marzipan idea and opt instead for a skin-toned buttercream. Tabby starts cleaning up, and I'm almost finished frosting when the bell over the door rings again.

"What is this, Grand Central?" Tabby mutters.

"How's it hanging, girls?"

"Jesus!" Tabby jerks around with a gasp, running to meet Betty Pepper, Oceanside Village's busiest of the ancient busybodies.

"Hi, Miss B!" she calls too loudly, intercepting the old woman. "What brings you to the store this evening?"

Betty glances around. "You should have items to sell if it's a store."

"Soon, Miss B... Just you wait," I call out. I've finished frosting the balls, and I reach for the bowl of dark chocolate shavings to sprinkle over them.

"How's my order coming?" Betty asks, and I'm pretty sure Tabs swallows her gum.

"Just finishing now," I call over my shoulder.

"Wait!" Tabby holds out her hand. "Hold the phone. Betty Pepper ordered that?"

The squat octogenarian pushes my rockabilly roommate aside and joins me at the massive, weathered-wood table where I work.

"Oh," she gasps. "Emberly Rose!"

Tabby's right behind her. "*You* ordered the penis cake?"

"Oh, *yes*!" BP clutches her chest.

"Well, don't have a heart attack," my friend snarks.

Stepping back, I survey the raunchy masterpiece. "I think it needs a vein." I pinch a bit of fondant and roll it into a long, skinny column, laying it along the shaft.

Once it's in place, I add the last bit of vanilla cream at the tip.

Miss Betty's voice is thick with lust. "It's so *good*!"

My friend arches a perfect, black eyebrow. "How long has it been since you've seen one of these?"

"Get a life, Tabitha Green. I see what I want on the Internet," Betty says before turning to me. "I can't believe you did this without a mold."

"The frosting helps." I walk to the wall of cabinets and take down my vanilla extract and a small paintbrush. "I thought about putting a square cake around the bottom and molding jeans with the fly down... Painting it blue, like it's rising out of his pants?"

The old lady's eyes widen. "You can do that?"

Using the paintbrush, I lightly dab the dark-brown vanilla around the ridges, giving the cake more dimension. "It would take a few hours."

"Forget it, then. I need it for Donna's shower now." She carefully steps around me. "It's absolutely thrilling! Hopefully it'll loosen her up some."

Tabs and I exchange a glance. "I'm glad you like it."

"How much do I owe you?"

Tabby starts to speak, but I cut her off. "Two hundred." I don't miss my best friend's glare, but I'm not going to charge an old lady full-price, even if she is annoying as hell half the time.

I also know the old biddies gossip about how much I charge for my cakes. They might call me a genius, but they won't pay genius prices for something they think they can do at home.

"Two hundred dollars?" Her lust turns to shock.

"I'm sure you took up a collection," Tabby snaps.

She still hasn't gotten over Betty Pepper ratting her out for skinny-dipping in the Holiday Inn pool last year with Mayor Rhodes's out of town nephew. It was a pretty tame stunt for Tabs... until we found out the kid was only seventeen.

In my friend's defense, the boy had a tattoo, rode a Harley, and we all thought he was at least nineteen.

BP digs in her wallet and shows us a few twenties. "This is all I've got."

"Make it a hundred and fifty, then," I sigh.

"You can write a check," Tabby adds, irritation in her tone.

The old lady is huffy, but she pulls out her checkbook and starts to write. I lift the foil-covered cardboard tray and place it in a waiting gift box on the opposite counter. Her next words stop my breath.

"Bucky can't wait until your date next Friday."

Tabby gives me a horrified, *I smell sour-milk* face, and I cringe. "Whaaat is this about?" she asks.

"Emberly is such a dear." Betty pats my forearm. "Bucky said after that brat Cheryl Ann dumped him last week, you talked to him for an hour at the Tuna Tiki."

"How could you stand it?" my roommate says. "And what were you doing at Tuna Tiki?"

"I wanted sushi," I say.

Betty pushes on undeterred. "Then she agreed to have dinner with him."

"You did not!" Tabby grabs my arm.

"It wasn't... quite like that." I step away, untying my apron and wiping my hands with it.

"He said you were. Are you not going to dinner with Bucky on Friday?" Betty cries.

"No. You are *not* going to dinner with Bucky on Friday," Tabby says.

"Why would you say something like that, Tabitha? Just because my Bucky isn't some pot-smoking, Harley Davidson riding—"

"I'll have you know, Betty Pepper, I've only dated three guys who smoked pot—"

"You know what?" I shout before those two start throwing punches. "It's just dinner. I'm glad to do it if it helps Bucky get over Cheryl... or whatever."

"You are *not* glad to do it. Bucky Pepper is a—
Ouch!"

I release her flesh from my sly pinch and pull the pin out of my dark hair, letting it fall down my back. "Thank you so much, Miss Betty."

"It's too bad you won't be joining us for cake." The old lady prances to the door, and I lean against the counter. The bell tinkles, and she's gone.

Tabby turns, arms crossed to glare at me. "What. The fuck. Bucky Pepper smells like formaldehyde!"

"He's a taxidermist."

"He's the shape of a coke bottle, and he'll probably give you a stuffed squirrel!"

I can't help a laugh. "It's better than herpes."

"Jesus, don't even joke about sleeping with him." Tabby does a full-body shiver. "His breath is like… like…"

I think a minute then it hits me. "Deviled eggs." Nodding, I collect my ingredients and carry them to the shelves, where I arrange them neatly in order. "I just realized it smells like deviled eggs."

"Good lord, Ember." My friend lowers her gaze. "I cannot in good faith let you go out with that… that…"

Reaching out, I squeeze her arm. "So I go out with Bucky the stinky taxidermist. He gives me stuffed road-kill. It's one night."

"I heard he tried to grab Cheryl Ann's cooch on their very first date. That's why she ditched him. She should've slapped him into next week." Tabby puts a hand on her hip and does her best Jane Russell glare. "What will you do if Bucky tries to grab you?"

"I'll throw ice water in his face and go home." Stepping forward I kiss her cheek. "See you tomorrow."

"There's no shame in pretending you don't hear him knocking."

"Goodnight, Tabs."

She grumbles as she leaves, and I walk slowly to the back of the old store where stairs lead to my loft apartment above. After my aunt died, she left this old five and dime store to me. Tabby helped me sell or trash all the shelves and retail furnishings, and I've been scrubbing and painting ever since.

Weathered wood painted white makes up the walls of shelves where I keep my meager baking ingredients. Two vintage chandeliers, fake branches, and driftwood arranged in vases are the start of my interior design. One day I imagine having a garland of multi-colored spring roses like Peggy Porschen's at the entrance.

"One day," I say softly, dreaming of the lavish London bakery and the lady who owns it.

The only piece of furniture I've been able to buy is the heavy wooden table where I do all my mixing, kneading, arranging, decorating...

I kept my aunt's register and checkout counter for front reception. Slowly, slowly I'm saving up to add a refrigerated case. Last month, I was finally able to buy a second oven so I can cook two cakes at once.

"Just keep swimming." I push open the heavy door leading to the upstairs where Coco and I will live.

When Mr. Lockwood developed that old stretch of sand, all the tourists moved away from our little village down to the beachfront property. I hope my cakes lure them back here—at least to shop—and if they do, I'll be a small-town hero pulling tourist dollars back into Our Town.

I walk over to my small table and pick up the photo of me on the beach, looking up, holding my little girl. "That's the plan, Coco Bean," I whisper.

I'll have my daughter and my cake shop, and that's all I need. One foot in front of the other, and before I know it, my dreams coming true.

Chapter 3

Jack

"I need the whole thing painted. All three storefronts." Wyatt Jones scrubs his nails in his scruffy grey beard and cocks an eyebrow at me. "You up for that?"

The door on the orange Ford step-side I bought off a used-car salesman in Madison makes a loud popping sound when I pull it open. "It'll take me at least a week. Maybe two. That okay?"

"You working alone?"

"Unless I can find a kid who needs a summer job."

"Summer's over around here."

My lips curl into a frown—I didn't think anything changed in Oceanside Village. "It's still August." *Dog days…*

"Kids started back August first," Wyatt says. "Keeps 'em out of trouble."

He narrows one eye at me, and I choose to let his insinuation pass as I climb into the hot cab of The Beast. "I'll start tomorrow."

"Tomorrow's Sunday, son."

With another loud pop, I slam the door shut. Every noise is a reaffirmation of my new reality. No more plush vacuum seals. No more buttery, conditioned leather. I'm hard edges and steel.

Plain and simple…

Paint and sweat…

Lots of sweat.

"I guess some things haven't changed."

"If that's the case, I won't save you a seat." He does a snarky grin.

"No thanks." I have no interest in attending service at the First Church of Marjorie Warren. The only thing that ever lured me to that shout-fest presided over by the town matriarch was Emberly.

Emberly…

A flicker of some old sentiment moves through my chest, but it's only a ghost. She's long gone, and those days are ancient history.

Wyatt rocks back on his heels, his thick brows rising with the corners of his mouth. The cock-eyed grin makes me uneasy.

"Welcome home, Jackson Cane."

"Lockwood."

"You're using Lockwood now?"

"It's my name."

"Oh, I know it." He chuckles. "I remember you as a little guy. Your daddy used to bust your chops, but you were tough enough. You're more like him now."

My shoulders tighten. I haven't talked to my father since I left my firm. I haven't talked to anyone besides Wyatt and a used-car salesman. "I'll see you Monday."

"You staying at the cottage?"

Nodding, I prop my arm on the open window of the door.

"All right, then." Wyatt clears his throat and starts off at a brisk pace toward his hardware store. "Monday morning. Bright and early.

Nodding, I turn the key. "Every day," I repeat under my breath.

It's all I want — hard work and no trouble.

* * *

Pushing through the door of the cottage, I flick the light switch and survey the weathered wood and white interior. Dad sold his house in Oceanside and relocated to the city after I started law school. He never wanted to have anything to do with this town again. He made his millions and got out.

I cross the yellow pine floors to the grayish-brown farm table. At first I'm confused. When I left the cottage was nothing more than an abandoned shack. I'd expected to find it closed up and empty. Instead, it's polished and clean and completely renovated.

I switch a quiet window unit on high and continue down the hall, past a smaller, office room, to the master bedroom. A king-sized bed is covered in a white Matelassé spread and matching pillows. It's all very Cape Cod and very new. *Am I in the right house?*

The sudden ring of a phone startles me, and I look around the place. A white cordless phone is on the bedside table.

Reaching slowly, I lift the receiver. "Hello?"

"Who is this?" I recognize the forceful male voice on the other end of the line at once.

"Dad?"

"Jackson? What the hell are you doing at the cottage?"

For a moment, I hesitate. I hadn't intended to have this conversation with him so soon — at least not until I'd sorted it out in my own mind.

"Well, my original plan was to clean it out, fix it up, and live here for a little while."

"I've already done all of that."

"I see you have." Walking through the two thousand square-foot residence, I take in the elegant décor — white paint, navy and white striped fabrics, driftwood accent pieces. "It's nice."

"I've been using it as a rental property. The manager just called to ask if I'd rented it without telling her. I didn't even know you still had a key."

Pinching the bridge of my nose, I try to think. "I can stay somewhere else."

"What the hell are you doing in Oceanside? You're supposed to be at work."

Here we go. "I took a job here."

"A job? Doing what? Wills and estates?"

"Painting. Wyatt Jones has these three old storefronts he needs repainted. I expect it'll take me at least a week to finish. Maybe longer."

"You're doing *what*?" His voice is a rasp. "What is the meaning of this? You're the newest partner at Wagner and Bancroft — the youngest partner they've ever taken on. I just read the fucking article last spring! It's unprecedented."

"I resigned."

"You can't resign!"

"Actually, I can, and I did. I'm sorry, I assumed my mother's cottage would be empty. I'll clear out and find somewhere else to stay in town while I work."

The line is silent for several long seconds. I'm about to say goodbye and disconnect when my father speaks again, his voice grave. "Are you in trouble, son?"

My muscles clench, and I take a deep breath. I'm not ready to talk about this with him. I'm still working out what I'm going to do. It's why I came here — to do manual labor and sort out my thoughts, decide what needs to happen next.

Still, to answer his question, "I'm not in trouble."

He's quiet a beat longer, and I can tell he's trying to decide whether to believe me.

"It's the end of the season. I can have Claire take the cottage off the market for a while. As long as you need."

"You don't have to —"

"I insist. Technically it's your place anyway. It was left to you in her will. Why do you think I never sold it?"

Because you loved her? The thought enters unbidden in my mind, as if my father has a sentimental bone in his body. I don't even know if it was ever true. I don't even believe in love like that anymore.

"Because it's a good investment property," I answer.

"Damn right it is." He exhales loudly. "However, if you'd rather use it as a residence, that can be arranged. I've been keeping whatever profits it makes in a separate account. It's all yours."

Stepping over to a small closet in the corner of the bedroom, I try the knob. It's locked. "I'll stay, but only for a little while. Don't change your plans because of me."

Again we're quiet, and I'm ready to end the call. My father and I are both take-charge individuals. Giving orders and expecting them to be followed is our most comfortable way of relating to the world — not this quiet concern.

"Let me know if you need anything."

"I will."

I'm just about to disconnect when he adds, "You'll find the things you left behind in a small locked closet in the bedroom. I put the key in the hall safe. The combination is the same."

"Thanks." I put the receiver back on the plastic cradle and stand for a moment listening to the sound of bugs screeching outside the window.

When this place was just an abandoned shack in the woods, it was my fortress of solitude — at least that's how I imagined it as a little kid. Later it became something else, a place I could take girls... one girl.

One girl, so many memories.

Tapping in the code, I find more than a key in the hall safe. Several small boxes are also inside, but I'll save those for later. I'm more curious to see what of my things my father chose to preserve. I hope it's what I'm looking for.

Back in the bedroom, I unlock the small closet. It's short and deep, a glorified crawl space with a door. I bend down and pull the string hanging from a bare bulb. At once the space floods with light, and I see them. It looks like they're all here, leaning against the wall.

Quickly I pull the long canvases out of the stuffy space. It takes a moment or two to arrange them around the room. They're my paintings — acrylic on canvass.

Some are brilliantly colorful: orange skies at twilight, a bridge over black water, a towering oak with small leaves and a labyrinthine root system.

None of them are what I'm looking for. My chest tightens, and I fear it's gone. Moving away the last box, I see it. I don't know why it's separated from the rest, but I'm glad. It isn't damaged or distressed, and I turn it once to the side so the tall end points up.

Here she is in all her petite, magical glory. Sitting with her legs strategically crossed, her hands in her lap. Her face is turned to the side, showing her profile, her full lips. Her torso faces front, her creamy shoulders straight and her perfectly rounded breasts bare. One lock of glossy brown hair is arranged so that it swoops down, the ends curling around the tip of her dark nipple.

Tightness moves low in my belly... An old familiar tightness of desire registers in my cock. I get a semi just looking at her. I thought I knew what it would mean to be her first. I had no idea. The way she looked at me when I kissed her, her eyes full of so much trust. When she looked at me, I believed I could do anything.

We were so damn young—she was even younger. I'd known her since we were little kids, but that summer everything changed. It was my last summer here...

It was our first summer together.

I can still see her on the beach, long wavy hair whipping in the breeze, dark eyes sparkling with magic and mischief and fun. She'd never been kissed, and she insisted I teach her. It wasn't long before I'd teach her everything. Then it became impossible to keep our hands off each other, which led to this day.

I remember it so well...

It was raining steadily. We were here in this cottage—only in those days, we didn't have a fancy bed or elegant furnishings. She'd sat on my T-shirt on the floor.

I remember telling her how to sit. How to hold her hands in her lap, turn her head to the side, lower her chin, raise her shoulder...

She was so fucking beautiful.

I was hypnotized by her breasts, distracted by her narrow waist, mouth watering at the sparse dusting of soft hair on her pussy...

Ember Rose.

My chest burns at the sight. I can still taste her clean, ocean-water flavor. Her body is still the most beautiful thing I've ever seen. Sketching her, painting her had been electric. It had been like taking her body all over again, but even more intimately, if that's possible.

My fingers tingled with each stroke of my pencil, as if the lines were laced with electricity. Her full lips had trembled as if she could feel me drawing them, shading them, caressing them with my fingertips.

Every curve, every shadow, every intimate place... She would melt when I touched her.

I remember touching her...

When we touch, everything grows brighter, hotter, faster, more desperate.

I'd painted her in warm gold, bright yellow, pure cream, and deep brown, and on the back I'd hastily written *Shine Like Ember*.

Her eyes glowed. She loved it, but at the same time, she'd been afraid. She was worried someone would find it. I'd promised her no one but me would ever see it.

Tearing my eyes away from her beauty, I look around the transformed cottage, and I realize I didn't keep that promise. We didn't keep a lot of promises. Still, why didn't I take this with me?

I know why.

I had always thought I'd come back for her. I had thought we would live here, and this painting was here waiting for that vision to become reality.

"Grow up, Jackson," I say, clearing the thickness from my throat.

Adjusting my fly, I lift the canvas and push it back inside the crawl-space closet, jerking the string to kill the light, hiding its magic.

Those days are over.

Daydreams are for children. I need a drink.

* * *

I'm out on the strand, alone, entering the Tuna Tiki on a Saturday night. It's as crowded as it ever was and equally cheesy, and just as I pass through the entrance, a big guy in a damp tee bumps into me. I move him away, forward into the crowd, and somebody cheers. Nobody seems to care.

"Drunk tourists," I mutter under my breath, hating what's become of this once pristine landscape. I guess I have my dad to thank for it... and he has all his money to show for it.

It's an open-air bar, so the constant breeze keeps us cool while covering us in fresh salt. Music drifts around me. It's Bob Marley, but it doesn't sound like one of his millions of familiar recordings. Lifting my chin, I try to see if there's a live band. That would be a switch from eleven years ago. I can't see anything from this spot in the crowd.

The sky is deep royal blue, and the lights from the bar drown out the stars. I don't expect to see anyone I know here. It's been too long, and when I left, nobody came out to the strand from Oceanside Village. They were all so bitter and angry that it destroyed the town. That's what they said... I'm not sure that's true. They might not have come here to socialize, but this place brought tons of jobs to the area.

I'm not looking to make amends for the past, so I push up through the barstools, a twenty flagging in my fingers.

The bartender is heavy-set with dark hair and a bright red lei necklace. A hibiscus is behind his ear, and he's clearly Latino. Still, they're going for a Hawaiian vibe, and I'm willing to bet everyone thinks he's Samoan. Either way, he's moving fast, mixing drinks, monitoring draft beers, and taking orders.

He sees me, and I lift my chin. "Vodka rocks, twist of lime," I shout.

A chin up, and I know he's got my order. I lean back against the bamboo countertop to wait as I check out the crowd. I was barely old enough to come here when this place opened eleven years ago, but if all's the same, they have pretty decent drinks, and I need something strong to kill the memories.

I almost asked for Fireball since I've always been partial to cinnamon, but I'd like to get out of bed in the morning. I don't know what I was thinking coming back to Oceanside — did I think she'd be waiting?

I know she's gone.

I remember what my dad said.

I remember how it kicked my guts out and set me on the path to what I am now. My dream was over. Might as well live out my dad's dream for me.

Only, now that dream is all fucked up, too.

A new song begins, and sure enough, a live band is situated in the back corner. Three guys strum acoustic guitars while one is on a small drum kit. A tap on my arm, and Pablo hands me my vodka. I give him the twenty and turn back to watch the show. I'm just collecting my change when I see her.

Jet-black hair swept up in a red kerchief, severe bangs, and blood-red velvet lips. An hourglass figure wrapped in a tight red dress...Tabitha Green is across the bar swaying her hips to "Jamming," holding the arm of some guy I don't recognize and laughing. She hasn't changed a bit.

For a moment, I'm frozen, unsure where to go or if she'll even recognize me.

It doesn't matter. The moment her green eyes land on mine, they blink twice quickly, then widen so big I can see the whites around them.

Her chin jerks forward as if she choked on her drink, and I try to fall back, to disappear into the crowd, but my back is against the bar. I'm trapped. This is happening, and Tabby never walks away from a showdown.

"Jackson Cane?" Her voice cuts through the din. The party doesn't even pause.

She crosses the small space to where I'm caught in the rope swings. Squaring my shoulders, I get ready. I'm not afraid of this ghost.

"What the fuck are you doing here?" Perfect black brows pull together over her eyes, which are shooting sparks.

"Hi, Tabby," I say, taking a sip of my drink and doing my best to act casual. "I didn't expect to see you."

"Why not? I live here."

"At the Tuna Tiki?" I give her a wink. In my experience, it disarms angry women, although I know Tabby better than that... or I used to.

"Are you flirting with me, Jackson Cane?"

"I'm trying to be friendly. I haven't seen you in ten years."

"No shit, Sherlock. Why are you here?"

"Well, despite this warm welcome, I like to think of Oceanside as my home." I exhale and take another sip of vodka. "I grew up here. My mother grew up here."

"You've got a lot of nerve coming back like this."

This adversarial bullshit is pissing me off. "I don't know what you're talking about."

"That's just what a lying bastard would say, isn't it?"

"I'm not a liar." My jaw tightens as anger flares in my chest. "If this is about my dad, I can assure you he didn't expect business to centralize out here the way it did. Mark it up to unintended consequences."

Her eyes flash like I just jerked her ponytail. "Your dad?" Her velvet lips part. "You don't..." For the first time I've ever known her, it appears Tabitha Green is at a loss for words.

Standing up straighter, I'm at my full six foot two, looking down on her. "I know this is part of your persona or whatever." I gesture to her Bettie Page getup. "Tough girl. But I'm just looking to have a quiet drink. Take it easy, Tab."

I slug the last of my vodka and leave her standing there gasping like a fish out of water. I guess coming back to Oceanside I thought I'd find peace and quiet, home and comfort, a place to sort out what's become of my career.

My gut led me here... I'm starting to think I shouldn't trust my gut.

Chapter 4

Ember

The day after Jackson left for college, my nightmare returned.

Water rushing in all around me, pouring in the windows, rising from the floor, filling the small space where I'm strapped down. It comes in faster than I can breathe, faster than I can scream for help.

I've always loved the ocean, but this dream is different.

This water wants to kill me.

I stopped having it when Jackson and I were together. That summer, I had three months of pure, uninterrupted sleep.

Sleep in which my only dreams were of his strong arms around me, his full lips tracing lines along my ribs, inhaling my scent, making the tiny hairs on my body rise. His mouth would close in a pucker over my straining nipple, and with a gentle tug, a flash of heat would register straight to my core. I would wake up so wet for him, I'd slide my hand between my thighs for relief.

Those dreams were luscious and decadent and wickedly sinful.

Those dreams were my life.

He left, and the nightmare returned.

To this day, every few months for no clear reason, I'm panicked out of a deep sleep by the force of rushing water. I wake up only to find I'm in my bed, in a wide-open space, completely dry.

It's early Sunday morning, and my small oven blasts heat in my face when I pull open the door to slide the cupcake tin inside. Every fan in my non-air-conditioned apartment is on high, but still a bead of sweat traces down my neck. I'll have to shower before I dress for church.

I've been up since six working on Coco's purple monster number three. I started by mixing yellow cake with blueberries and the slightest pinch of cayenne pepper for the monster bite. I've made a deep purple buttercream frosting by mixing confectioner's sugar with red and blue food coloring.

I try to imagine what it would be like if she were here right now. She'd love adding the colors and watching it all slowly thicken and turn purple... I can't wait for those days to come.

When my aunt died and left me this place, I'd gotten to work renovating what was once attic storage as fast as my budget and time would allow. The upstairs had been in worse shape than the downstairs, but after nine months of elbow grease, it's a clean, partially painted, partially furnished enormous studio apartment.

Honestly, it looks a lot like my "store" downstairs.

"I'll have things to sell, Betty Pepper, don't you worry." I twist my long, heavy hair onto my head and shove a pencil in to hold it.

In the late summer, it can be hot as blazes up here, even with all the fans blasting. Still, it's only truly unbearable for about a month. Then, with the French doors open across the front balcony and the small windows open in the back, I catch the sea breeze, and every night I fall asleep to the sounds of the surf crashing just a few miles away.

Coco can spend the night here once it cools off, since I have a radiator for heat in the winter. It's just during these summer days she does better staying in my old room...

Pictures of us together mixed with her preschool drawings are pinned all over the walls. My favorite is a framed one of the two of us on a swing, our long hair blowing back in the breeze. Her brown eyes look so much like mine...

"You'll be here with Mommy soon," I say, tracing my finger down her chubby cheek. "Just a few more weeks."

A glance at the clock sends me hopping. I dash to my small bathroom area and take as cool of a shower as I can stand.

Church starts at nine, and the days of me sleeping in, blowing off that weekly ritual are gone — it's one of the conditions of my mother keeping Coco in a plush, air-conditioned home and paying for her preschool.

Even more motivation to work faster. I step out, wrapping an old white towel around my body. My phone buzzes, and I scoop it up quickly when I see the name on the screen.

"If Sunday is the day of rest, why does church start so damn early?" Tabby is not a morning person.

"I've been up since six." I turn to the side in front of a full-length mirror in an antique picture frame leaning against the wall.

"You have a sickness."

"I'm admiring my tattoo," I say, getting closer to the glass and tracing my finger over the colorful blue-green mermaid scales on my hip.

"Has Marjorie seen it?"

"Of course not." Tapping my finger on the speaker button, I put the phone on my dresser and grab my thong. "Does this mean you're coming to church today?"

A loud groan fills my room. "It's my ten percent agreement with Uncle Bob."

"Explain to me how that works again." Throwing a blue rayon sundress over my head, I grab the phone and dash to the kitchen.

"I go ten percent of the Sundays, or five Sundays a year. It's a time-tithe."

Snatching up the hot pad, I open the oven and pull out perfectly golden cupcakes. I'll have just enough time to cool and frost them purple.

Holding the phone on my shoulder, I run to the mirror again with my makeup bag. "Then shouldn't it be thirty-six Sundays a year?"

"What?" Tabby's voice is a shriek, and I pull the phone away quickly.

"There are 365 days in a year. If you're tithing the days, then ten percent would be... Actually thirty seven if you round up."

"Who the fuck's side are you on?"

Laughing, I dust powder on my nose. "I'm just trying to follow your logic."

"This is math, not logic. I'm tithing my *Sundays*."

"Hmm," I say, reaching for my eyeliner. Just a touch at the corners. "If you only have to go five times, why now? I'd start on the Sunday after Thanksgiving and finish out the year—those are the fun ones."

"If church is fun, you're doing it wrong," my friend announces loudly.

"I feel like there's more to this story."

She's quiet a minute before she says, "Chad pulled me over last night."

I pause in my mascara application to give myself a knowing look. "Now we're getting somewhere. What did you do this time?"

"I was going forty in town."

"Tabs! That's dangerous!"

"I wanted to get home," she whines. "Anyway, who's out walking at 2 a.m.?"

"Sleepwalkers... Alzheimer's victims."

"I know every person in this town, and none of them fit those categories."

"Medical emergencies?"

"You'd make a great cop. I'll ask Chad to give you an application next time I see him," she grumbles.

"Why does getting pulled over mean you're going to church today?"

"I promised to be in church if he didn't give me a ticket."

"So it's a penance service?"

She takes a loud sip of what I'm sure is coffee. "Something like that."

"So you still have to go one more time to make your tithe."

"Forget cop. You'd make a better lawyer."

The word makes me wince, but I blow it off. *It's only a word.*

"I'm hanging up now," I say. "I've got to get these cupcakes to Mom's. If you're ready in ten minutes, we can walk together."

"Wait for me."

I trade my phone for the bowl of purple frosting. The cooled cupcakes are quickly covered, and I've molded chocolate 3s for the tops of each. I transfer them to a square Rubbermaid dish, and I'm out the door.

Tabby is waiting when I arrive at my mother's house. The door is unlocked but the house is empty. I place Coco's present in the refrigerator and hurry back out. We arrive at the small wooden building just as the organ music begins.

First Christian Church of Oceanside Village is a one-room building with a back door that leads straight into the sanctuary. The door creaks so loudly it echoes when we enter, and a few people turn to scowl at us. I smile at Betty Pepper, who clutches her hymnal to her chest and gives me a thumbs-up, mouthing, *It was delicious.*

Right next to her is Stinky Bucky, and he gives me a lecherous grin. I blink away fast, feeling sick that I'm trapped into going out with him on Friday. I've got to stop being so nice.

Tabby pulls me into a pew two rows behind Chad.

"I don't think he saw you," I sing in tune, holding the red hymnal open to the wrong page.

Tabby isn't looking forward, though. She's glancing over her shoulder, scanning the room. I do likewise, but it's all the same thirty or so faces we see every week.

"Who are you looking for?" I'm right at her ear, and she jumps.

"Nobody! Why would I be looking for anybody?"

That's suspicious. "Good question. I thought you were here for Chad."

"I am!" Her voice is too loud, and we get a glare from one of the old biddies in front of us.

I join in at the chorus, which is the only part I know. "Crown him with many crowns…"

Tabs continues in tune with the melody. "I don't see him back there…"

Nodding, I give her an elbow, but she only briefly glances at Oceanside's lone deputy sheriff two rows in front of us. She's still surveying the place like it's the wondrous cross—the hymn we've moved onto.

"You can say hello after church," I sing.

Song service ended, we sit and get comfortable as Tabby's uncle takes the two steps up the lectern and gazes down on us with a disgusted frown.

"*Idolatry!*" he shouts, and an old man nodding in front of us snorts awake. "Sex and idolatry are the workings of the flesh, and in the last days they will grow stronger and stronger amongst the children of men…"

He continues blasting about how lustful and depraved we all are. Then he moves on to the Ten Commandments and putting God first in all things.

I spot my mother in the front with her chin lifted. So pious. Her hair is a perfect blonde helmet, and the faintest hint of a smile is on her face. Occasionally she nods when he says something particularly loud. My nose automatically scrunches.

Scanning the other faces in the room, I observe how they respond. Some shift in their seats, while others look at their hands or study their Bibles.

Two years ago, when I was searching for an email from Coco's preschool teacher, I found an email conversation between my mother and Pastor Green.

I was snooping, I know I'm going to hell, but he thanked her for her insightful notes on the text. He wrote that he looked forward to incorporating them into Sunday's message.

Curiosity piqued, I glanced down her folders on the side of the screen and saw one labeled "Sunday sermons." Clicking it open, I found all his sermons going back years, since I'd rejoined the congregation after having Coco and briefly moving back home.

When I was a little girl, I'd seen the movie *Pollyanna*. I didn't understand the part about "nobody owns a church" until that moment. My grandfather had been one of the richest men in Oceanside Village before he died. He was the first city council president. My mother was an only child, and when her parents died, she inherited their big house in the middle of town and their legacy of leadership.

After my father was killed in the car wreck that also took Minnie, she kind of lost it. For weeks she stayed in her bedroom with the door closed, and I stayed at Tabby's house.

When she finally emerged, she was different. It was like she decided their deaths were God's way of punishing her for not doing more to keep everyone on the straight and narrow.

Now all I see are my mother's eyes judging all our shortcomings and delivering instructions on how to address them via Pastor Green each week.

I haven't cared for Bob Green's sermons ever since.

"...and you shall be saved," he ends ominously. "Let us pray and beg the Father to expose our hidden sins and save us from ourselves."

"That's what I call church," Tabby says, leaning forward. "Anxiety and upset stomach for the rest of the day."

I elbow her in the ribs. I know the source of that fire and brimstone, and I feel fine. It's simply another of my mother's methods for trying to control me — forcing me to be here, to listen to her judgmental bullshit coming from Marjorie's mouthpiece.

"Just a little while longer," I whisper.

It's Coco's last year of preschool, I'm making enough money to keep us clothed and fed. My daughter will be back with me in just a few short weeks, and I'll start sleeping in on Sundays again.

We're finally released, and Tabby and I are the first ones out the back door. I linger around on the front lawn a few minutes, waiting for my mother to appear with Coco.

"My advice on sex and idolatry is 'don't mix tequila with Googling your ex,'" I say, looking up at the small but imposing structure and remembering the one time five years ago when I entered *Jack Lockwood* in the search bar on Tabby's laptop.

"That was a crazy night," Tabby says, giving me a grin. "You were wild."

I was miserable.

With a rueful smile, I quote, "Beer makes you pee, wine makes you cry, tequila makes you pregnant."

"At least Coco's dad was a gentleman and went away."

I cut my eyes at her just as Betty Pepper makes a beeline for me with Bucky on her heels. "Ember Rose, that cake you made was the star of Donna's party!"

"I'm so glad!" I give her a hug.

"Hello, jump back!" Tabby calls, and I step away quickly when I see Bucky coming in for his turn to hug me.

He's dressed in cornflower-blue polyester suit with a shiny gold tie. I glance up to his face, and it's not *awful*. He's just so... weird. He has been since we were kids.

"Hi, Emberly," he says, and he moves his eyebrows in a way I'm sure he thinks is flirty, but it's totally creepy.

"Hi, Bucky."

"You have to make another one," Betty continues, and her son's pale blue eyes ogle my boobs.

Like, seriously.

In front of his mother.

"My store manager Thelma's anniversary is next Friday." Betty finally notices her son's inappropriate gaze. "Bucky! Go get the car!" He jumps and scampers off, and the old woman leans in close. "He's got quite the package—"

"What!" I pull back startled.

"Thelma's husband!" she scolds. "It's the dark chocolate variety, if you know what I mean."

"I know André." I'm just not sure about this repeat business.

"Just wait til all the guys find out you're baking their junk," Tabby teases, jabbing my ribs. "You'll be the most popular girl in town."

My mother appears at the top of the steps, and I feel my face go red. Even though I'm too old to believe it, I'm convinced she has a radar for when I'm "sinning."

Coco saves me. As soon as she spots me, she throws my mother's hand aside and runs straight to me. "Mommy!"

"Coco bean!" I swing her up onto my hip laughing, her purple and white gingham dress swooshing around us.

Her dark curls are brushed smooth down her little back, and the very top is gathered in a white grosgrain bow as big as her head.

"How did you sleep last night?" I ask when she presses her head against my shoulder.

I only get a shrug. "Granny made me go to bed early with no treats."

"No treats?" My brows pull together in a frown. "How come?"

"She said you were bringing me too many cupcakes today." Her little head pops up. "Did you bring me too many cupcakes?"

"I brought six purple monster three cupcakes, and you can eat them all if you want." Cutting my eyes back toward the church, I see my mother in a chaste conversation with the minister.

"Just save one for me." Tabby pats her little back and drifts away to where Chad stands talking to one of the parishioners.

Betty Pepper has me by the arm again. "Can you take an order for it now?"

Blinking back at her, I'm momentarily confused. "For what?"

Her eyebrows rise, and she makes her eyes big. "For the *humpht* cake."

When she says *humpht* she wobbles her head and jabs her index finger straight up — I imagine like a springing erection.

I grab it in my fist quickly. "How soon do you need it?"

"Friday. You know, the same night you're going out with Bucky."

"Right." As if I could ever forget that good deed gone wrong.

"Are you making a cake, Mommy?" Coco's head is up, and she's lifting my hair around my shoulders. Her sadness over last night is ancient history now that too many cupcakes are waiting for her.

"I need to be making more," I say, looking over the crowd.

Tabby gives Chad a little wave and starts back, but just before he slides those aviator sunglasses up his straight nose, I see his eyes linger on my best friend's ass. The muscle in his square jaw moves, and it's pure lust.

It's also pure busted when he sees me. I give him a little wink, and he turns quickly. I just laugh. Poor Chad. He's been in love with Tabs since the town hired him, and she won't give him the time of day. She says he's too "law-abiding." I call bullshit. I think she knows what I know... Chad Tucker would have a ring on her hand faster than she could say *I'm not that kind of girl.*

"What's that smug expression about?" she asks once she reaches our little huddle.

"I see Officer Tucker punched your church card."

"My what?" Her black brow arches. "Oh. Right. Yeah."

"You'll also be happy to know Betty here just placed another order for a *humpht* cake. Chocolate this time."

Tabby's eyes widen even more. "Who the hell-"

"Coco bean!" I cut her off loudly. "Run tell Granny you're walking home with Aunt Tabby and me."

My daughter does a little hop on my hip, and she's out of my arms, running top speed in the direction of the church.

BP leans closer. "I put the word out you made the cake. You should have a few more orders across the week."

"Thanks, but remember to tell them I do legitimate baking as well. Birthday cakes, wedding cakes, anniversary cakes you can serve your pastor..."

"What's the fun in that?" The old woman clutches her purse against her lavender suit and starts down the lane leading to where her son sits in the car waiting, leering at me.

I can't help a shiver. I'm waiting for Tabby's snarky response, but she doesn't even notice. My best friend is so distracted, I honestly can't take it anymore.

"What is on your mind, Tabitha?"

"Don't call me that," she says absently. "Chad calls me that."

"Well, it's your name."

Cocoa charges back to us, blowing air through her lips like a loud little motor, and grabs both our hands. We set off at a leisurely pace in the direction of my mother's house.

"Speaking of Chad, he's rocking that suit today." I cock an eyebrow in her direction. "Has he been working out?"

Coco takes off ahead of us chanting, "Work out... turn to the left! Work out... turn to the right!"

"Is that Supermodel?" My friend snorts.

"Her teacher's using it to teach them left and right."

"Shi—oot, all we got was the hokey pokey. I demand a RuPaul do-over!"

63

We take a few more steps with only the sounds of my energetic preschooler filling the air between us.

"Hey, Em?"

I glance up at the change in her tone. "What is it?"

"How would you feel if... say... I don't know... Just for instance, if you were to bump into Jackson Cane?"

I stop walking. It's like I've been electrocuted. My heart is flying in my chest, and I automatically the painful space. "Of all the things..." I whisper. "Why would you ask me that?"

Green eyes flicker to mine. "Just... he broke your heart when he left, and —"

"No," I shake my head, needing to keep the history accurate. "He left to go to college. He needed to leave. It broke my heart when he never came back."

I start walking again, albeit slower, and my hand moves from my chest to my stomach. Now I have heartburn.

Jackson Cane left me holding onto a promise, and after a few months, he just disappeared. He stopped calling, he never wrote, he never answered my calls or letters...

He was gone.

And I was left to pick up the pieces.

The shards.

"So if he were to come back —" Tabby's voice is slower.

"Why would he do that?"

"I don't know."

We're at the steps leading up to Mom's front porch, and I'm angry. I can't believe my best friend would bring this up. She knows his name only hurts me.

"What if he did?" I snap before following my daughter into the house. "I've moved on."

I'm just passing through the door, when I hear Tabby say behind me. "Have you?"

I'm still mad at Tabby a half-hour later when my mother launches into her weekly post-service postmortem over our usual fried chicken lunch.

"I thought the pastor's words on lasciviousness were particularly well-timed with all that's going on in the world today," she says.

It takes every ounce of willpower to hold my gaze on my chicken and not roll my eyes at her. Like I don't know this is a direct reference to the penis cake.

"That's a word I've never been able to spell," Tabby jumps in, saving me. "*Lasciviousness... Lascivious. Ness.* What does it mean?"

"It means lustful... smutty... obsessed with s-e-x."

"Oh!" Tabby's face brightens, and she shoves a huge spoonful of lumpy mashed potatoes into her mouth. "I can spell *smutty.*"

I choke on my sweet tea and almost laugh, my anger at my best friend forgotten. If anyone can deflect my mother's obnoxious, judgmental statements, it's her.

Naturally, I get a stern glare before my mother continues talking about her favorite parts of her sermon. I'm so tempted to say, *I know you wrote the whole damn thing!*

Instead, I turn my attention to Coco, who's creating a mountain out of her potatoes, complete with a moat in the middle for the gravy to run through.

"Looks like you're finished!" I cheerfully hop up and take her plate, cutting my mother off mid-sentence. "Who's ready for purple monster number three?"

"Me! Me! Meeeee!" Coco squeals holding her hand high and shaking it.

I laugh and go to the refrigerator to grab the square container. "I made one for each of us with two left over."

Coco gets the first one, and she dives in smearing purple frosting all over her nose and chin.

"Mm!" she squeals. "Chocolate and purple. It's hot!"

"That's the dragon's breath," I say with ominous glee.

"None for me, thank you." My mother's affected tone is like some old antebellum woman. Again, eye-roll suppressed.

"Split one with me," Tabby says. "I haven't exercised enough this week for a whole one."

"Having a little dry spell?" I tease. "Officer Tucker would be happy to help you out with that, I'm sure."

"I like a man who's faster than me," she says, taking a pinch of purple. "Chad Tucker is too slow to catch me."

"Sometimes slow can be nice."

"Is that crude talk?" Momma snaps. "On the Lord's day?"

"What? No!" I act innocent as I sit down. It only reminds me of Betty's order after church today. "Speaking of slow, I've got to get more orders coming in. I don't know what to do."

Tabby leans forward on her elbows. "I told you. We've got to get your website up. Online orders are the hot new thing! And a delivery guy…"

"I'm not interested in spending all my time online." My last venture into cyberspace landed me a baby. A baby I love, but still.

"Have you considered handing out fliers on the strand? I'm sure people out there are having birthdays, anniversaries… Maybe they just want cake by the ocean!"

Shaking my head, I watch her take a bite of spicy chocolate. "I did that a few times this summer. It didn't seem to make a difference."

"This is so delicious!" she cries. Just as fast, her eyes go wide. "I have an idea!" She's out of her seat, taking my cupcake out of my hand and putting it in the box beside the remaining four.

"What are you doing?"

"Grab CC and the fliers. We have a cute baby and a beautiful Sunday afternoon. We need to hand out samples!"

"I'm not a baby!" Coco cries, and I laugh. Her angry face is covered in purple.

"It's not a bad idea." I go to the sink and pick up a washcloth.

"It's a great idea!" Tabby has me by the arm, pulling me to the door. Coco's behind us doing her kangaroo hop again. "Coco! Stop hopping. Walk with purpose!"

"You called me a baby," my little girl fusses, and I know we're pushing naptime.

"I expect a raise once the money starts rolling in!" Tabby leads us to her car, the box of cupcakes in her hand.

I scoop up my daughter and follow her. "I don't pay you now."

"Exactly."

Chapter 5

Jack

I read somewhere the earth is round so we can't see too far down the road. Opening my eyes mid-morning Sunday, the first thing I see is my hard-on tenting the elegant Matelassé blanket over me. The second thing I see is Ember across the room.

It takes me a few seconds of blinking before I remember coming home last night after my run-in with Tabby and having a few more drinks. Then, possibly a little drunk, I dug her portrait out of the closet again.

"Fuck," I growl, sitting up and rubbing my face. "No more midnight cocktails."

Throwing the blanket aside, I stalk down the hall toward the bathroom. My feet make dull thudding noises on the soft pine floors.

This place is really nice, I think, entering the sparkling bathroom. Bracing myself with one hand against the wall, I reach down and ease my erection toward the bowl so I don't paint the elegant ceiling yellow.

Out in the kitchen, I open and close the empty cabinets realizing quickly I forgot a few important things. I don't even have coffee.

"Dammit," I growl, heading for the bedroom to put on clothes. I jerk faded jeans over my hips and a gray tee over my head. Scooping up a baseball cap, I'm out the door.

Two minutes later I steer The Beast into town, searching for coffee and sustenance. It's deserted, of course, since half the population is at church and the other half is sleeping it off. When I was a kid, the closest grocery store was two towns over. Thankfully, someone's opened one here since then.

I pull up outside the building I'll be painting tomorrow. The sign reads, "Pack n Save Poboy Shop," and it's adjacent to the hardware store.

A little bell rings over the door when I enter, but the place is empty. Only a guy in a ball cap sits behind the register studying his phone. I grab a plastic basket and make my way through the aisles quickly, grabbing a loaf of bread, coffee, filters. The refrigerated section has a limited supply, but I grab a package of ground beef, sausages, what looks like a decent steak. Cheese and a carton of cream, and I return to the front.

The guy puts his phone down and quickly rings me up, placing my items in the plastic bags hanging beside him. I look up and read the menu. The listing is a full range of specialty sandwiches from pastrami on rye; to turkey, apple, Brie, and bacon; to New Orleans muffulettas; and Cajun shrimp and oysters.

My stomach growls just reading it.

"Hey," I say, giving the guy a nod.

"How's it going," he answers without looking up.

"How long has this place been open?"

He doesn't smile. "'bout five years."

"You the owner?"

Dark eyes evaluate me. "No."

He goes back to scanning, and it looks like that's all I'm getting.

I try again. "I'll be honest, when I lived here, there weren't many people of color in Oceanside Village."

"Still aren't."

I think a moment, and as a last-ditch effort, I hold out my hand. "Jackson Cane. I used to live here. I'll be painting your storefront starting tomorrow."

Brown eyes move from my outstretched hand to my face. "It's not my storefront."

I think he's going to leave me hanging, but he catches my hand in a firm shake. "André Fontenot."

"Good to meet you, André." I motion to the sign. "You make the sandwiches?"

"Yep." I'm all bagged up. His work is done. "Thirty-two fifty."

Digging in my pocket, I pull out two twenties and hand them over. "I'll stop in tomorrow and try one. Which do you recommend?"

"Depends on what you're in the mood for."

"Fair enough." I nod, heading for the door. "I'll be working every day for a week at least. Maybe I'll try them all."

"Suit yourself."

His answer makes me chuckle. I'm getting nothing out of André I don't earn.

Pausing for a moment, I look up at the two-story buildings — my project. The paint's flaking off all of them, and I'd like to give them a good once-over before I start tomorrow.

I'll come back after I've had a cup of coffee and eaten something. Pulling the driver's side door, I'm greeted with the usual *pop!* It's a far cry from my

Audi, but I couldn't give a shit. I place the bag on the bench seat and slide in.

* * *

It's early afternoon when I make it back into town. I've left the truck at home, and I'm on foot this time. It's not far enough to drive unless you're carrying perishables.

The sun beats down strong, and sweat traces a line down the center of my back. I'll need to get an early start tomorrow if I'm going to beat the hottest part of the day. I'm keeping construction-worker hours now, not lawyer hours.

Stopping at the first building, I peer through the leaded-glass windows. When I was a kid, this was a five and dime store. Emberly's aunt owned it, and I remember she kept a barrel of candy at the front register. She'd told me why once, but I can't remember. Something about a book she'd read... *Little House on the Prairie* shit.

The main thing I remember is it was full of hard candy, similar to Jolly Ranchers but a homemade variety. I was addicted to the cinnamon ones, and even though they were a nickel, she'd let me have them for free. I must've eaten twenty of those damn things a day. My mouth was always on fire.

Cupping my hands over my eyes, I see the place has been completely cleaned out except for the front register. A heavy wooden table is positioned against the back wall, and the shelves that extend to the ceiling are full of what look like baking supplies.

A large farm-style sink is beside two ovens stacked against the wall and on the other side is a refrigerator. It looks like somebody's opening a bakeshop, and it's pretty damn girlie—all whitewash and ribbons and dried flowers and twig clusters everywhere.

Wyatt gave me three different colors for the buildings—light blue, a peachy beige, and sand with black shutters. This place should be the peachy beige, I think.

Moving down to the hardware store, a few customers are inside. Wyatt is behind the counter bagging an order. I'm surprised. When I lived here nothing was open on Sundays. A quick glance tells me noon to six for this place today. Every other day begins at ten.

My new boss catches my eye, and I give him a nod. He waves for me to come inside, and I go up to the counter. The person he's helping grabs his bags and takes off out the door.

"Ready to start tomorrow?" Wyatt asks.

"Yep, bright and early." Motioning with the swatches, I say, "Peachy beige for the cake place. Light blue for you, and this fleshy sand for the poboy shop."

He nods. "Works for me."

"I'll need to get the supplies. You here early?"

He frowns and holds up a finger. I wait as he reaches under the counter, taking out a small metal box. A set of keys is inside, and he pulls one off and hands it to me.

"Lose this, and I'll dock your pay a hundred dollars."

I almost laugh. "You own a hardware store. You can make a new key for free."

"But I'll have to change all the locks, and that's a pain in the ass."

A quick nod, and I take it. "Understood." Stepping back, I motion next door. "I'll set up the scaffolding and arrange it so it doesn't impede your business."

"Good thinking." He gives me that weird, knowing look he gave me earlier. It makes me uncomfortable, like he has some secret on me, and he's going to whip it out when I'm not looking.

"Okay, then." I back toward the door. "I'll let you get back to your customers."

Out on the street, I walk in the direction of the poboy shop. I've got the cottage pretty stocked, but a muffuletta and a glass of pinot sound good for tonight.

André is inside, and he's slammed. It's early for dinner, so I keep walking further into the old neighborhood. It's a road I remember well, and my chest grows tighter with each step. Without realizing, I've put myself on a path down memory lane.

Everything changes as I get closer to the main cluster of houses forming the tiny garden district. The town is laid out around a collection of twenty or so houses in a four-block radius. It's where the original "founders" planned a neighborhood village. The stragglers, newcomers, transients, and business-owners planted their cottages and shotgun houses on the fringes or they lived over the businesses they owned.

My hands are in the pockets of my jeans as I follow the sidewalk. The trees are ancient and otherworldly. Their trunks are dark wood, nearly black, and thicker, as big around as two adults. The branches are heavy and curved, almost reaching to the ground, and covered in dark green leaves.

I'm thinking about painting, stretching a canvas, when I look up, and I'm at the corner.

It hits me like a gut punch. The old house takes up the entire block with its curved porches and arched latticework. The yard is pristine as always — crepe myrtles and gardenia bushes. It's too late for the gardenias, but the bushes are thick with leaves. Other bushes are dotted with cranberry-red clusters of flowers.

My breath is shallow as my eyes rise higher to the cedar shake roof, to her old window hidden behind the tall oak tree. One thick branch extends like a ramp from the ledge to the ground. I involuntarily clutch my stomach as a phantom memory assaults my mind.

I can see Ember swinging over that narrow gap between the roof and the tree. She was quick and nimble. She moved like a dancer, sure and strong...

"Hello! You there?" The strong female voice cuts through my internal distress.

It's stern and authoritative. It's so familiar.

"Young man!" she insists. "This is private property!"

Pushing off the painted fence, I turn to see the woman I remember well. From her startled expression and the way her eyebrows shoot up, I can tell she remembers me, too.

"Jack?" It's just above a whisper. "Jack Lockwood?"

"Hello, Miss Marjorie." I gesture to her fence. "I'm sorry. I didn't mean to be on your land. I just... I..."

I don't know what to say to her. She never wanted me here. Anytime I was, I was sneaking around, or I would sit in my car out there at the

75

corner, waiting until I saw Ember dash across the road and into the woods just beyond the settlement.

The wild woods with the path that led all the way to the shore, to our place. The place where we would meet.

"What are you doing here?"

I have to confess, I don't know why everyone keeps asking me the same question. "It's my home. I came back to see if anything has changed." *That's a new reason. Is it true?*

"You weren't supposed to come back."

She's never looked this way in my memory— confused, anxious... afraid? I don't care about this woman standing in front of me. I didn't care about her as a teen, and I sure as hell haven't changed my mind. Only one question is burning in the top of my mind.

"How is she?" Nostalgia, longing, regret... all the feelings of loss twist together in my chest.

Her mother's lips tighten, and I see her fear turn to fury. "The same as she ever was."

"What does that mean?" I don't intend for my tone to be forceful. Still, it came out as a challenge.

"It means she's still better off without you." With that, Marjorie Warren turns on her heel and storms into her enormous home, slamming the door.

I'm left staring at the mansion, knowing the words aren't right. They can't be right.

Only... what made Ember start believing them? At some point after I left, something changed. I remember that night, talking to my father, seeing the proof it was over...

I slowly return the way I came. Passing the poboy shop, I decide I'm not hungry. Talking to Marjorie has left me feeling exhausted and beat down. Everyone keeps asking me the same question — why am I here?

I'd thought it was to clear my head, get some perspective on work, but now I'm thinking I came here for another reason. Something in me needs to put the past to rest. I need to close this door. I need to write the end to this chapter of my life.

Back in the cottage, I pull out my laptop and do something I've fought against for years. I open a search engine and type the name Emberly Rose Warren. My finger actually hesitates before I hit Enter and wait.

In a blink, the page fills with entries, but none of them are her. One is a stripper, which almost makes me laugh. Clicking the Images tab turns up nothing. She's not here.

The answer to my question won't be found that easily.

Chapter 6

Ember

Inside the narrow box, I'm strapped down, unable to move. A loud noise and a sudden jerk forward, my head snaps up while my shoulders are held firmly in place. Sound is muffled. The darkness is green, with only flickers of iridescent turquoise like the sun on fish scales or headlights in the rain.

I cry for my dad. I cry for my sister, but no one answers.

Then the water comes.

It streams in through the walls in smooth arcs. It rises up from the floor, a black torrent touching my feet, my ankles…

It comes so fast my breathing is tight with panic.

It's at my knees.

It's at my waist.

It's at my chest…

Strong hands grip me, pulling me out of the watery grave. My eyes squeeze tightly shut, and I hold onto my savior's neck. It's a man. He smells like cedar and cinnamon…

Cinnamon.

It's not a man.

It's a boy.

I sit on his lap, my legs around his waist, and he holds me tightly against his chest. We're both naked, and our skin is flush against each other's. It's soothing and warm. My fingers lightly trace the lines on his back, and I press my lips against his neck, tasting the salt on his skin.

He holds me, one hand at the back of my head, fingers threaded in my hair. The other is around my back, holding me steady.

Something incredible just happened, something powerful and life changing. Together we climbed a mountain and jumped off into the expanse. We flew through the air and touched the stars, let the rainbows slip through our fingers...

Blinking slowly, I open my eyes to a hazy awareness. In this place between consciousness and dreams, I feel him so distinctly inside of me. I taste him so clearly. My body hums with the energy of my fading orgasm, and his scent lingers in my nose. It takes several seconds to recover, to understand where I am.

To realize it was only a dream.

I blink at the painted wood walls, the fan turning slowly, the long shadows tracing up the corners of the room with each oscillation.

Reality hits me all at once like a punch to the heart. I sit up and look around. I'm dressed in a thin white tank and panties, and it's early morning.

"Oh my God." I drop my head into my hands with a groan.

I haven't dreamed of Jackson in... well, a week, I guess.

Damn him.

Ripping the sheets aside, I climb out of bed and walk slowly to the kitchen area of my studio apartment. My legs tremble like I've just run a mile, but it's all in my mind. He's not here.

"Get a grip, Emberly," I mutter, picking up the kettle and filling it with tap water. I set it on the small stovetop and flick the heat to high.

I won't do this again. I won't dwell on the past because my present is actually pretty great. Tabby's idea of taking Coco to hand out samples on the boardwalk yesterday paid off, and I have five orders for this week alone.

"Five!" I whisper to no one.

I should get a cat...

Either way, one woman asked for a three-tiered chocolate-pepper cake with elaborate, buttercream rose decorations for a dinner party of thirty. That's three hundred dollars plus a seventy-five dollar delivery charge!

Two other people wanted simple six-inch rounds for the week's dessert. Another man wanted a fruit tart. Combined with Betty Pepper's penis, I could make a thousand dollars this week. Granted, my profit after supplies wouldn't be that much, but still.

Holding the coffee press, I do the *I'm making money* dance. A loud banging outside my open window makes me squeal and almost throw grounds everywhere.

Shit! I forgot—Wyatt shoved a slip of paper under my door last week saying he'd hired someone to paint the storefronts. It's about time. The three of us pay a tiny fee each month for "beautification," and I swear, I was beginning to think he'd pocketed that money.

Tiptoeing to the balcony, I peek around the corner to see what's happening. Down below, on the opposite end of the row, a tallish guy in an ancient-looking grey tee, jeans, and a baseball cap is assembling scaffolding in front of Betty's market/poboy shop. I can't see his face, but his arms flex as he twists and hammers the metal rods. *Nice physique...*

Not that I give a shit.

I only care about two things right now — making my business a huge success and making a home for Coco and me. Men are off my list for the duration.

The shrill whistle of the kettle breaks my concentration, and I skip over to pour the boiling water over the coffee grounds before I head to the bathroom for a quick shower. It's bright and early, and I've got to get busy if I'm going to meet the demand of being a soon to be regionally famous baker.

* * *

Two hours later, all three of the sponges for the spicy chocolate cake are waiting on the cooling rack, and I'm leaning over the heavy wooden table studying a book of decorative frosting techniques when the little bell over my door rings.

Tabby flies inside. "Are you okay?"

She crosses the room reaching for my hands, and the fear in her enormous eyes makes my stomach plunge. Terror shoots through my chest, and I pass her, rushing to the door.

"What happened?" The apron is over my head, and I'm grabbing my shoes. "Is Coco okay? What's going on?"

"What?" Confusion lines her face. "Coco's fine — I mean, as far as I know..."

Stopping at the door, I turn and glare at her as my arm drops. "Tabby! What the hell are you thinking barging in here like that and scaring me to death?"

I lean against the glass door, trying to calm my breathing and feeling super annoyed. My heart is beating so fast it hurts.

"Are you serious?" Tabby's crosses the room to where I stand, studying my expression.

"What the hell, Tabs?"

"What have you been doing today?"

Pushing her hands away, I walk to the table where my book is open to the page on alternative piping nozzles for buttercream roses. "I've been working on this cake order since seven. I need a Wilton 2D star tip, but I'd have to order it online..."

She watches me chewing her lip, and I frown. "What small-town drama has you so wound up?"

The bell rings above the door, and in walks my mother holding Coco's hand, stopping just inside. Her eyes are strained as well.

"Mommy, cake! Let's make cake!" Coco chants as she skips across the wood floor to me, her long hair bouncing all around.

She's wearing a bright yellow gingham dress with little strawberries around the smocked collar. I stand and swing her up on my hip.

"What are you doing here?" I give her a quick kiss on her rosebud lips.

"Granny said I can play with you today!"

"She did?" Frowning, I turn to my mother, who is peering through the window in the direction of Betty's shop. "Doesn't Coco have preschool?"

My mother's blue eyes slide from the glass to me, and she hesitates, her chin slightly lifted. She was acting weird last night when we got back from the strand, but Coco had fallen asleep on my shoulder. I didn't have time for whatever lecture she might offer, so I went straight to the bathroom, bathed my whining baby and put her to bed before saying a quick goodnight and heading back here to crash.

Walking slowly to where I stand with Coco on my hip, she clutches her square handbag tight against her stomach as if it's a shield. "I thought you might like to have her with you today."

"I want her with me every day, but you said preschool is important to get her ready for kindergarten." I don't add the tuition is outrageous.

"Missing one day won't hurt her." My mother looks at my best friend a moment.

They hold each other's gaze as if searching for something. I have no idea what, nor do I care. I meant it when I said I want Coco with me all the time, but of course, my mother picks the busiest week of my life to bend her rules.

"It's great to have her here, Mom, next time, just, you know, check with me first?" Putting my daughter down, I wrap my long brown apron over my denim cutoffs and white tee knotted at my waist.

My daughter walks around the large, open space while I face my mother, waiting to see if that's all she has to say. Again, she hesitates a few moments in silence as if she's waiting on me to do something.

"Is that all? Because I've got five cakes to make this week, and I need to get to work."

Her brow lowers, and she turns on her heel headed for the door. "I have to run a few errands. I'll come back and get her for lunch and naptime."

My jaw tightens at her words. "You don't have to. I can keep her and have her home after supper.

Unless she gets too hot. I'll text you."

Standing at the door, she shakes her blonde hair. "I'll be back." With that, she leaves, and I exchange a glance with Tabby.

"Keep an eye on her just a second." Apron off, I jog to the stairs leading up to my apartment.

Throwing open the closet, I drop to my knees and dig in the box of toys I keep for days like this. I need to shop for new ones now that she's started preschool. Still, a plastic bucket of assorted play-dough molds is inside — perfect! I dig deeper, pulling out several Ziploc bags holding different colors of the squishy stuff.

Hopping up, I hear the muffled sound of voices coming from below. It's early on a Monday, and I can't imagine who it could be. One is Tabby, but the other is deeper, a man's voice. *Could it be the fellow who wanted the fruit tart?*

Hurrying down, I'm at the bottom of the steps reaching for the door…

I'm still in the dim-lit hall, my hand grasping the cool metal knob, when the world shifts into slow motion.

That voice…

Momentum carries me forward and I push the door aside and my eyes lock with his.

I can't breathe. All the air disappears from the room. I grip the door handle. My knees are liquid… I'm going to fall.

The plastic bucket slips from my grip, and it lands on the wood floor with a loud crash and a rippling clatter as everything spills out.

"Play-dough!" Coco cries, oblivious to my distress.

She dashes across the room to retrieve her toys, but I haven't looked away from Jackson Cane standing in the middle of my bakery.

Last night he was in my bed, in my dreams.

He's only ever been in my dreams — for more than ten years.

Now he's standing in front of me, flesh and bone, in the middle of my store.

Like he can just walk back into my life…

Out of the past…

Just like that.

He doesn't move. He only blinks at me, seeming stunned. He reaches up and slowly pulls the cap off his head. He cut his hair.

All of these things happen so fast, until my daughter's words break the spell. "Can I play, Mommy?"

Jackson's blue eyes move down to her and up to me again, down and up as if putting us together.

"Yes," I say softly.

She scoops up the plastic bucket, marching to the large table like nothing is happening, like I'm not spiraling through space. In my peripheral vision, I see Tabby's hand cover her mouth, but my brain still hasn't recovered from the lightning strike. It takes a few more breaths before I'm able to speak.

We both speak at once. "What are you doing here?"

His voice adds a depth to my softer one. It's a vibration that echoes in my core. My breath comes in pants, but from somewhere inside me rises a strength I didn't know I possessed.

I take a step to the center of the room, in his direction.

"I never left." An edge is in my voice.

He shakes his head, his eyes never leaving mine. "No. That's not right."

He looks to my daughter, who has climbed onto the long bench by the window, pulling her pretend baking dough out of the bags. Tabby moves to Coco and twists her long brunette curls into a cute little bun on her head. My daughter starts to sing one of her made-up songs as she pats the dough in her small hands.

She's pretending to be me. She's always pretending to be me, and I watch as his expression turns slowly to confusion and then anger. My teeth clench and all the past is consumed in a tidal wave of protective rage rolling through my chest.

"It's time for you to go." My voice is level, and his eyes are back on mine. I'm not smiling. "I don't know why you're in Oceanside, but there's nothing for you here. Not anymore."

The words twist pain in my stomach, and I watch as he passes a large hand over his mouth. The muscle in his jaw flexes, and he puts the cap back on his head, going to the door. It's only then that I recognize the faded jeans, the beat up gray tee... the cap. He's the man working for Wyatt.

Why the hell would he be working for Wyatt?

He's through the door and out of my bakery just as I sink to my knees, then to my butt, right there on the floor in the middle of my shop.

Tabby runs to me, dropping to sit in front of me. Her green eyes are round, and she's holding both of my hands as the waves of emotion rise and fall, crashing and churning in my chest.

"Jackson's back," she says.

"He's painting the building."

Painting...

My eyes slide closed, and the tears fall.

Chapter 7

Jack

Storming out of her shop in a rage, I almost flatten Wyatt standing on the porch unlocking his door. "Sorry," I growl, hopping off the walkway and onto the street.

"Where you going?" he calls after me.

"I'll be right back." I'm walking fast in the direction of the cottage.

I'm furious, but I can't put my finger on one single reason why.

I'd walked up to the door for a courtesy call—just to let the business owner know I would be painting and setting up scaffolding.

Just to give a heads up.

When I'd seen Tabby inside with the little girl, I'd gone in and been greeted with a repeat performance of Saturday night—inexplicable bitchiness. I wasn't putting up with it anymore, and I told her as much...

Then everything changed.

Ember walked in the room looking like everything good in the world I'd ever lost as a nervous teen starting out on my own in a new city. She was the only dream I'd ever wanted. She was the only thing I'd ever regretted leaving behind, and she was just as beautiful as ever.

Her dark hair hung in waves around her shoulders, and her brown eyes flecked with caramel held mine. Her body was covered up by some brown apron-thing, but her slim arms were bare, her long legs were bare, her bare feet... Her skin still so smooth, my fingers longed to touch her. She was still so damn perfect.

Slamming open the door to the cottage, I snatch the phone off the base and hit call back. It rings twice before my father answers.

"Randall speaking," he says, a hint of annoyance in his tone.

"It's me, Jackson."

"Oh, hello, son, what's on your mind?"

"She's here, Dad. Living in Oceanside. She has a business and a child. She never left." Even I can hear the rage seething in my tone. I'm ready to rip someone limb from limb. I'm just trying to figure out who. "Why did you lie to me?"

"I don't know what you're talking about." His casual tone fuels my anger.

"Emberly Warren. I just saw her. She's here in Oceanside."

"So what?" He exhales a dismissive laugh. "You're there in Oceanside. Are you trying to say *you* never left?"

"You told me she was sent away after I went to college. Her mother had arranged for her to marry a preacher's kid or some kind of bullshit, and she'd moved on without me."

"I told you the same story I was given." His condescension is almost more than I can tolerate right now, but he continues. "Either way, it's in the past. That town gave you nothing but grief—"

"And you made millions destroying it."

"Karma is a bitch." He has the nerve to gloat.

"Don't act like you did it for me. I never took a dime of that money —"

"Still, you left Oceanside poised for greatness. You focused on your studies and made it all the way to the top of your class. You went to one of the most prestigious law schools in the country and became the youngest partner to join the ranks of the oldest firm on the East Coast. Do you think you would have done all those things holding onto a little girl back home?"

I don't need him to recite my résumé to me. He can't begin to understand what I wanted when I left this place. Only Ember knew. She's the only one who listened to me when I talked and looked at me like I could rule the world — even if it was just from a little bedroom community on the coast.

My father thinks I want all these things. He has no idea how once I'd lost her I didn't have anything else. He'll never understand how I buried the pain in the grind of studies and research and cases and claims.

"She wasn't meant for you," he concludes.

It's the only thing I might possibly accept — if I were in the mood to accept any of this.

"She has a little girl." My voice is quieter, my mind returning to the small child leaning over the table.

Her dark hair and eyes are just like Ember's. The sun shining through the window had lit her porcelain skin, highlighting her olive features chiaroscuro.

"It must be his. Perhaps it's why she's back in Oceanside. To be near her mother." He says it like it's the logical response.

Only it's not logical.

Ember never got along with her mother.

None of this is logical.

None of it makes sense.

When I saw her today, she looked at me with all the shock and pain and hurt and anger I've felt these last ten years as though *I'd* betrayed *her*. There's more to this story.

"I'm going to find out what happened." My voice is calm, but I hear the edge. I know he hears it as well.

"I love you, son."

"I'll be in touch."

I slam the phone down and walk the short distance to town fast, burning off the excess anger. I can't talk to her now — she doesn't want to talk. Her words burn in my stomach like acid. *There's nothing here for you. Not anymore.*

I'm at the Pack n Save, and my pulse has slowed. Pausing, I look toward the cake shop. It's quiet and still, in direct opposition to how I feel inside, to what I'm sure is happening behind those walls. It takes all my willpower not to storm in there and take her, pull her in my arms and force her to tell me the truth, tell me what happened, what made her give up on us.

The tension is back, burning hot in my chest, and I start walking again. Following the road, I make quick progress to the end of the short strip of businesses. I pass the small bank that's been here since I was a kid, a little retail and knickknack store, an antiques store, and the post office. The last building on the corner is a gas station. I hesitate long enough for a car to pull up to one of the pumps, then turning on my heel, I storm all the way back up the street.

My head is full of thoughts — ten years is a long time. While I spent it losing myself in work, neither of us are teenagers anymore. Ember has always been smart and strong. She's always known what she wanted. I remember how she was with me. Telling me to kiss her. Telling me to teach her everything. I won't take that for granted.

She's a mom...

My stomach burns when I think of how I felt when I left here. I had planned to come back and marry her after college. She was supposed to have *my* baby. A low growl rises in my throat, and I'm back at the scaffolding.

Wyatt is out on his porch. "I'm not paying you to walk around. I'm paying you to paint."

Glaring at him, I bite my tongue to keep from lashing out with all the fury ripping through my chest.

Instead, I pick up the brush and climb the scaffolding to the second floor where I left everything. I crack open a gallon of sandy beige and get started.

* * *

My arm aches, and I'm covered in sweat when I finish the second floor exterior. Hours have passed, the sun is directly overhead, and my mind hasn't stopped turning over what happened this morning.

Hour after hour.

Over and over.

Glancing up, a bead of sweat rolls down my cheek. The heat is blasting like an oven. It's too hot to keep working, so I head down to get food from André.

I can't stop my eyes from flickering in the direction of the third building on the row. It's quiet. No one has come in or out since this morning. As much as I tried to stop, I kept watching for a crack in the door.

Grabbing a rag, I wipe my face and step into the poboy shop. André is in his usual spot behind the register, only this time his expression is slightly more approachable.

"Jackson Cane," he says, holding out a bottle of water. "You're working hard."

"Thanks." I take it and twist the top off, finishing it in one long gulp. "What's the special for today?"

"Today is California Reuben, or what some people call a Rachel."

"A Rachel?"

"Roasted turkey and Swiss on rye with sauerkraut and Russian dressing."

My eyebrows rise. "I'll take it."

He walks down behind the glass case and lifts a large sandwich into wax paper, placing it in a white bag with a paper napkin and a fork.

"Side of pickle," he holds up what looks like a kosher spear in a skinny bag. "And a pot of my famous potato salad."

"Damn," I say with a laugh. "When word gets out, you won't be able to stay here."

"Then how will we keep this place integrated?"

I glance up, and his brow is lowered. "Yeah, sorry about that," I say, feeling like an ass. "It was kind of a boneheaded thing to say."

He stares at me a moment longer, until finally a crack in the wall. "I won't hold it against you."

"Thanks."

I dig in my pocket to pay him for the food. "Throw in a Coke and how much for the water?"

"Water's on the house. Don't want you dying of heat stroke out there." He punches the register and hands me back my change. "So you're from Oceanside?"

"Grew up here. Just me and my dad."

"Is he still around?"

"He moved to Connecticut when I was in college."

The bell rings, and none other than Betty Pepper walks through the door. Her jaw immediately drops, and I notice she clutches her purse. "As I live and breathe. Jack Lockwood?"

"Hi, Mrs. Pepper."

She doesn't move from the doorway. "When did you get back in town? Are you staying in the cottage? Does your father know you're here? Does Marjorie?"

She speaks so fast, I'm surprised she doesn't hyperventilate.

"I think that's a..." Looking at the ceiling, I run through her list of questions. "Yes to all. You've got fifteen more to go."

Her brow wrinkles. "Fifteen?"

"Questions."

A short laugh turns into a throat clearing behind the counter. Betty scowls, and André leans back against the wall, arms crossed.

"Good morning, André," she says, giving him a nod. "Is Thelma coming in today?"

"Yes, ma'am, she'll be in after lunch. Any minute now, I guess."

The old lady turns to me again, her eyes quickly scanning my clothes, my paint-stained hands. "Are you the man Wyatt hired to paint the buildings?" Her voice is pure astonishment. "Why aren't you off somewhere being a lawyer?"

"I missed home," I say, walking toward her to the door. She jumps out of my way quickly. "I saw the flier up at the gas station and asked Wyatt for the job. Since I was on the paint crew in high school, he knew I could do it."

"When is the last time you painted anything?"

"Ten minutes ago." My hand is on the doorknob, and I'm ready to end the inquisition. *Twelve left.*

Her eyes narrow. "I meant before today."

Movement outside catches my eye. I look in time to see Ember placing her daughter in the back seat of a bike and fastening her belt. A large box is in the front basket.

"Is she married?" The question is out before I can stop it.

"Who?" Betty steps forward and peers out the window. "Emberly? Why, no. She never married."

My lips tighten, and something shifts in my chest. I watch her climb on the bike, her toned legs flexing as she pedals. My throat catches, and I want to stop her.

She's still dressed in denim cutoffs, but her white tee is gone. She's wearing a maroon tank top with a short-sleeved cardigan over it. Just as I step out onto the long porch, she dashes past, standing in the pedals and disappearing quickly up the street in the direction of Oceanside Beach.

I watch as she disappears, not looking back. I'm left standing in front of the store, staring at the dirt rising from her tires.

Chapter 8

Ember

Staying down is not what I do. I only sit on the floor bracing against the pain radiating from my still-shattered heart one minute before I'm pushing up, angrily wiping the tears away, and getting back to business.

"Look, Mommy!" Coco holds up a flower made of scraps of Play-dough. "Roses!"

"It's beautiful." I swallow the torrent of emotions in my chest. "You just gave mommy an idea."

Taking small strips of wax paper, I put them on my lazy Susan and proceed to make a lavender rose using my regular piping tip and short strips of icing, round and round.

"That's really smart," Tabby says, watching as she takes the round sponge cakes from the cooling rack. "We'll have to rename the place Ember and Co."

"Coco!" My daughter cries, smashing her rose into a pancake with her palm. "Ember and Coco."

"I like it," I say, taking a cleansing breath and stepping to the side to kiss the top of her head. "Mommy's assistant."

"So I should check the want ads?" Tabby teases.

"Of course not." I shake my head and return to work.

Beside me are bags of lavender, pink, and green buttercream. My insides are still shaky, but I'm glad to have the distractions of work and these two. The wreath cake is finished and in the refrigerator by eleven, leaving just enough time to assemble one of the smaller, two-tiered rounds needed for this afternoon.

"I'll take these down and leave a few more fliers at the hotel front desks," I say, tying them together. "If you see my momma, tell her I took Coco with me."

"It's so hot." Tabby walks with me to the door. "Think you'll make it without them melting?"

Coco is on my hip, and I lean into the glass, looking up the scaffolding. My insides are tight, but I see it's empty. The porch is also empty. No sign of him.

"I'll move fast."

She follows me out, and we quickly load the cakes in my front basket. "If orders like these keep coming in, you'll have to invest in a car."

"No." I quickly buckle Coco into her seat behind mine. "I'll figure out a way to make Dixie work. See you tomorrow."

"Are you coming back here tonight?"

Chewing my lip, I look at the scaffolding again then up to my open balcony. "I don't know."

She nods, and I stand in the pedals to get momentum. I'm pushing hard, doing my best to pick up speed when a tall form emerges from the poboy shop.

My heart plunges, and I push harder. We fly past, making our way quickly through the four-block garden district, past my mother's house on the corner, and onto the trail leading out to the strand.

I leave nothing but dust on the road behind us.

* * *

Both of my new customers are impressed and bragging about their cakes when I leave them. They offer to recommend me to friends in the area, which I desperately need to keep my business growing. I also get permission to leave fliers at two of the more expensive resorts. I take business cards for the head chefs at the restaurants, although I'm repeatedly told they handle desserts in-house.

"Ups and downs," I say with a sigh, holding Coco's hand and walking to my bike Dixie. "Nobody said starting a business was easy."

Coco back in her place, I pedal us a little closer up the coast to a portion of beach hidden from the tourist traffic. I park Dixie and unpack the picnic lunch Tabby made for us while I decorated the cakes.

Sitting on my towel, I can't help remembering how I know this little cove. Jackson had taken me here. It's where we'd meet when we didn't want to go all the way out to the strand.

I watch Coco running up and down, chasing the waves rushing in and out, and my mind travels to when it would be me out there in the surf, dancing to show off for him in my itsy bitsy bikini. He'd sit on the sand, dark skin shimmering in the sun, looking like a god. He'd smile, and my stomach would flip.

I'd dance up in front of him and kick the sprays of water. The little drops would hit his heated skin, and he'd be up on one fluid movement, chasing me. I couldn't outrun him, and he'd toss me over his shoulder, carrying me out into the swirling cold breakers. I'd squeal as if I didn't love it, and he'd lower me. Our lips would meet, and it would be salt water and cinnamon. Bathing suits pushed aside, thumbs sliding back and forth across beaded nipples. My breath would catch as hard muscle met slippery heat...

Coco runs into my arms like a little bird, and I slip bite-sized crackers into her mouth. She only stays until the edge is off her hunger, then she's right out in the waves again. She's as much of a water bug as I ever was.

I thought I could depend on Jackson in those days, but he broke me. He ripped out my heart and left me bleeding and devastated. Resting my cheek on my knees, I watch my daughter play and do my best to blink away my tears, to put the memories in the past where they belong.

I owe Coco stability, a mother who can't be broken.

I have to be strong.

It doesn't matter if he's back.

* * *

It's late when Coco and I arrive at my mother's house. The sun is hidden low in the trees, and blue-green shadows stretch over the sidewalks. Hopping off the bike, I maneuver it through the low, white fence surrounding the yard, keeping a hand on my daughter.

Taking her out of her seat, I leave the bike parked at the gate. Her sleepy head is on my shoulder, and her arms and legs go around my waist. I can't help thinking of a baby koala, and the warmth filling my chest soothes that old wound.

"Emberly?" My mother quickly steps into the foyer when we enter.

I gesture to Coco asleep on my shoulder, and she gives me a tight-lipped nod. Impatience tightens my throat, and I reconsider my earlier plan to spend the night here. The idea of waking up alone in my bed with the balcony doors wide open and Jackson right outside sends my imagination down a rabbit-hole of impossible possibilities.

Not going there.

At the same time…

Not going there with my mother either.

She silently hated Jackson when he was here the first time, and her hatred turned verbal after he left. The last thing I can cope with on top of everything else is the nonstop lecturing, warning, badgering, questioning.

Without hesitation, I step into the shower with Coco in my arms. She whines in my ear, and her little arms tighten over my shoulders. I tilt the showerhead so it's not pointing in her face and wash the salt water out of our hair.

I read somewhere ocean water is actually really good for your skin and hair. It's probably fiction, but I decide tonight to believe it and don't bother with the soap or lathering us up too much.

Grit gone, I wrap us in a thick, expensive towel and head to bed.

* * *

"I guess she has to go to preschool today," I say, carrying Coco into the kitchen where my mother sits at the small table immaculately dressed and holding a cup of coffee.

I, by contrast, am in my cutoffs and the maroon tank I wore yesterday. My hair is twisted up in a messy bun, and Coco is on my hip, complaining that she can't spend the day "baking," riding bikes, and swimming in the sea with me.

My mother studies me. "I thought you might need her with you yesterday."

"Why?" I deposit my daughter in a chair at the table and step over to pour myself a cup of coffee.

As much as I hate to admit it, I do appreciate having coffee ready when I wake up... in an air-conditioned bedroom with my little girl's foot against my face.

"I thought he might try to see you." Momma is still watching me, and those words pull me up short.

"You knew he was back?"

"He stopped by the house Sunday evening."

Betrayal flashes in my chest. "You didn't tell me?"

"I didn't see the point." She sets down her cup and leans back in her chair. "I knew he'd find you eventually."

Eventually... She could have fucking warned me. She could have saved me that lightning strike.

Sarcasm drips in my tone. "I'm surprised you risked her being around such a negative influence."

She sniffs and lifts her coffee. "Most men are put off by other men's children."

I try to swallow the knot in my throat. I always knew Marjorie Warren was sneaky. Now I'm convinced she's just plain evil.

"Colette will go to school today." That gets a whine out of my daughter. My mother's response is firm, albeit far more gentle with her granddaughter. "There is more to life than baking."

I let that jab go, turning to my baby instead. "I can't wait to hear all about the new monster." I hug her tightly, rubbing her back and kissing her little shoulder. "I'll make a cupcake for him."

Suddenly Coco is far more interested in returning to school. I pick up my bag and give my mother one final glare before leaving.

If I thought it would sell, I'd create an ass cake with her face in the center. As it is, I have a penis to make. And some other, more respectable items.

Either I'm lucky or he's inside one of the buildings. I see no sign of Jackson when I arrive at my place. Wheeling Dixie into the alley, I quickly fasten the chain, though it's not really necessary in Oceanside, and enter through the back door.

A few moments later, my apron is on, and I'm shaking out the flour to make the puff pastry crust for the fruit tart. I left a list of ingredients with Tabby yesterday. A quick check in the refrigerator, and I see she bought them all.

Raspberries, strawberries, kiwis, blackberries, and blueberries sit in pretty little green baskets on the shelves. The bell over the door rings and I look up to see my best friend checking over her shoulder as she dashes inside.

Today she's wearing a red and white gingham blouse with the sleeves rolled up. Her dark hair is pinned up around her head in curls, like a classic 1950s pinup. Her eyes are dramatically outlined, and her lips are red velvet — as usual.

"I should keep more fruit in here," I say, looking in the refrigerator again. "For Coco."

"Where did you sleep last night?" Tabby actually sounds concerned.

"I stayed at Mom's." Closing the door, the ingredients for the custard filling are in my hands. "We didn't get back until late."

"Thank goodness." Her shoulders fall with her exhale. "I was worried."

"About what?" Pressing my lips together, I give her a frown. *As if.*

"Don't look at me like that." She pulls out the stool beside me. "I remember how you two were in high school. Now he's suddenly back, and looking... as good as ever."

A little growl is in my throat. "I have more important things to focus on now. Like Coco and this shop."

"Doesn't mean he isn't still out there." She nods to my torso. "Or in there."

Heat filters through my chest. "How are you managing to pay bills on all the money I pay you?"

"What money?"

"Exactly." I nod, returning to my pastry dough. "Maybe you should get a real job."

"Rude!" She drops her large hobo bag in the corner. "Are you going to talk to him?"

"Who?"

Her eyes say *Bitch, please.*

"There's nothing to say, Tabby. We broke up. Or at least we moved on." I'm kneading the pastry dough a little too hard. "Everybody else needs to move on as well."

The doorbell tings, and we look up to see both Betty Pepper and Donna White entering the store.

"Saved by the bell," I mutter.

"Don't ever say I don't deliver," Betty announces. "You say you need business, and I bring you business."

"Hey, Miss Betty." I nod, reaching for my twelve-inch tart pan and lowering the rolled crust into it. "How's it going, Donna?"

"Hi, Emberly, Tabby."

Donna White is such the demure wallflower. I confess, I was surprised Betty Pepper got her something as bold as a penis cake for her shower. I wonder if she also gave her toys...

"What can I do for you ladies?" I smile as I carefully press the dough into the tin, paying careful attention to the corners.

"Donna wants to order her wedding cake from you." Betty holds her hands up as if it's a victory. "I'm here about... what we talked about at church."

Tabby frowns like she can't remember. "What did we talk about at church? My uncle's sermon on lasciviousness?"

"Tabitha Green, you know very well that isn't a real word." Betty snaps.

"I know what you need, Miss B," I say. "Chocolate, right?"

Her eyes twinkle. "Right, but I want to be sure you have the proper fillings. The one you made last time was a little on the plain side."

"Oh!" I'm slightly taken aback. "I'm sorry. I guess, considering what it was, I didn't think you'd want a lot of extra... things."

"Obviously, we don't want anything red or yellow inside," she carries on, oblivious to my best friend turning green in the face.

Donna is blissfully ignorant of what we're discussing... at least I think she is. She walks over to the windows and looks out and to the left. I don't allow my mind to wonder what she's seeing.

"I made a cayenne pepper and chocolate cake over the weekend—"

Tabby jumps in. "Oh! That sounds perfect! Hot chocolate for a hot cake?"

Betty's nose wrinkles. "I'm not sure. I get the reflux, you know."

"Um... in that case..." I pull out my chocolate combinations cheat sheet. "I've done a chocolate cake with chocolate mousse filling and chocolate buttercream or fondant... Devil's food with coconut pecan buttercream filling and dark chocolate ganache frosting—"

"That one!" Tabby cries. "Do that one. Trust me, BP, that is the cake you want. It is so good. So good."

The older woman's lips curl. "I'm not sure about coconut. That might look like something nobody wants to see."

"It's not flaked coconut," I explain. "It's coconut flavor."

She smacks the counter with her palm. "Book it."

I scribble down the order on my notepad, and the short little lady scoots up closer. Her shoulder is just under my armpit. "How are you holding up?" Her voice is low and full of concern.

"I'm doing just fine, thanks." I nod, without meeting her eyes. "Why do you ask?"

"I swear, the whole town's buzzing." She steps back and starts pacing. "Jack Lockwood slipping in like that under cover of night... and the nerve of Wyatt giving him a job. As if the Lockwoods haven't taken enough money out of this town—"

"Isn't he staying at his mom's old cottage a few blocks away?" Donna asks, still staring through the glass.

I wish she wouldn't do that.

"That's just it," Betty continues. "His mother was a good, local girl. Your own mother's best friend." She nods to me. "And Randall Lockwood just ruined her. And Oceanside—"

"And we're working hard to bring it back," I cut her off, brightly, already sick of this conversation. "Me and Daisy with her antiques... and André! His sandwich creations are as good as anything you'd get on the strand or anywhere!"

"André's a good boy." Betty nods, and I wince. "It's why I'm having this party for his and Thelma's anniversary! I love those two like they were my own kids."

Tabby and I exchange a hopeless look, and I press my lips together. This old woman has no idea how wrong her words are—on so many levels.

"Well, I'd better get back to the store." She waddles to the door. "Donna, you stay and tell Emberly what all you want on your wedding cake. Then you come right back. I need your help with the inventory."

"Yes, ma'am," Donna says in her shy voice.

"And Emberly." Betty holds the door wide open, as she's shouting at me. "Don't you worry one bit about that Jack Lockwood. My Bucky will take good care of you."

My jaw drops as my body flashes hot and cold. I don't have time to say a single word before that old lady pulls the door shut behind her with a slam, and we watch the top of her teased grey hair marching past the window outside, headed in the direction of her store.

Chapter 9

Jack

Curtains are the first thing I see when I arrive to paint. I'm working on Wyatt's hardware store today, and sheer, white-lace curtains have appeared in all the downstairs windows of Ember's place.

It's possible she'd already planned this addition to her interior design, but I can't help thinking it has something to do with me. And I don't like it.

Light blue paint, up and down.

It's hotter than it was two days ago. My muscles have adjusted to the manual labor, and even though I'm using sunscreen and working early in the day, my skin is darker.

All three balconies have shutters, which are painted black. Betty and Wyatt's second floors are dusty and full of boxes and old fixtures — something you can't see from the street. Ember's windows are open. I'll start there tomorrow.

Light blue.

Up and down.

Sweat runs down my cheek, and my thoughts drift between my unfinished business here and the unfinished business I left behind.

First one, then the other.

Up and down.

Waves on the ocean.

Yesterday afternoon, I walked down to the little cove just outside of town. It's between here and the developed coastline of Oceanside Beach, not too far to walk or ride a bike.

Thick pine trees surround it and narrow creeks cut through the landscape. A few little footbridges are dotted around, but you have to be careful. They're old and can break without warning. The terrain keeps it from being interesting to real estate guys like my dad, but it's as beautiful as any other spot in this area.

It's where I used to take her.

Desire pulls in my chest when I remember those days. Being there felt like we were the only two people on Earth, and we acted like it. Pausing in my brush stroke, I glance down at her shop remembering all the public decency laws we broke on that little secluded stretch of beach.

Last night, I couldn't sleep. I walked up the path and stood in the street in front of these buildings. Her windows were open, and standing there, in the moonlight, I imagined how it used to be when I would come for her at night.

I've only been aware of her presence a few days, but I've noticed she's always alone. No other cars are parked around her building. It's only her and her daughter.

Light blue.

Up and down.

I'm at the end of Wyatt's building. I've done both floors, upstairs and down. All that's left are the shutters, but it's late. I'm ahead of schedule and hungry as a horse. André has been keeping me fed since I met him, and I try a new sandwich every meal. Yesterday I tried the turkey, apple, and Brie, and when I said I didn't like it, he was pissed. I tried to explain I'm not much of a Brie fan, but...

Laughing to myself, I climb down through the steel bars. When I drop to my feet, I almost shout. Ember is standing right in front of me holding a large pink box.

"Oh!" She almost falls, jerking to avoid me.

"Hey!" I reach out and catch her arm. "Were you trying to sneak past me?"

"Of course not. I didn't even know you were still here." Her cute little chin lifts and she tries to look superior.

I've seen her mother do this before, but it's all wrong on Ember. It makes me laugh, a scratchy rough-voiced noise from working in the heat and not speaking all day.

"Are you saying you wouldn't have come out if you'd thought I was still here?" Placing one hand on the wall of her building, I lean closer, inhaling lavender and cedar.

"What are you doing?" A slight tremble is in her voice.

Do I affect her as much as she does me? Are her panties wet?

"I'll start on your place tomorrow," I say. "Early."

Her slender throat moves as she swallows. "Should I stay away until you're finished?"

"You don't have to. It doesn't seem like you have a lot of customers."

"I have customers."

"Sorry." Straightening, I lower my arm and step back. "I only meant the scaffolding shouldn't be in your way. You're free to work or do whatever you need to do."

She nods and takes a wide path around me. "Thanks for letting me know."

I watch a moment as she continues up the walk, her round ass swaying in those cutoffs, her long dark waves swishing down the back of her white shirt. It's so much like something she would've worn in high school. Her top has little flowers on it...

"Ember," I call out.

She stops, but she doesn't turn around immediately. I jog the few steps to where she stands between Wyatt's and Betty's buildings. Her teeth are clenched, and I can tell she's doing her best to be stern.

"I'd like to talk to you. We need to talk." Looking down, I survey my sweaty clothes, the paint on the back of my knuckles. "I'm kind of a mess right now. Would you have dinner with me?"

"Tonight?" Her beautiful brown eyes blink wide, and I can see the caramel flecks in her irises.

"Or tomorrow?" I smile, hoping to ease the tension. "It's Friday. Date night."

Again, her brow lowers. "I have a date tomorrow night."

Now it's my turn to frown. "With who?"

"None of your business," she snaps, starting to walk again. I step in front of her, blocking her path.

"Hey — I'm sorry." My tone is gentler. "I didn't mean it like that."

"I think you did. But even if you didn't, I wouldn't go out with you. Not if you were the last man on Earth."

She tries to step around me, but I catch her shoulders to stop her. "Why not?"

"You know why not. Now let me go, Jackson Cane."

"I can't do that." Sliding my hands off her shoulders, I drop my chin. "I thought I could, but I can't."

Fire simmers in her eyes. "Is that so? So you came back thinking I'd be sitting here waiting for you?"

"No—I didn't..."

"That's right. I'm not. I have more important things than you in my life. You can keep on driving for all I care."

She pushes past me and goes into the poboy shop. I fall against the side of the building then swear. Light blue is all up the side of my back, and I've fucked up the paint on the hardware store... among other things.

Chapter 10

Ember

My insides are all shaky, and I almost dropped Betty's penis cake. "Damn Jackson Cane," I say under my breath. "Hi, André." I wave to the poboy maestro behind the counter.

"Ember Rose!" he calls out in his smooth voice. "Something for me?"

"Oh, um…" My cheeks flame red. Damn Betty Pepper and her perverted orders. "Not exactly. Is Betty in the back?" I hurry down the aisle to the door at the back of the store before he can ask to see what's in the box.

Since we both work in the food trade, André and I are always sharing our latest creations.

"Should be." The front door starts to open, and I can tell by the baseball cap it's Jackson.

"Thanks!" I push through Betty's office door, shutting it quickly behind me.

For a moment, I lean my forehead against it and listen. I'm breathing fast, and sure enough, Jackson's voice fills the store. It sounds like he and André are having a lively conversation… complete with laughter.

Jerk. I can't believe he can just stand out there and laugh and act like nothing has changed. Like he can waltz back into Oceanside, and I'll be waiting to fall at his feet. The more I think about it, the madder I get.

Turning slowly, my jaw is tight as I look around the room. The space is about the size of a small kitchen with paper and office supplies filling a tall set of metal shelves dividing it in half. Betty's wooden desk is situated in the back corner. It appears to be empty.

"Hello?" I call, and Donna White sticks her head around the corner.

"Oh, hey, Emberly. I'm just finishing this inventory."

I go to where she's sitting on a high stool holding a clipboard and a box of ballpoint pens. "Where's Miss Betty?"

"She went down to make a deposit and mail some stuff."

Hesitating, I can still hear the voices out front. "Mind if I hang out and wait for her?"

"Sure!" She leans back and returns to counting. "You have her cake?"

"Yeah." I walk around to the other side of the room. "Does she have a refrigerator or anything I can store it in? It's kind of stuffy. I don't want the icing to melt."

Donna hops down and motions for me to follow. "She has a spot cleared in the back of the refrigerated section you can use."

"So long as André doesn't see it."

We pause in front of the silver metal door. "Can I see it?" she whispers.

"Sure." I lift the lid, and inside is the dark-chocolate confection. "I tempered the chocolate to make it shine."

"It's so *big*!" Donna's face goes from bright red to pale in a matter of seconds.

"Betty said to make a cake for twenty people."

She blinks at it several more seconds then she bursts into giggles. "Oh!" She sniffs, wiping her eyes. "I'm sorry. I just... It's so shiny!" She immediately starts giggling again. "It looks so real!"

"It's what Betty wanted," I say, trying to defend myself. "And it's a paycheck for me."

"Oh, Ember..." She laughs a little more, but then her mood starts to change. "Oh, Ember," she says again, walking to her stool and slumping her shoulders.

Now I'm really confused. "Are you crying?"

"I'm sorry," she repeats, wiping her eyes quickly. "I'm just feeling a little emotional these days."

Rubbing her arm, I smile. "Well, that's normal. You're about to get married. It's a big transition."

Nodding quickly, she wipes her face with a tissue. "Right. I know you're right."

We're quiet a moment, and I leave my NC17 dessert in Betty's fridge. I don't hear voices out front anymore, but I'm not sure I should leave Donna alone.

"Is there anything else on your mind?"

She looks up at me, her watery eyes round. "Actually..." Her cheeks go pink again. "Well, I mean, you've had sex before, right?"

"Uh, yeah... I have a daughter."

"Right." She nods fast, picking up the clipboard. "And here you are. Just fine!"

The uncertain reassurance in her voice almost makes me laugh. "That's right. I am fine. Is that what you're worried about? Giving birth?"

119

Hopping off the stool, she runs to the door and locks it. Then she comes back and clasps both my hands in hers.

"Ember! I'm so scared! I've waited and waited. I told Liam I was waiting to have sex until we were married because that's what God wants us to do, but the truth is I don't want to have sex with him at all!"

Her voice rises to a shriek, and I hold my hand just in front of her lips. "Shh! André will come back here."

She's breathing fast, but the shrieking stops. Chewing my lip, I'm not exactly sure if Donna is trying to tell me she's a lesbian or if she's really just that scared of penises.

And I'm totally going to hell, because I'm also thinking about her $500 wedding cake order.

"What exactly is on your mind?" I say instead.

She starts to pace, slapping her palms on her thighs as she speaks. "First, the way it's done! It has to go in there!" She slaps her leg. "And Liam is a big guy! I can only imagine his, you know…" She wiggles her hand in front of her like a fish. "Is equally big."

"Okay, well first, it doesn't move like that." I put my arm around her shoulder. "And there are ways to manage size differences in the beginning."

I don't add she might not mind it so much down the road. Instead, I press for a little more information. "Is that the only thing you're worried about? Or is there something more… fundamentally wrong?"

I don't know how else to put it.

"I've heard it hurts really bad even when the guy is small." Her voice is quiet now. "So here I am.

I don't even use tampons! And on top of that, I pick the most enormous man to marry."

My lip is between my teeth again, and I decide to just go for it. "Okay, well, I can give you some tips, I guess."

She spins under my arm to face me. "Oh, would you?"

I guess it's okay to talk about this with her. "So you know Jackson was my first. He's pretty well-endowed."

"Did it hurt really bad? What did you do?"

"Well..." Maybe I shouldn't tell her I was so horny I tried to climb him like a tree. "It helps if you're really wet, you know?"

"Like in the shower? Oh! Or in the ocean?"

"No... that's actually counter-productive because those liquids can wash away your own, personal wetness."

"Oh!" She frowns. "You mean... like urine?"

"Good grief, Donna, don't you know anything about sex?" I don't mean to shout, but what are they teaching in school these days? My mind travels to Coco Bean and what she might or might not know at twenty-two.

"I was home schooled," she says mournfully. "I got home from school one day and asked my mother what F-U-C-K spelled... It was written on the bathroom wall, and she pulled me out of public school."

Pressing my lips together, I study her a moment. "That shouldn't have made a difference. Your mother made you, after all." The things parents don't tell their children. "Okay," I continue, and for the next few minutes I give her a basic lesson on anatomy and foreplay until she seems less panicked about it all.

"Communication is critical," I finish. "Tell Liam your fears. If he loves you, he'll work with you. Do you love him?"

She nods her head quickly. "Very much."

"That's the most important thing." My phone buzzes, and I lift it, studying the text message from my mother.

Polly's mother invited Colette to spend the night for her birthday. I think it's okay. They're a good, Christian family.

Frowning at the last sentence, I go slowly to the door and unlock it. "I've got to head back now, but I'm just down the way if you have any other questions."

"Thanks, Ember." Donna is quiet.

I glance up and give her a smile. Outside the door, I wave to André, who's helping a customer. Studying my mother's words, I decide there are worse things than having a sleepover with a good, Christian family. Anyway, I know Polly's mom. She's nice.

"Who's side am I on?" I say as I tap out my reply.

I'm sure she'll have fun. Thx.

I lower my phone and look up to see none other than Jackson heading down the lane. His back is to me, and he's apparently walking to the cottage. I quickly scan the deserted street to be sure no one sees me watching as he goes. I can't help noticing he hasn't changed. His shoulders are still broad and his arms are still naturally sculpted. His ass is still tight and perfect in those jeans.

His hair is shorter. I guess lawyers don't have shaggy hair, which is kind of sad. Still, thinking back to our earlier encounter, I kind of like his polished look, or polished meets scruffy under a baseball cap, unshaven, and sweaty from working hard.

Chewing my lip, I can't stop the onslaught of memories of our first night together. The flinty determination in his eyes this afternoon mixed with my talk with Donna unearthed all those feelings I'd been wrestling to keep tightly packed away.

I'd been in love with Jackson Cane since I was old enough to know what love was, and I'd wanted to be his since my hormones kicked in and my body started changing.

He resisted me because of our age difference. He was almost eighteen, and I took full advantage of the *almost* that summer. I knew it was my last chance before the steel wall of the law slammed down, cutting off any possible romance between us.

Pushing my door open, I cross the empty space to the back stairs. I'd convinced him to teach me how to kiss... I'd felt what he wanted in that kiss, and if the clock ticking had made me desperate, the fire in his lips made me fearless.

My entire body is hot, and I go to my refrigerator. I don't normally have wine during the week because of Coco, but tonight, I pour a decent-sized glass of Chardonnay and take a long drink.

Chapter 11

Jack

Dinner at last, is the Italian muffuletta with a pinot I brought with me from my apartment in the city. André says it's too hot for muffulettas, but he guarantees I will love this masterpiece. I'm inclined to agree with him because it smells like everything delicious.

I also convinced him to go out with me tomorrow night. Since it's Friday and Ember has a fucking *date* and I can't hang around this cottage wanting to put my fist through the wall, I suggested it.

He'd mentioned his wife is getting together with Betty Pepper and a bunch of women for the eve of their twentieth wedding anniversary, and it came to me. We can head down to the Tuna Tiki and have a beer and take in some live music.

Leaving the sandwich on the counter, I dig in my pocket for a piece of cinnamon candy. That old barrel of candy I remember from Ember's aunt's store is now in Betty's place, and I couldn't resist grabbing a handful. The flavor fills my mouth, burning my tongue, and I remember why I was so damn skinny back then. My taste buds were scalded off.

With a chuckle, I take the piece from my mouth and set it on a dish I carry with me into the small room off the kitchen. When I got here, it was furnished to be an office, but I've cleared the furniture away and placed an easel in the center. I still haven't stretched a canvas, but I found a large sketchpad and some of my old charcoal pencils in the bottom of that closet in the bedroom.

A few tubes of acrylic paint I never opened are still like new, but the problem is they were shitty colors. It's why I'd never opened them. I'll have to hop online and order what I need to do any real painting.

Pulling off my shirt, I put the cinnamon candy in my mouth and pick up the black charcoal pencil and return to Ember. I have a rough outline of her body standing like a petite statue. It's the image of her I'll never forget — the first time I saw her again after ten years apart.

She's standing in the doorway with the staircase behind her. I now know it leads to her bedroom. I've made it more mysterious, however. This is Ember Rose bursting out of the recesses of my past, walking out from the happiest place I buried in the deepest part of my heart.

Tilting the pencil to the side, I shade the side of her cheek, the line in her chin. Her hair is a mixture of deep brown, lighter chestnut, and tips of gold. One dark lock curves over her right eye, and her gaze is set.

Her expression is seductive defiance. Just within reach is the fiery vixen who captured me. I wanted her in those days so bad it hurt. I remember lying awake in my bed aching for her. I knew we were months away from missing out on everything, and I was prepared to concede.

Ember took our age deadline and set it on fire. I longed for her, but she demanded me. She was the persuasive innocent. She knew nothing, but she knew I would teach her. She knew once I taught her, I could never let her go. She would have me forever.

With the tip of my thumb, I smudge the shading on her bottom lip. My tongue slips out and touches my bottom lip. My insides hum with wanting her.

"I don't care what you say, Ember Rose," I whisper. "I'm not going anywhere."

Sitting back, I look at her beautiful image. I've been at it for hours, and the sun is gone. It's purple haze outside, and the moon is only getting bigger. Pushing off the floor, I walk through the cottage straight out the door.

A damp breeze sweeps around me. I'm barefoot, no shirt, only my jeans from earlier today as I walk through the trees to the street. I don't know what I'm planning to do. I only know I can't be this close to her and stay away.

Another, stronger gust whips past me as I step out onto the open street in front of her building. It's going to rain. I can smell the precipitation in the air. It's on my skin, mixing with the remainder of the day.

Long, thin clouds sweep quickly across the moon. Everything about this night is disturbed and restless, heavy with what's to come. I'm breathing hard, my chest rising and falling from how fast I walked here.

Faint light flickers from her windows, and I see the long curtains moving in the breeze. She sleeps with those balcony French doors open. The scaffolding stands beside it like a temptation, daring me to resist.

"Ember," I say in a voice just louder than normal.

I'm on fire, driven by lust, desire, need. My heart is beating so fast, I couldn't leave if I wanted to.

"Ember Rose," I say a touch louder.

Shadows move in the windows above. A lone figure catches the moving curtains and holds them apart. My chest tightens, and I'm sure it's her. She holds the long sheer in her hand, tight against her side and steps into the window. She's not on the balcony, but she's there in the shadows looking down on me.

I'm standing in the street looking up at her, my chest rising and falling fast, waiting for one word.

"What do you want, Jackson?" Her voice is hushed, but loud enough for me to hear clearly.

"Tell me to come up," I say in the same tone.

My muscles strain for her. I don't know if anyone is around. I don't think they are as most of the residents live further north in the old neighborhood part of town. It's just like Ember to choose this place to live. She's always been just outside their rules.

"No," she says, but I hear the waver in her voice. "Go home."

"You are my home."

She's quiet, but she doesn't go away. She doesn't close the doors and shut me out. It's a start—a tiny one, but one I'll take.

Without hesitation, I go to the scaffolding and climb. I'm on her balcony in seconds. Standing on the balcony, I'm feverish with anticipation of what might happen next.

She's inside the room watching me through the open door.

"Come to me," I say in a low voice.

It's quieter with her so close, but the hush only makes it more intimate. A cloud moves across the moon, and the world goes dark. She's lit from behind, and I see she's only wearing a thin white tank and panties. I'm consumed with longing. My cock twitches in the darkness, and I want to bury it deep in her clenching heat. I want to kiss her pussy and make her come. I want to hear the moans that have haunted me for a decade. The cloud slides away and she disappears in the moonlight.

"Ember," my voice cracks. "Please. Let me touch you."

A quiet noise, a hesitation.

Suspense is a painful knot in my throat.

The slightest movement, and she steps forward into the silvery light. Her shirt is thin, and I can make out the dark tips of her nipples, beaded and pointing at me. I lift my hand, holding it palm up to her. It feels like an eternity, but she slowly places her hand in mine.

Our fingers thread, and the fist in my chest relaxes. I exhale a groan as I pull her to me, covering her small body with mine. Her face is at my sternum, and I hold her, wrapping her in my arms. Small hands touch my lower back, and I feel her tremble.

"Are you afraid?" I speak against her hair, kissing it, kissing the side of her head, inhaling deep breaths of her delicate lavender scent.

"Yes," she whispers, and I lean back.

Her hands are still on my waist, and I cup her cheeks, looking deep into her brown eyes. They glisten in the moonlight, and I kiss them gently, left, right, salt on my tongue.

"Don't fear me."

She's off her feet in a sweep, her back against the wall. Her legs are around my waist, and our mouths collide. Pushing her lips apart, I find her tongue. Oceans of warmth flood my veins.

Yes.

Home.

Ember.

I hold her by the ass, using my chest pressed against hers for balance. Our stomachs press together, skin against skin, and it feels so damn good.

A little moan slips from her mouth into mine. Her hands are on my neck, her thumb touching my jaw, moving to our mouths. She's kissing me with as much need as I feel. I move away, and she follows, holding onto me and whimpering.

Heat burns where my erection is pressed against her core. Only a thin scrap of silk and my jeans stand between us.

Kissing her deeper, I taste her mouth. She's oaky Chardonnay and saltwater sweet. She's pulling my lips with hers, and I rock my erection against her clit.

Her head drops back and she moans, "Oh, God, Jackson."

I trace my tongue up her slim neck to her jaw. "I want you so much." I kiss her again. "I want you so much it hurts."

She kisses me again, but something changes. As if waking from a dream, I feel her retreating, her kisses growing shallower. Her hands fist against the tops of my bare shoulders, moving down to my arms.

"Stop," she gasps. "Put me down, Jackson."

"No," I groan.

I go in for another kiss, sweeping my tongue into her mouth, finding hers and claiming it. Her hands return to my face briefly before moving to my shoulders again.

"I said stop." Her voice is stronger. "Put me down."

She arches her back away, unhooking her legs from around my hips. She exhales a noise, and when her feet touch the wooden floor, she places her palm flat against my chest.

"I shouldn't have done that." Her voice trembles when she speaks. "I won't... I won't do this with you. Not again."

She won't meet my eyes. Her breasts rise and fall, her luscious curves straining beneath thin cotton. Her words are like knives slicing through my abdomen, the pain of having her so close, yet not having her.

"Ember..." My voice is a ragged whisper. "Please don't send me away."

"You have to go now. Don't come here again."

She slips through the open door into the darkness of her room. A lamp is shining from the top of a shelf, but she has gone somewhere I can't see her.

I won't cross her threshold. I won't force her to be with me when she asks me to leave this way.

"You've got to talk to me, Ember," I say, straining my eyes into the darkness. "You have to hear me out. There's more to our story. I—I need you to talk to me."

Silence is the only reply.

I know she hears me, but she's withdrawn. I won't get any further with her tonight. My shoulders drop, and I go to the end of the porch. Lifting one leg over, I look back at the shadows in her room.

"Goodnight, my Ember Rose," I say softly, and with that, I climb back down the way I came.

Chapter 12

Ember

Sitting on the floor in the darkness, I hold my hands over my ears and weep. My body shakes. Pain radiates from my chest out through my limbs, and I can't stop crying.

He kissed me the way he always did, demanding, possessive, take no prisoners. It was so good. It hurt so bad. He even tasted the same. It was Jackson. It destroyed my already broken heart.

"No," I whisper, shaking my head. "I must be strong."

With a hiccupped breath, I crawl weakly to my empty bed. He can't do this. He can't come back and snap his fingers and I fall into his lap, onto his dick.

Lying on my back in the darkness, I listen as the rain begins to fall, mixed with low, rumbling thunder. The long curtains hanging beside my French doors billow and stretch out in the breeze. The fans push the cooler air around me, and I pull the blankets higher seeking comfort.

Red-hot cinnamon fills my mouth, tears are in my eyes, and my core is achy and wet. My nipples tingle and my whole body is lit like a firecracker.

Damn you, Jackson Cane.

His scent is on my skin. I can still feel his large hands gripping my ass, his chest pressed against mine, strong and hard. Skin against skin, my thighs wrapped around his waist. I'd held him and kissed him like I'd been lost in the desert and he was a cool drink of water.

I've never been able to move past Jackson Cane.

My teenage dreams rush back on the damp air. I'd wanted him to fill me. I felt him straining to make us one, but self-preservation broke through the haze of lust.

Pain and heartbreak rose like an iron rod inside me to push him away. I can't go down that road again.

The first time I lost him, I didn't think I'd survive it. I didn't want to survive it. I had Tabby, of course, and my mother... my constant source of shaming. I'd given him everything, and he'd taken it and left.

The worst part was never knowing why. It had been in that time just on the edge of everyone having cell phones and easy Internet access — not that I would have had those things in high school. Marjorie would never have tolerated that much freedom for her one remaining daughter.

So I sat in silence, cut off, confused, and broken.

I was so sure what we'd had was real. I was so shattered and miserable.

And time passed...

Eventually, I had to live without him. I gave in to my mother's pressure to find other interests, to volunteer at the church. I'd go out with Tabby. It distracted me, but it never filled the hole in my chest.

Nothing filled it until Coco... which is why I won't be going down that road again. My daughter needs me, and I have plans.

Clutching a pillow to my chest, I roll over and force myself to think of her. Her sweet scent, her velvety cheeks, her little hands, and enormous personality. Coco is my world now.

Her and this store.

They're all that matter.

* * *

"Polly's mommy's cake is gooey." Coco is on my lap at my mother's table. Beside her is a bowl of dry Cheerios and a glass of milk. "She said it comes in a box."

Gathering my little girl's hair in my hands, I kiss the side of her neck and take a long sniff. "It's faster that way. And cheaper."

"You look tired." My mother takes her seat at the opposite end of the table, coffee in hand.

"The rain kept me awake." I don't look up when I answer.

Or smile.

Words that would be kind from anyone else always have a tinge of judgment when they come from her mouth.

"The thunder went *Boom!*" Coco raises one hand over her head.

"Did it keep you awake?" I ask, twisting a tie around her thin ponytail.

"Nope." Coco is focused on stacking her Cheerios. "Polly's daddy said God was rolling his barrels."

"Polly's daddy is wrong," my mother snips. "God doesn't have barrels."

"He does, too!" Coco argues, adding a round cereal to the stack. "Barrels of beer."

I bite back a laugh, thinking of my mother's text from yesterday.

135

"Colette Corinne Warren. That's blasphemous."

Coco climbs onto her knees. "Blasperous!" she growls, smashing her Cheerio tower. "Blasperous!" She holds out her little hands.

I can't stop my snort at this point. My mother cuts her eyes at me, and I stand, sweeping my girl onto my hip. "She's finished. We're going to the shop."

"She is not finished!" My mother snaps. "She needs to drink that milk."

Scooping up the glass, I carry it to the kitchen and transfer the liquid into a small plastic sippy cup. "Here," I say, handing it to Coco. "I'll have her back for supper."

We're out the door while my mother is still fussing. I'm just strapping Coco into her seat and putting on her little helmet when someone calls my name. Looking up, I see Betty Pepper is headed my way.

"Emberly! That cake you made was absolutely drool-worthy!" She waddles across the median to where I stand holding Dixie.

"Thanks, Miss Betty." I walk the bike to meet her. "Are you headed to work?"

"You know I'm retired," she says, holding her enormous purse. "I want to see if that rain damaged the paint last night."

"Oh..." I frown looking up ahead. "I hadn't thought about the paint."

"Cause he hasn't gotten to your store yet. It's probably fine." We walk a bit further before she shifts gears. "Bucky said he's picking you up tonight at seven."

"That's what he said," I say with a sigh. You'd think she was taking me out as much as she talks about it.

"Is Tabby watching Lola for you?"

"Coco," I gently correct her. "No, she'll be here at my momma's."

"Good of her to help you the way she does."

"My momma likes to be in control of things." I do my best to keep my tone light.

Betty nods, pressing her lips together. "You are so right there. That is one thing Marjorie has always done. Controlled things, bless your heart."

I was right with her up until the last part. "What do you mean?"

"It'll be the first time you've dated anyone since... Mason Green? A major breakthrough if you ask me."

"I didn't really date Mason. He took me to a few dances."

"You've never really dated anyone since..." She arches her brow in a knowing way, but I'm not discussing my love life with Busybody Pepper.

"I guess I'm frigid," I tease.

"Oh, you're not frigid. You've got too much of your daddy in you for that." She pats my forearm. "Yes, you got that Warren fire from him—and your strength. He was a strong man." We're just entering the small business district, and my shoulders tense when I see Jackson touching up the paint on the hardware store. "Although, I guess he did have one weakness, didn't he." The old woman gives me the side-eye then shrugs. "I suppose that's what drew you two together. Genes."

I stop walking. "Betty Pepper, I have no idea what you're talking about."

She does a little jump as if I've startled her. "You don't? Well..." Pulling her giant purse closer to her, she starts up her front steps. "Maybe you'll figure it out."

She storms through her door, and I'm left standing in the middle of the street staring after her wondering what the hell. A low voice from above snaps me out of it.

"Good morning," Jackson calls down.

I don't look up.

Coco, by contrast, is eager to return any greeting. "Good morning, painter man!" she cries, waving her hands frantically.

I pick up the pace, practically jogging us past the hardware store and my bakery, around the corner and into the alley.

"Zoom!" Coco hums as I get her out of the seat. The moment her feet touch the ground, she takes off headed for the corner. "Zoom!"

She's running, but I catch her around the waist. "Hold up, speed racer. Give me that helmet."

Carrying her in through the back door, I drop her little helmet on a chair and set her on her feet. She takes off running to the front of the store, where her stash of "baking supplies" is still waiting from earlier in the week.

"What's our new monster?" I call, stopping to lift the apron over my head.

"Yellow monster says *cuatro*!"

"Hmm," I think about it. "I think zesty lemon for this monster."

"Yes!" she cries, dumping all the play-dough items on the wooden floor.

I head for the refrigerator. All but the final two-tiered dessert cake and Donna's wedding cake are left on my schedule. The dessert cake needs to be done by the weekend, but I have a month to work on Donna's.

As I take out the ingredients, my mind bounces from my conversation with her to the strange conversation I just had with BP. My phone buzzes, and I place the eggs, milk, and butter on the heavy wooden table where I work.

"Who's texting me?" I lift the device then do a little shiver. "Probably Bucky Pepper."

I'm sorry if I went too far last night.

Frowning, my eyes go to the door.

Who is this?

I text back, looking at the windows. I notice bits of the scaffolding have moved closer to my building. Fluttery nerves tighten my stomach. It's as if the metal bars surrounding me are a trap.

I hope you'll let me see you again. We need to talk.

How did you get this number?

Several seconds pass, and the only noise is Coco humming as she assembles her brightly colored dough. I don't see any little dots or indication a reply is on the way.

"Jackson Cane," I say under my breath. "You'd better answer me."

Just then the bell over the door rings, and my best friend enters. I don't miss her nodding to someone outside.

"Good morning!" Tabby calls out happily.

"Aunt Tabby!" Coco shouts. "I'm making yellow monster *cuatro*!"

"Yellow monster *cuatro*! Let me guess... He's number four?"

"*Cuatro*!" Coco cries as if she's at the bullfights.

"*Cuatro*!" my friend echoes.

I'm standing at the table, arms crossed and waiting.

"What's twisting your panties?" Tabby drops her bag on the opposite end of the counter.

"I just got a text from someone who shouldn't have my number."

"Telemarketer?" With a little skip, she pulls out a notepad and a pen. "Speaking of which, I was thinking I'd get started on your online store. I'll need pictures... What else? Let's discuss."

"Okay, for starters why did you give Jackson Cane my number without my permission?"

"I don't know what you're talking about," she says with a little laugh as she continues scribbling on her notepad.

My phone buzzes again.

Don't be mad at Tabby.

"Don't..." I turn to the window, and electricity flashes when my eyes meet Jackson's. He gives me a wink, and my mouth drops open.

Tabby frowns and looks over her shoulder, spotting him. "Talk about throwing people under the bus," she mutters.

She flips him the bird then all I see are legs as he continues up the scaffolding. "He's starting on the balcony?" I look at the ceiling overhead. "I thought he would start at the bottom!"

Chewing my lip, I try to remember how I left the place this morning.

"Underwear all over the floor?" Tabby teases.

I wave frantically at her. "Keep your voice down. He can hear everything we say."

"I wouldn't be surprised if this building takes him a week to finish."

Her teasing is making me furious, and I pull her closer over the table. "Why are you being so flippant? I thought you were on my side in this."

"I'm always on your side," she hisses. "I just bumped into him at the store, and he told me something I didn't know."

"What?" I step back and fix my eyes on the table.

She shrugs. "He didn't tell me much, but I think the two of you need to have a conversation."

Pressing my lips together, I try not to growl. "What did he say?"

"What if Jackson thought you were the one who left? What if he was given the same line as you?"

"I wasn't given a line. A line would have been great. I wasn't given anything." I storm over to the mixer and pull out the large glass bowl. "I got radio silence."

My KitchenAid mixer was the first appliance I ever bought, and it wiped me out for three months. Still, I don't regret the decision. Reaching for the flour, baking soda, and eggs, I start the process of making the cake.

"I'm sorry," Tabby says, carrying the cocoa to where I stand. "I should have asked your permission first."

"Yes, you should have."

"I only want you to be happy, Em. I remember what it was like when you were with Jackson. You were pretty young, but still… you just glowed."

Heat fills my eyes, and I blink it away quickly. "I've got more important things to worry about now."

"You have to make time for your needs, too."

"I have to think about Coco and what *she* needs and this store and what *it* needs."

"You need to prioritize you. Remember that thing about putting on your own oxygen mask before helping someone else?"

Arching my eyebrows, I look up at her. "You've never been this philosophical as long as I've known you."

"I don't want to see you end up with Bucky Pepper."

"Oh, God," I groan, wiping a tendril of hair off my forehead and focusing on the batter. "Hand me that spoonula, would you? Start mixing up the buttercream. I'll let you run this over to the strand once it's done. And keep half for yourself. It's time I started paying you."

She grins and sashays to the refrigerator. I can never stay mad at Tabby, and shit, a wriggling part of me says she might be right.

* * *

Lemon zest cupcakes made, lunches eaten, I purposely prolonged the decoration of the round dessert cake until I'd seen Jackson climbing down the scaffolding and briefly glancing in the window. Of course, I quickly turned my back.

Tabby took the order in her car and headed out to Oceanside Beach. I carried my sleepy toddler to the bike and pedaled her home along with her box of Yellow Monster Number Fours.

Now I'm back at my place dusting on makeup and trying to drum up the smallest bit of interest in Bucky the deviled-egg-smelling taxidermist. My phone rings, and I hit the speaker button.

"Where is he taking you?" Tabby's voice fills the open space.

"He didn't say, but I'm guessing it'll be Tuna Tiki. He seems to love it there."

"It's the live music."

"And the cheap beer," I add, outlining the corners of my eyes.

"I'm going to Thelma's party, but I'll slip out and head over after about an hour."

I carefully brush on mascara. "You don't have to do that. I'll be fine."

"Emberly, you know what happened with Cheryl Ann." Her tone is ominous, and the tiniest warning goes off in my chest.

"Cheryl Ann can be a little flighty. He probably thought he was being flirty and he was really being inappropriate."

"Is that supposed to make it better?"

"No! I'm just saying. His mother and I are friends. He knows this. I think it'll be a good deterrent."

"Bucky Pepper is an idiot, and I'll be there to back you up if you need it. Don't worry."

"Hopefully, the date won't last that long."

Makeup done, we say our goodbyes, and I shake my long hair out with my fingers. I'm wearing a white romper short set with a long, floral black kimono on top. My sandals are flat, since Bucky is only an inch taller than me. Overall, it's a very conservative look. I pick up my small clutch just as the knocking starts downstairs on the door.

"Coming!" I jog down the stairs and head for the front entrance. "Hi, Bucky," I say, stopping right at the door.

"Hey, Emberly." He steps back and smiles. His eyes widen behind his oversized glasses, and sure enough, he pulls out a box.

"I made this for you." It's a medium-sized, pink cardboard box.

It's similar to what I'd pack one of my cakes in... and examining it further, I'm pretty sure it's the box I used for Thelma's.

"You didn't have to," I say sincerely, taking it with a sigh.

"Go ahead and peek. See what you think."

Turning around in the doorway, I carry the heavy-ish item inside and set it on the counter. I'm glad Tabby's not here to gloat as I lift the lid, squinting my eyes almost-closed.

"No!" I jump back from what looks like the teeth of an attacking squirrel.

Bucky laughs through his nose. It's sort of an adenoidal, honking sound. He lifts the disturbing statue out of the box. It's two squirrel torsos rising out of the base of one set of legs. The squirrel on the left is reaching forward while the squirrel torso on the right is holding a large acorn away, teeth bared.

"Are they conjoined twins?"

"Naw, I designed it to look like they're fighting over that nut." More honking laughter. "It's funny, right?"

I force a terrified smile. "It's... interesting."

"You'd be amazed how many dead squirrels you can find."

My smile melts into a grimace. "You don't kill them yourself?"

"Sometimes. These two I found off in the grass near the highway."

I quickly move the monstrosity from my counter over to the window. "I'll just put it there. Better sunlight."

When I turn around, I catch Bucky's eyes going from my ass to my breasts, where they linger. "Ready for some seafood? I love eating tuna... all kinds of tuna."

Do not gag. Do not gag. Do not gag.

"Let me guess," I say, doing my best to smile and breathe through my mouth. "You're taking me to the Tuna Tiki?"

"Where else?" He lifts his arm to put it around my shoulders.

"Oh!" I accidentally breathed through my nose. Trying to hide it with a cough, I step away. "I mean Oh! It's my favorite place for sushi."

He's only slightly discouraged as I take the lead, rushing out the door to where his truck is waiting in front of the shop. Once he's outside, I quickly turn the key. I don't even bother waiting for him to open the truck door. I'm ready for this evening to be over and done with, and for me to be back home.

Bucky climbs in and waggles his eyebrows at me while stretching his arm across the top of the bench seat.

"Want to sit in the middle? I have a third seatbelt."

"Oh, no!" I sing out. "I'd better stay here with the shoulder strap. Safer."

He nods and again checks out my boobs before turning to the front and starting the engine. It takes about fifteen minutes to get to the Tuna Tiki. The soft, melodic strains of Bob Marley greet us at the door. It's the live house band playing all their standard tunes. I've only been to the Tiki a few times, but they're always playing that same old list.

"We'd like a seat near the stage." Bucky leans across the hostess's counter, and she recoils frowning.

"Oh my goodness!" Her eyes fly to me, and my frown matches hers. "Right this way."

The nice thing about the Tiki is it's outdoors. The ocean breeze sweeps Bucky's deviled-egg, formaldehyde, body odor up, up, and away, and the proximity to the band makes talking difficult.

My date orders us a pitcher of Natural Light on tap. I mentally calculate that's probably three dollars total. Oh well, I'm not here to be spoiled. I'm honoring a commitment—and making another commitment to myself *never* to get in this predicament again.

A waitress puts the watery beer in front of us and we shout our orders to her. I get the California roll with a side of tuna sashimi. Bucky orders the grilled tuna sandwich, and waggles his eyebrows in that creepy way.

If he thinks he's getting anywhere near my tuna...

The song ends, and the band takes a break. House music fills the air, and sadly it's too quiet for us not to have a conversation. I wrack my brains trying to think of anything I might want to know about Bucky Pepper that I don't already.

He's leering at me with that weird smile.

"So," I begin, lifting the small plastic cup of beer in front of me. "How did you get interested in taxidermy?"

"My dad did it."

I've just taken a big gulp of watery brew, and I realize that's it. He's done. The house music drifts between us. Shit, I would've thought that would at least buy me a few minutes.

"Okay... that thing you made for me. The squirrel, or squirrels —"

"I invented it. It was my own creation." He smiles again, and I nod.

"I thought you must have made it." As if. "Is that a specialized technique? Fusing two bodies together like that?"

"It's just stitchin and stuffin."

Heaven help me. I look around for Tabby, wondering when an hour from the start of that party might roll around. Trying again. "Did you see a squirrel like that in a book, or did you —"

"I imagined it."

"Okay..." It's like I'm on a date with Slingblade. Only Slingblade was slightly more interesting. "How old were you when you stuffed your first animal?"

"About ten or eleven. My daddy was working on an eight-point buck, and I asked if I could help him. The rest is history."

I almost do a fist pump. I just got a whole three sentences that time. "What's the strangest thing you've ever stuffed?"

As soon as the words leave my mouth, I wish I could take them back. No telling what he might say. I need to slow down on the beer.

"One time an old lady wanted angel's wings on her dead cat. She wanted it to look like it was jumping through the air."

I'm totally buzzed, because that answer makes me start to giggle. The server appears just in time to block me with the tray, placing our orders in front of us. I'm still snorting when she finishes and relieved to get some food in my stomach.

"Can I get y'all anything else?" the girl asks.

"Another pitcher'd be good," Bucky says, and she nods before I can say no thank you.

Taking the chopsticks, I snap them apart and hurry to get something in my mouth. Thankfully, the band returns to the stage and after some brief chatter, they launch into a Grateful Dead tune. Bucky takes a bite of his tuna sandwich and smiles at me again, and I make the decision to leave with Tabby once she gets here.

The dark red sashimi dipped in soy sauce is delicious, tangy and fresh, and I'm transporting a slice of California roll to my mouth when my eyes land on Jackson. My chopsticks flip and I drop the piece right in my lap.

"Shit!" I scoop it out of my napkin hoping the dark brown sauce didn't bleed through onto the crotch of my white shorts.

Another glance, and I see he's glaring at me from the bar where he's standing next to André.

"Would you like to dance?" Bucky shouts across the table.

He holds out a hand, and I'm paralyzed. On the one hand, I do not want to be clutched against Stinky Bucky. On the other hand, I don't want Jackson thinking I'm just sitting around at home waiting for him to show up in the middle of the night and kiss my lips off.

"Sure," I say slowly.

Bucky's eyes light and he stands, waiting for me beside my chair. I rise and clutch both his hands in mine, keeping them down and away from my torso. He tries to lift them, and I clutch his wrists tighter, holding our hands straight down and swaying side to side.

"You're not a very good dancer, are you?" he asks.

"My mother doesn't approve of sinful hugging," I lie, although it's probably true. I've never asked her.

We stand in front of each other on the dance floor, surrounded by couples clutched up and writhing, with our hands straight down doing the sway. My brain is slightly fuzzy from too much cheap beer. I don't even notice Jackson approaching from the bar until he's right beside us.

"I'm cutting in," he says, catching Bucky by the shoulder.

"That's not how it works here!" my date protests.

It doesn't matter. Jackson wraps an arm possessively around my waist and pulls me to him. My soft breasts flatten against his hard chest, and my entire body floods with heat.

One strong arm is tight around my waist. The other holds my hand close in his. The whisper of his breath is against my brow, and it sends electricity humming in my veins.

With every rapid inhale, my senses are filled with leather, soap, and Jackson — a scent I remember too well. The song is beachy, free and easy. I recognize the tune, but I don't know the words. All I know is the molding of my body against his in perfect time.

"Why are you here with Bucky?" His voice is against my skin, and my eyes close.

I'm too light and buzzed, and after our kiss last night, it's very possible I might kiss him again. A few deep breaths, and I force myself to remember through the haze. I have very good reasons for staying away from Jackson Cane. I force my racing heart to steady.

"We're on a date, not that it's any of your business." My voice sounds so much calmer than I feel.

He doesn't reply. Instead, his hand on my back moves lower, pulling me closer against his body. The song merges into something new, and we're quiet, swaying. I'm holding his shoulder, and my fingers are white from clutching his firm muscles.

"Let me go, Jackson," I say those words again, but this time, they seem to have less conviction.

Again, no immediate response. The hand on my back moves higher, to my waist, tightens briefly before relaxing, releasing me.

"I don't like to see you dancing with another guy." Blue eyes sear into mine, and his possessive words are like warm caramel in my veins.

I should argue with him. I should tell him I'll dance with whomever I want.

But he's the only person I want to dance with...

It's always been him.

He returns to the bar next to André, but his eyes stay on me. I walk slowly to the table, where my sushi waits beside the half-finished cup of watery beer. My insides are so mixed up. I want to collapse into the chair and cry. I want to go home, get away from this noise and confusion. I have to think about

Coco and refocus my mind on my plans, what's important.

Tabby's words that my needs are important float around in my mind, and I sneak another glance. My eyes meet Jackson's, and it's a flash of lightning to my core. He isn't smiling. He's watching me.

Bucky takes another big slug of beer. "Jackson Cane thinks he can just come back here, take over..."

Blinking to my date, I notice he's talking more, and I wonder if he's too buzzed to get me home. "Would you take me home now?"

His eyes widen briefly, and that leering smile returns. "I'd be happy to. I'll be right back."

He's on his feet, his eyes dipping to my breasts once more. He's gone, searching for our waitress before I have the chance to offer to pay for my half. I truly have no interest in Bucky whatsoever. It only seems fair.

Taking my clutch off the table, I start slowly for the door when a small ruckus bursts out onto the patio. Tabby is in the lead, and she has Donna White and André's wife Thelma with her. When she sees me she makes a beeline to where I stand.

"Ember! We got here as fast as we could." She looks around, and when Thelma goes to her husband at the bar, she spins around fast, clutching my arm.

"Ouch!" I cry.

"Did you see Jackson at the bar?" Tabby's so close her lips graze my ear.

"Yes. He broke in when I was dancing with Bucky."

"Ew!" Tabby jerks back. "You danced with Bucky? How could you stand it?"

"We just sort of... held hands and swayed side to side."

She snorts. "I'm sure that was something to see."

"It kept the odor contained."

She starts to laugh more as Donna joins us. "Ember! I've been wanting to talk to you about… the thing." Her eyes go round.

I do a half-frown, thinking about her cake. "Any better?"

"Yes!" Her voice is breathy, and her eyes take on a glow. "Liam was so happy when I told him how I felt. We've been experimenting. I have so many questions for you."

Just then my date returns. "Hello, Tabitha. Hello Donna." He says the words in a melodic tone, like he's a radio announcer, and all three of us grimace in unison. "Emberly, if you're ready."

"Wait!" Tabby grabs my arm again. "You're not leaving?"

"Tabs, I have to." My traitorous eyes flicker to the bar again, and my insides flash. He's still watching. "I can't stay here with him looking at me like that."

A smile curls her lips, but I start shaking my head the moment I see it. "No."

"No?" Her eyebrows arch, and she tilts her head to the side making puppy dog eyes.

Exasperation fills my lungs, and I blow it out on a loud sigh. "Goodnight."

Bucky smiles and tries to wrap his arm around me, but I sidestep him, picking up the pace and trotting into the restaurant. I don't stop until I'm out the door and at his truck.

Chapter 13

Jack

Watching Ember walk out the door with Bucky Pepper makes my blood hot. She says what she does is none of my business. She says to let her go.

Not happening.

Holding her in my arms, dancing just now, the world was right. She tasted like cheap beer, but she smelled like my girl, lavender and citrus, fresh and earthy.

"You okay?" André asks, breaking my glowering into my beer.

"Yeah, sorry." I give him an unconvincing smile.

He only frowns back. "I wouldn't be okay if I saw my woman leaving with another guy. Especially someone like that."

"I don't know what she's doing with him." Turning my back to the bar, I watch the band and the couples dancing, but my mind is following her home.

"When I met Thelma, she was dating this guy... he was so far beneath her, I nearly couldn't take it." He does a little chuckle into his tumbler of scotch.

"Where was that?" I turn to face him.

"New Orleans. I grew up there."

"I figured as much. Did you work in a restaurant?"

He gives me a wry smile. "I was a musician."

"Yeah? What instrument?"

"Guitar, trumpet, drums. I graduated from UNO in music, sat in with a few of the greats at the House of Blues, Deacon John, Wayne Sanchez..."

"You played with Deacon John?"

André laughs at me. "I was just a kid. He let me play with him at Tipitina's once."

"That's good shit. How the hell did you end up here making poboys?"

Shaking his head, he takes another pull off his drink. I follow his gaze down the bar to where Thelma is talking and laughing with Tabby and Donna. She's a beautiful lady.

"Love will make you do some crazy shit," he says, his voice thick with love.

"It's true." I turn to face the bar again, thinking about ordering another drink and really wanting to be with Ember. "So Thelma dragged you here?"

"I guess you could say I followed her." A twinkle is in his eye. "She always wanted to move here. Had an uncle from Madison."

"And the poboys?"

He exhales. "You can't grow up in New Orleans and not know food. I got here and realized I wasn't going to earn a living in the music business."

I can't resist teasing him. "Not interested in sitting in with these guys?"

He laughs. "I don't mind beach music. The Dead, Marley."

"It's the lack of soul you can't get onboard with?"

That gets me a bigger laugh. "There's some blue-eyed soul happening." Pointing to the fellow on bass, he nods. "He's hitting some interesting licks."

"Okay." I nod, hoping he's aware I'm totally out of my league talking reggae music versus traditional New Orleans blues.

"All this place needed was some good food. I figured I'd give it to them."

"I'm a believer. You're a master."

"Except for the brie."

"Somebody will love that brie shit. Just not me."

"Just not you," he says it at the same time, and we both laugh.

For a minute, we listen to the band putting their spin on "Santeria" by Sublime. A few couples are out on the floor doing a two-step. I think about living in this town, being able to hop down to the beach, surf, love on Ember whenever I get a chance. The simple life of Oceanside always appealed to me. It was my father who demanded I be "better," whatever the fuck that means. I already had what made me happy, what made me complete.

"It's not a bad place to live." I don't state the obvious—I'm here and my presence is solely dependent on what happens with Ember. I can't imagine living here without her.

"Not much different from what I'm used to," he says, polishing off his drink. "Pristine, idyllic beaches meet meddling gossipers and busybodies."

That makes me laugh. "You sound like a local."

Tabby is over at the other end of the bar with Thelma and Donna White. They're chatting, but Ember's friend is facing me. She's frozen me out since I got here, but two nights ago at the poboy shop I managed to get her to let her guard down and listen to me. It's how I got Ember's phone number. It's what gave me hope. When our eyes meet, she walks down to where I'm standing.

"How's it going?" she says. "Made any progress?"

My eyes go to the empty bottle in my hand, and my mind goes to my girl leaving here with Bucky Pepper of all people. "She's really defensive."

"You really hurt her."

Frustration tightens my throat. "I was really hurt—"

"So you say," Tabby cuts me off, green eyes flashing. "I'm not sure what's true, but I'm willing to take a chance if it'll help her. You'd better not make me regret it."

"If things go the way I imagine, there will be no regrets. Ever." I mean the words with all the determination tightening in my chest.

"Then what are you still doing here?" She gives me a look. "You saw her walk out with Bucky Pepper, right?"

Sighing, I place both forearms on the bar. "I can't keep forcing her. I have to give her space to come to me."

"Ember is only with him to fulfill an obligation." A quiet voice comes from behind Tabby, and I look up to see Thelma has joined us. "She promised his mother. Ember's one of the nicest people in town."

I hold out my hand. "Hi, I'm Jackson, Jack—"

"I know who you are, Jack Lockwood. André's told me all about you." She does a little laugh and rests her face against her husband's chest. His strong arm goes around her shoulders.

"Did I see Ember leave with Bucky?" Donna appears beside Tabby, asking as if she's trying not to let me overhear.

"She said she was tired," Tabby says, equally low.

156

Donna's mousey brown eyes widen. "Do you think that's a good idea?"

I don't like the implication of her words. "What does that mean?"

She seems to grow even smaller, looking down at her feet. "I don't like to spread gossip."

"What does *that* mean?" The knot in my throat has moved to my chest.

Tabby makes a face. "Cheryl Ann said Bucky... Well, she said he grabbed her inappropriately, but I'm not sure how much of that you can trust."

She continues talking, but my vision has tunneled. I'm waving at the bartender trying to get his attention.

"My question is why would she go out with him in the first place?" Tabby continues.

Donna's voice is still soft, but her words slice through me like a knife. "They say women never lie about things like that. I believe Cheryl Ann."

"Sorry, man, I hate to leave you like this." I shove a twenty in André's hand. "Use that to pay for my beer and call a Lyft home."

He's instantly on alert. "What's wrong? Did something happen?"

"It better not have." I'm moving fast for the door with murder on my mind.

Chapter 14

Ember

Our drive back to my place is mostly silent. Bucky has the radio on a country music station, and I look out the window doing my very best not to let my mind replay the feeling of Jackson's strong arms around me, his scent...

As we're entering Oceanside Village, my phone buzzes in my purse. It's a text, and I freeze. Jackson has my number now. I saved him to my contacts. Clenching my hands together, I look out the window, not wanting to be rude, even if this is just a courtesy date.

Bucky parks the truck in front of my building, and before I can say anything, he's out and jogging around to help me. We walk the few steps up to the front door, and I stop and face him.

"Thanks so much, Bucky. I really appreciated dinner." I smile and hold out my hand.

"Don't say thank you." He bypasses it, circling around and getting between the door and me. "It was like I always dreamed it would be."

"You... dreamed it?" I do a little frowny-smile trying not to think too much about Bucky dreaming about dating me.

"It's awful early, don't you think?" His leery smile turns tentative. "I sure would love to have a slice of your amazing cake."

Another tiny alarm bell goes off in the back of my mind. "You know what?" I walk toward the truck hoping he'll follow me away from my door. "I don't really keep cakes for walk-in business yet. Everything I make is for hire."

Instead of following me, he peers through the glass. "Well, what are those little things? Right there on the counter?"

"What?" Breathing through my mouth, I go to where he's standing and look into the shop. "Oh, sweet baby Jane..." I left half of the Yellow Monster Number Four cakes under the glass in plain sight. "I'm sorry, Bucky, we can't eat those."

He smiles, and I'm sure he doesn't mean it, but it creeps me out. "I bet we can have just one... we can share it! And a little coffee, too. It'll be nice."

My nose wrinkles. "Ahh... Tell you what. I'll pack one up for you, and you can take it back to your place and have it with a cup of coffee before bed."

His smile morphs into a crooked frown. "I guess. If that's the best I can do."

With a deep sigh, I turn the lock and lead us inside, headed straight to the case. I hear the door shut behind me, and the lock clicks. It stops me before I even uncover the dish.

"Now that wasn't so hard, was it?" Bucky's voice has changed. I spin around, and my eyes go huge when I see the glint of lust in his. "You know, we never got to finish our dance. That damned Jackson Cane cut in on me."

Backing up, my legs hit the counter and I stop, holding out my hand. "Bucky... I'm too tired for dancing."

"We don't have to do anything fancy. We can just sway like before. I liked having you in my arms."

"No. I'm sorry. It's too... I don't want to lead you on."

"You've just never thought of me that way, Ember Rose." He reaches out to catch my hand. I try to pull it back, but his grip is a vise.

"Bucky," my voice is firm. "What are you doing?"

"I want to help you Emberly."

"Help me how?"

"My mamma said you're like caged heat. She said you're smoldering fire burning under ice."

A knot is in my throat. "That's a really inappropriate thing for your mother to tell you about me!"

"Oh, she didn't tell me. I heard her telling one of her friends on the phone."

"Of all the—" I can't decide if I'm furious or embarrassed. Or both. Betty Pepper! What kind of stories is that dirty old lady spreading around town about me? "That's really inappropriate for her to say to anybody!"

"Your aura is calling to me." Bucky's voice is low, possibly what he considers seductive, and he steps forward, still gripping my wrist. "Don't fight it, Emberly Rose. It's what your body needs..."

"Gross!" My hand is behind me now, feeling around on the counter for anything I can use as a weapon, my spoonula, my cake pan, my knife...

"Mamma said you haven't been with a man in a long time. Let me help you with that. Use me, sweet Emberly..."

Swallowing the bile in my throat, I push hard against his stomach. He doesn't budge. Instead he starts leaning forward, eyes closed, lips extended in a pucker.

I dodge his kiss and grunt as I try to push him to the side. "No, thank you!"

"You're so beautiful, Ember." His clammy hands are on the backs of my thighs now, moving up and over my ass. "Let me eat your tuna. I'll eat it so good, you'll beg me for more. I'll make you so wet—"

"Get off me!" I throw all my weight at him and scream, punching my fists against him until he grabs them both in one hand.

I scream louder, trying to jerk my hands away. Just then a banging noise starts on the door. Bucky jumps and looks over his shoulder. His grip loosens, and I jerk my hands, slipping out of his grasp and away from him.

"Get your fucking hands off her *now*!" Jackson's voice is loud and raging, and Bucky makes an audible gasp. "Ember, unlock this door!"

I try to run to him, but Bucky catches me around the waist. "You get away from there, Jack Lockwood!" he shouts back. "You leave us alone. Emberly wants to be with me!"

"I do not!" I shout, furious about this whole idiotic turn of events. "Jackson! Help!"

I watch him look around the door, hesitating only a moment before disappearing. *Where's he going?*

Bucky's face is in my hair, and my eyes fly around my workstation. "That's right. Get rid of that Jack Lockwood. He hurt you. I would never hurt you, Emberly." He runs his tongue up the side of my neck, and I flinch, seeing what I need. "I'll keep you coming. You'll come so hard, you'll be screaming my name—"

My fist closes over my heavy rolling pin, and I'm about to whack Bucky into next month when his voice turns into a gagging noise and his grip on me goes slack. Spinning around, I see Jackson has him by the throat and is dragging him to the door. My rolling pin hits the table with a clatter as Bucky's boots kick on the floor, making loud, scuffling sounds. Catching my breath, I take a few steps in their direction, not sure what's about to happen.

"Let me go!" Bucky's cry is garbled from Jackson's fist around his neck.

Jackson pauses to unlock the door then continues dragging him outside. I creep forward a few more steps just in time to see Jackson throw Bucky off the porch onto the dusty street. Bucky lands flat on his back with a loud *Oof!* But Jackson isn't done. He hops off the porch right onto Bucky's chest and starts punching.

"No means no, asshole!" Jackson's fists fly, but I can't see Bucky on the ground from where I stand.

I hear grunts mixed with spitting mixed with wet coughing and shrieks. "Stop! Jack, stop!" Bucky cries.

I rush out the door, into the dim night where Jackson is beating the shit out of him.

"Jackson! Wait!" Reaching forward, my hands spin in the air as I try to catch his flying fists.

He pauses and looks up at me, blue eyes throwing fire and jaw clenched. "Don't kill him. Then you'll be in trouble!"

He's breathing hard, but he stops beating Bucky. Pushing off the ground, he steps back, shoulders hunched. His shoulders rise and fall quickly, and his hands are clenched into fists. His expression is so wild, I'm afraid he's going to start kicking. I've never seen murder in someone's eyes until this moment.

Bucky is whining from the ground. "Oooo... I think you broke my face."

"Don't you ever touch my girl again." Jackson's voice is hoarse.

My insides flash at his words, and I carefully reach for him again. "Jackson? Come inside. I'll call Chad. The deputy sheriff."

He blinks those blue eyes up at me, and they change from fury to concern. "Are you okay?"

"Yeah." I nod, reaching for him. "He didn't hurt me. Come inside. Chad'll take him to jail."

He stands for a moment longer, looking down at the moaning heap of potential date-rapist garbage on the ground. His leg twitches, and I know he wants to kick him.

"Come on now," I say gently.

The muscle in his jaw moves, and he hesitates a beat longer before stepping back and moving in my direction. I already have my phone out, and I'm dialing Chad's cell number.

"Ember? You okay?" Chad sounds worried. He gave me his number once he found out I lived alone above the store—even though I told him I don't have any money in the register and nobody comes into town anyway.

"We've had a bit of excitement..." I glance up at Jackson, and he's watching me with so much intensity, it makes my stomach flutter. "I was with Bucky Pepper, and well... he sort of got a little handsy."

"Did he hurt you?"

"No—I'm okay. Jackson was here, and he kind of, ahh, he kind of beat him up a little bit." *Gross exaggeration.*

"I'm sure he did. I'm surprised he didn't kill him."

"Anyway, Bucky's outside—" The noise of squealing tires echoes through my door.

Jackson spins around and jogs to where we left my attacker. "He drove away."

"Strike that," I say to Chad. "He must not've been hurt that bad. He was able to climb into his truck and drive away."

"I'll go by his mamma's house and pick him up. You come down to the station tomorrow and press charges. We'll take care of this."

"Thank you, Chad."

I end the call, and it seems so quiet in my shop. Jackson stands by the door looking back at me. One small lamp is on inside, and everything is cast in a yellowish glow.

"I guess you want me to go." He hesitates. "Are you sure you're okay?"

"I'm okay." I nod. He turns and opens the door, and I quickly speak. "Wait..."

My insides are all mixed up. I don't want him to go, not at all, no matter what my survival instincts have been screaming at me since the first day he appeared in town.

"I could make some coffee if you want," I continue. Looking around, I see the dish of cupcakes still waiting. "I have these. They're lemon curd with a pinch of cayenne pepper."

His brow relaxes with a smile, and he pushes the door shut. "That sounds really good."

165

The idea of feeding him cake gives me an unexpected rush. "I read about how in Mexico they sprinkle red pepper on fruit or have it with chocolate. I was just experimenting."

He walks slowly closer to where I'm standing, and my heart beats faster with every step. "You're a baker now," he says with a smile.

"I try," I say with a little shrug.

"Looks like more than a trial." He looks around the store, and my eyes move from his square jaw, over his full lips, down his neck.

Finally, his blue eyes return to mine, and I lose my breath. "Thank you," I manage to say.

"For what?" He takes another step closer, and I can smell that amazing leather and cedar and Jackson scent.

"For saving me."

"Oh." He nods, looking down at his hands. I do the same, and I see one of his fists is cut open and bleeding slightly.

"Jackson! You're hurt." I start to go to the sink, but he stops me.

"Hang on." His voice is firm but gentle, and his touch on my arm becomes the focus of my attention. I love his warm, strong grip on me. "I really do want to talk to you. We could do it here or we could go to the cottage if that's more comfortable?"

"We can talk here." Looking around, I realize I don't have anywhere to sit in the store besides the stools around the worktable. "I have a couch and chairs upstairs."

The faintest hint of a smile ghosts across his lips, and I turn, leading him to the door at the back of the room — the same one he must've come through when he saved me from Bucky. The fire in his eyes, his determination to protect me, all of it is branded in my memory.

We walk slowly up the staircase to my apartment. I rush quickly and turn on a few lamps so we have light, although it's still pretty glowy and atmospheric. When I turn around, he's looking at the pictures of Coco and me at the beach.

My chest clenches as I remember my mother's words. *Most men are put off by other men's children.*

"She looks like you as a little girl." My defenses melt when he smiles at me, warmth in his eyes. "She's beautiful."

"She's feisty," I say, and he exhales a laugh.

"I guess she acts like you, too." He walks around to look at more pictures and finishes softly. "Watch out, little boys."

I'm completely disarmed, and I don't know what to do. Jackson is standing here filling my vast, empty apartment with his presence, the dream I gave up so long ago.

"She's been the best thing in my life for four years."

He nods, looking down. "Is she Mason's?"

"Mason?" I'm confused.

He looks up to me. "Mason Green? Isn't that who…" His words trail off, and his expression is like finding the last piece to a challenging puzzle.

"What did you want to talk about?" I ask.

He comes to where I'm standing, and I see the thoughts moving behind his eyes. He pauses. It seems like he might touch me, but he hesitates. I want him to touch me. My skin aches for his touch.

He blinks down briefly, and when our eyes meet again, his smolder. "I don't know what happened or why. I only know you'll tell me the truth, and we need to know the truth."

"The truth about what?" My voice is as solemn as his.

We've reached an important moment.

A moment of truth.

Another step closer, and my heart beats harder.

"When I left... It seems so long ago." With a bitter laugh, he runs an injured hand over his mouth. "I never wanted to let you go, Em," his voice changes. His eyes are burning, intense. "Leaving you was the hardest thing I've ever done in my life. Still, it was important. I went to school thinking I'd work hard, double up on my hours, finish early so I could get back here sooner..."

My stomach cramps. All of those days fly back, assaulting my memory like a riptide. Blinking fast, I watch as he struggles with the words.

"When I found out you weren't waiting, that you were with someone else, I didn't know what to do." He clears his throat, blinking his gaze to the side. "I kind of lost it for a little while."

"But..." My brow clutches, my chest tight. "I wasn't... Why did you think that?"

He shakes his head. "It never occurred to me that my dad would lie. He says he didn't. He says it's the information he was given."

"Given by who?" The words pass through my lips on a whisper, but as I say them, I know the answer.

I know who wanted to keep us apart.

"You didn't just leave me here... to fade into your past."

He shakes his head. "I thought you didn't want me." Blue eyes capture mine, and like a magnet, I'm drawn to him. I go straight into his arms, and they open, catching me, clasping me to his chest, holding me, surrounding me in the warmth and security I thought I'd lost.

In that single moment, everything melts away. The walls melt, all the things that kept us apart dissolve like sand in the sea. Lifting my head, I find his eyes, and he smiles, smoothing his palms along my cheeks, tracing my jawline with his thumbs.

"I want you back, Ember Rose. I want it all back."

I nod, my eyes heating. "I want that, too."

Leaning forward, he kisses me softly, just a nip of his lips against mine. It's fire in my veins. "I thought I came here to get away, to find peace, but I came for you." He speaks against my skin, kissing and inhaling. "You drew me here. I don't care about the lies. I don't care what we were told. They won't keep us apart anymore. You're mine."

"Yes," I repeat, my lips parting as his return to mine.

His tongue sweeps inside, and warmth floods my stomach. A bubble of happiness expands in my chest. Our kisses consume, and the jagged lines of the chasm in my heart slowly meld together.

"Jackson..." His grip on me is strong but gentle, firm and possessive as he carries me to the bed.

It's only us.

The scars are gone.

Sitting on the edge of the bed, he holds my back in his hand. His lips are on my shoulder, tracing a line and leaving chills in his wake. I shiver and look down, heat flooding my panties.

"I want you now." His voice is thick with hunger, and all I can do is nod, touching his face.

169

Reaching up, I lower the spaghetti straps of my top. They fall down around my upper arms, and he kisses across the top of my chest, moving lower to pull a beaded nipple into his mouth.

"Oh, yes!" I gasp as my back arches.

It's been so long.

I want him so bad.

He pulls my sensitive skin between his teeth then soothes it with his kiss, and I move like a wave, following the progress of his mouth.

Bending forward, I kiss his head, his soft hair, and he rises to cover my mouth as his hand covers my breast.

I catch his shirt and pull. My hands are on his body, smoothing the planes and lines, tracing the rippling muscles with my fingers. I feel him tighten with a groan.

"Ember," he whispers, lifting me to stand and sliding the remainder of my clothes to the floor.

I hold his cheeks as his mouth moves across my navel to my hip.

"Oh, God," I gasp as his fingers touch my core, looping in my panties and ripping them away.

The first pass of his tongue over my clit causes my knees to buckle. "Oh..." I moan.

"So good," he speaks against my sensitive skin, his scruffy cheek roughing my inner thigh.

I catch his shoulders to find my balance, but he's not letting up. He's not slowing down. He's hungry. He grips my thighs, pulling me closer, kissing and sucking eagerly at my clit, twisting feverish desire in my belly.

"Jackson... Jackson..." I chant his name as streaks of pleasure climb my legs like vines, centering in my core, drawing tighter with every pass of his tongue.

Fluttering starts in my feet, and I feel my wetness on my thighs. My hands are on his shoulders, and my fingers clench as the orgasm grows tighter...

Tighter...

Unbearably tighter...

Until it explodes.

I cry as the shudders wrack my body.

He's kissing me now, slower, soothing passes. My fingers flex and release, and my legs tremble as he cups my ass, gently rotating me so I'm lying back on the bed.

I'm buzzing with aftershocks, and I watch with hazy eyes as he pulls his shirt over his head, leaving his dark hair in a silky mess. Next, he shoves his jeans down, allowing his erection to spring free. It's thick and straining, just like I remember.

He doesn't hesitate to come to me, kneeling on the bed and moving my thighs apart. His blue eyes are navy with hunger, and in one fluid move, he's inside me.

"Oh, God," I gasp.

"Yes..." His voice is at my ear.

Holding my cheek, he kisses my neck, my shoulder, as the thrusting grows faster, stronger. My knees rise, and he holds the back of my thigh, plunging deeper, impossibly deep as our bodies rock in time. The pace increases. He's pumping hard, and little noises ache from my throat with every hit. It's so good, my second orgasm burns hotter than the first. Stars shoot behind my closed eyes. My insides erupt in shimmering spasms of pleasure as I come.

"Fuck, yes." His back arches, and with a low groan he holds me, steadying himself as I feel him break, pulsing and filling me.

Reaching up, I slide my hands over his shoulders, down to his waist.

His kisses are soft, slow, on my shoulder, my neck. "Only you, Ember. Only you."

His heart beats against my breast.

Our hearts beat together.

We're one, like we were before.

Like we were always meant to be.

Chapter 15

Jack

Having Ember Rose in my arms is like winning the fucking lottery. It's like being named King of Everything. It's like...

I can't help a grin. My mind is a lovesick teenager.

I'm the boy who left ten years ago.

In adult terms, having her again is better than graduating with honors from the hardest law school in the country. It's better than winning the toughest case of my career. It's better than anything I've done since I left this place.

She has matured since I knew her last, but she's still so much the same. She's a woman now, a mother, and she moves with a confident grace she didn't have as a teen.

Still, holding her now, looking down into her dark eyes flecked with gold, I see the girl who stole my heart years ago. She's everything I always wanted. Her fingers trace along the tops of my shoulders, and I lean down to kiss her again, inhaling deeply of lavender and rose. We're lying, our bodies pressed together in her bed, and...

Fuck me, I'm suffocating.

"How do you sleep in this place?" Lines of sweat follow her fingertips down my back. "It's hot as hell."

She starts to laugh. "I don't usually have a human radiator generating heat in the bed with me."

"We can't sleep here." Sitting up, I pull her with me. Her dark hair falls around her shoulders, and for a moment, I forget my name.

She's sitting here naked, her small breasts round and full, her dark nipples peaked and straining. Her narrow waist leads down to her curved hips and bare legs with only the sheet tossed across her lap.

"Jesus, Ember," I whisper awestruck. "You're so beautiful."

Dark brown eyes lift to mine, and they're shining with emotion. I can't help cupping her cheek, sliding my thumb over her lips, moving my hand down her slim neck to her chest, her breast. I cup it, a perfect handful, rolling her nipple between my fingers. She inhales audibly, and my dick stirs. I want to be inside her again.

Her hand covers mine, fingers spreading before sliding up my arm. "You're the same boy who stole my breath the first time I saw you."

"Am I the same?" I grin. "I can think of a few differences."

White teeth appear when she smiles, and she traces her fingers along the line of my hair. "Your hair is shorter." Her bottom lip goes between her teeth. "You're more polished. You're a man now."

My stomach is tight, my whole body tense with lust. I'm a man who sees everything he wants in the world and who's ready to claim it.

"Come on," I say, clearing the thickness from my throat. "If we stay here much longer, I'll have to fuck you again."

That gets me a real laugh. "You're a little dirtier than you used to be."

Standing beside the bed, I pull her straight up against me, her soft curves melting against my hardness. "I'm a lot dirtier than I used to be."

I feel her body shiver, and her eyes darken. That's my Ember Rose, the girl who told me I would teach her to kiss. The girl who told me to teach her everything. The girl who eagerly went wherever I wanted to take her...

Remembering those days, the things we did, her innocence makes her more mine than any vows we might have made.

Stepping to the side, I hold her hand. "Get dressed. I'm taking you to my place."

I watch as she goes to an old armoire. Her ass is round and soft like a peach, and shit if I'm going to be able to get my dick in my pants if she keeps prancing around here naked. She takes out a filmy dress and drops it over her head. When she turns around, she does a little shrug.

"Ready?"

Fuck me. Knowing she's completely bare underneath is even sexier than her walking around this hotbox naked.

"I have an idea." My jeans are on, and I've pulled the shirt over my head again.

Taking her hand, I lead her down the stairs and out to my truck. We're moving fast and once inside, she scoots across the bench, leaning her head on my shoulder.

My insides are buzzing with joy, comfort, *completion*. Instinctively, I wrap my arm around her as I turn the wheel and take us up the street, through the quiet neighborhoods and out of town.

"Where are we going?" she asks, her hand tracing lines along the top of my thigh, an action that fuels my desire.

"I thought we could go to our place." I'm thinking of washing her in the ocean, making love to her, holding her bare body against mine as the waves roll around us.

Her cheek moves, and she smiles against my shoulder. It isn't long before we're there. I pull off the road, parking in the brush, behind a tree and two small bushes like I always did.

She's out the door before I've killed the engine, and I think of a night not so long ago near a lake with a different girl. I didn't give a shit about following that girl.

Tonight, nothing in this world could keep me away.

Tonight, I'm chasing the girl of my dreams to the place I can never forget.

Her dress is on the dry sand, and her moonlit body moves slowly into the water. For a moment, all I can do is watch as the water rises gradually to her knees, her waist. Her dark hair falls in thick ripples down her back, meeting the water and spreading out around her the deeper she goes.

The moonlight tips the dark water with silver, and the stars are points of light in the midnight-blue sky above. She's magical, a creature of the sea, an innocent seductress, and I'm bewitched by her beauty.

I quickly shed my jeans and tee and follow her, pushing through the surf, using my hands to help me move faster until I capture her in my arms.

"Hmm," she turns to face me. She wraps her arms over my shoulders, pressing her breasts against my chest, and I sigh deeply. "It's been so long since I've come here with anyone besides Coco."

"You bring your daughter here?" I try to imagine the two of them, so similar in this beautiful place. I've only seen her daughter twice, but already she feels as much a part of us as anything.

"It's the best place to get away from the crowds, to have some peace and quiet."

Leaning down, I kiss the top of her arm, loving the feel of our skin against skin, warm in the cool water. We came here so many times that summer, stealing away in the dead of night. I remember standing at the head of the path, straining my eyes in the darkness for her to appear on that damn bike.

"You would never ride in the car with me," I muse, sliding my hand down to cup her ass.

Her legs lift, wrapping around my waist and I walk us out further into the waves.

"I was so afraid of us getting caught together," she says against my neck. "My mother could make people disappear. I was afraid she would make you disappear."

"No one is making me disappear." I turn and kiss her lips.

She gasps slightly as my hand moves lower, dipping into her core, testing her wetness. Her voice grows silky, like honey. "But you did…"

Two fingers inside, she moans, and I pull at her lips. "Not anymore. I'm never letting you go, Ember Rose."

Happiness flickers across her face, but her mouth forms a little O. She's focused, needing me. Leaning into her, I seal my lips to hers, replacing my fingers with my dick. I hold her thighs and pull her to me, letting the motion of the waves assist in bringing her flush against my pelvis.

A moan is consumed into my mouth. Her muscles flex, her thighs tightening over me as she rocks. It's the closest thing to heaven on Earth, and it doesn't take long before we're soaring.

My release comes quickly, blanking my mind. I hear her moans of pleasure. Her core clenches rhythmically as she comes undone, and I wrap my arms tighter around her, holding us together in this reunion.

The water swirls around us. I hold her, and we drift together. I'm lazy and satisfied and already thinking about the future. I know what I want, and I'm ready to make it happen.

"Tell me about your daughter," I say, kissing her ear. "How old is she?"

Her head lifts, and her eyes are round. "I had her four years ago."

"What's the status of her..." I try to think of a delicate way to put it. "Father?"

Ember's eyes cloud, and something like worry fills her expression.

Reaching up, I slide a piece of hair behind her ear. "What's wrong?"

"Does it bother you?" She's studying my face, watching me closely.

"What?" A little wave crashes between us, sending salt into my mouth. I spit it out.

Her eyes flicker away, but I'm not having any more hiding. I give her a little shake. "What are you afraid of?"

"My mother said men don't like other men's children."

Heat tightens in my chest. It's becoming a regular occurrence whenever Marjorie Warren comes up. I'm mentally piecing together what happened after I left... The only unanswered question is why.

"Come on," I say, leading us out of the water. We walk up the shore to our clothes, the light breeze cooling our heated skin, and I think about my words. "Your daughter is as beautiful as you. I'd like to get to know her." Ember looks up at me, and I can tell she's not convinced. "I expect the two of you are a package deal."

She reaches down and quickly drops the sundress over her head. "I won't leave Coco behind." I don't miss the edge in her voice as she says it, almost like a challenge.

Jerking my jeans over my hips, I catch her around the waist as she tries to pass, pulling her to me. "I would never ask you to." Leaning forward, I kiss the corner of her mouth. "I'd like her to come with you. Is that possible?"

Her shoulders drop, and she relaxes in my arms. "It should be."

Releasing her, I scoop up my tee, shaking the sand out of it before dropping it over my head. "Tell me about her. Were you..." Unexpected jealousy hits me as I say the words. "Is her father someone you cared about?"

We reach the truck, and I help her inside before jogging around to climb in the driver's side. She tells me the story as we drive back to the cottage. Her voice is quiet, cautious, and I hang on every word.

"I'm embarrassed to say it was a drunk hookup, but it's the truth." She looks down at her hands, twisting in her lap. I want to reach out and cover them with mine. "I don't know what I'll tell her when she's older... about her dad."

"Wait to cross that bridge. If she knows how much you love her, she won't hold it against you."

She glances up at me, and her lips press into a sad little smile. "I only went out with one guy after you left..."

"Mason Green," I say, remembering the picture my father showed me.

The photo that killed all my dreams and changed the direction of my life.

"My mother wanted me to try. She said it wasn't good for me to pine away after a boy who wasn't coming back."

My fists tighten on the steering wheel, but I don't say the words in my head. "What made you believe her?"

She does a little shrug. "I guess I already feared it was true when you left. I knew I was only a kid. You were a man, smart and educated. It was easy for me to believe you wouldn't come back."

I feel as if I've been punched in the chest. "Was it?" Looking at her, I can't keep the frown off my face. "I thought you knew how I felt."

She chews her lip, and I can tell she's thinking something she's afraid to say. We drive through the neighborhoods of Oceanside Village in silence. We continue past her storefront, making the left turn headed north into the woods where my mother's cottage is located.

"We'll be more comfortable sleeping here," I say, holding the door for her as she slips out of the cab.

She's right in front of me, her head only reaching the center of my chest, and I cup her cheek. The shadows are thicker here, the moonlight more ambient. I press my lips gently to hers, and I feel the tension leave her body. When I pull away again, our eyes meet, and we're back.

I take her hand and continue to the house. "So you didn't date," I say, hoping to continue the story.

"After we graduated, Mason left to go to the mission field. I didn't want to go to college, but I wasn't sure what else I'd do."

I unlock the door, and we step inside. She gasps, and I smile. "I know, right?"

"It doesn't look anything like it used to." Her voice is a whisper as she walks carefully around the living room, touching the back of the couch, the pillows. "It was only a shack when we came here."

"Dad had it completely redone."

She nods. "I remember when it was happening. I... I never could bring myself to come back. Not after..."

"I know." I do know. We shared several firsts here. I painted her here. We can revisit those times later. "So you went to culinary school?"

That gets me a laugh, musical and soft. "No." She shakes her head. "I never went to culinary school. I did hair. I sold makeup, I sold leggings, I was a teller at the bank for about five minutes..."

"Jesus, you've done everything in Oceanside!" I laugh because my insides are warm with love.

"Not true," she laughs, leaning into me for a quick kiss. "I never painted houses. I never worked at the hardware store, and I never made poboys."

"What got you interested in cakes?" I push a lock of damp hair behind her ear. "How did that start?"

"When Coco had her first birthday, I'd planned this whole Little Mermaid theme." She sits on her knees on the couch, and I walk around to sit in front of her. "I wanted a cake with blue raspberry and strawberries and cookies for the clam shells…"

"What happened?" Her energy telling this story pulls me in.

"Everybody looked at me like I was crazy. If it wasn't a basic round, two tiered sponge, nobody knew how to do it."

She's already talking over my head, but I don't want her to stop. "So?"

"So I found a cake baking book and I did my research and I made it myself." She sits back, a smug look on her face.

"And it was good," I finish for her.

She leans forward as if letting me in on a secret. "It was really good." Her nose wrinkles, and she's fucking adorable. "My aunt Agnes—"

"The lady who owned the five and dime?"

"Yes!"

"She always gave me free candy."

A sly smile curls Ember's lips. "Cinnamon."

I can't resist. I lean forward and kiss her. "Tell me more about the cakes." We're catching up so fast, our conversations flying from one memory to the next seamlessly.

"Aunt Agnes believed in me from the start. She said I had a natural gift for baking. I started baking cakes for birthday parties, which led to special occasions, and eventually weddings. It started as a hobby until I read a magazine article about Peggy Porschen…"

I frown and shake my head, and she explains. "Peggy Porschen owns this super-famous bake shop in London. It's gorgeous. It has flowers everywhere and chandeliers and the whole front entrance is pink with a huge rose garland above the door…"

"I understand your interior design choices now," I tease, but she's serious.

"It's everything I aspire to be. I'm going to work my ass off, own my own shop, and take care of Coco and me... And maybe I can bring some business back to Oceanside."

Sliding my finger along the line of her cheek, I don't say aloud that I plan to be the one taking care of her and Coco. I love her dream, and she can bake as much as she wants. But now that I have her in my arms again, no one is taking her away from me — past or present. Ember Rose is mine from now on.

A shadow crosses her face, and my chest tightens. "What's wrong?"

"My mother says it's a ridiculous pursuit, especially as a career path. She doesn't believe anyone will pay enough for cake to support a family."

"I don't like to agree with your mother, but in this part of the country, where everyone bakes..."

She nods, grasping my forearm. "I know, but Aunt Agnes was looking ahead to the future, to where we are now. Things have changed so much so fast!"

"You're right." I nod, lacing our fingers. "In the city, a cake shop like yours could easily support your little family with plenty left over. Here, you might have to get more creative with your business plan."

"Tabby wants to set up a website for online orders, and as time passes, I'm getting more orders for things like birthday cakes, special occasion cakes... Women our age don't bake as much. It's becoming a specialized thing."

"It sounds like a great idea, and you're a natural. Right?"

Her chin drops, and she looks up at me through her lashes. "You've never had one of my cakes."

Leaning forward, I kiss her nose. "I've tasted other things of yours, and they're very good."

"Jackson!" She slaps my arm, which makes me laugh. "I don't make coochie cakes..." She pauses, and I see her thinking. "Only penis cakes."

"What?"

She laughs loudly at my surprise. "Betty Pepper orders penis cakes!"

My eyes go round, and I stand, pulling her to her feet. "Are you telling me you're a dirty Betty Crocker?"

She snorts loudly, and it makes me laugh. Scooping her off her feet, I throw her over my shoulder and start for the bedroom. "I'll give you penis cake..."

"Jackson! Put me down," she laughs, but I head down the hall to the bedroom. As we pass the smaller room I've been using for a studio, she starts wiggling out of my grasp. "Stop. Wait!"

I set her on her feet, and stand beside her as she looks into the room. The sketchpad is where I left it propped on the easel. Light from the doorway falls directly over the charcoal drawing I did of her, and the effect is dramatic.

Every curve and shadow seems more pronounced, and she walks slowly toward the image of her. It's a replica of my painting. Her legs are strategically crossed to cover her private parts, but from the waist up, she's exposed.

Her dark hair flows in ripples around her shoulders, and her beautiful breasts are on full display. I took my time on them, sliding my fingertips under the curves, over the nipples...

184

She reaches out and holds her hand above the lines and shades of her face. "When did you do this?" Wonder is in her voice, and my stomach tightens.

"Do you like it?"

Her chin lifts and she looks up at me. "It's so good. It's... like the other one."

Stepping behind her, I wrap my arms around her waist, leaning down so my chin is on her shoulder. She places one arm over mine.

"I couldn't get you out of my head any other way. I had to draw you."

"You still paint?"

We're both speaking as if we're in church, hushed and reverent. We're in the presence of my dreams, both of them married together on paper in front of us.

"I haven't painted in a long time. About ten years."

"But you sketch?" She steps out of my arms, turning to face me and hold both my hands in hers.

"This is the first sketch I've done in about as long."

Small lines crease her brow. "Why did you stop?"

Now it's my turn to look away. "I lost my inspiration when I lost you."

"And now you've found it again?" It's a quiet question, a question so full of meaning. It's the question of what will happen next.

"That depends..."

Mentally, I've already made a place for her and her daughter here. I have unfinished business, we have truths to sort out, but the outcome doesn't change. Ember belongs with me.

Lifting her fingers to my lips, I kiss the top of her hand. "I'd like to paint you again now, with all of your changes."

Her nose wrinkles. "Ten years older?"

Lowering her hand, I reach out and slide my finger under the strap of her dress. It drops down her arm, exposing her breast. My lips heat, and I lift my hand to touch her. Her breath catches in a soft gasp as I cup the weight, sliding my thumb over the tightening nipple.

"They're larger," I say in the same quiet voice.

I lift my other hand to do the same, lower the strap, expose her breast. Only this time the entire dress drops to the floor. The blood rushes below my waist, and my cock rises.

My eyes are fixed on her body, her beautiful curves in my hands. Her hips are more rounded. "You were only a girl when I painted you last time. Now you're a woman."

When I look up, I see her eyes are dark. Her lips are parted, then the bottom one is clutched below the tips of her white teeth. "I want you inside me."

Fuck. My hand drops between her legs, and she moans softly as I touch her.

"You're so wet."

"Please..." she hisses.

I don't have to be asked twice.

I quickly shove my jeans to the floor, allowing my cock to spring free. She grasps it, pulling gently, sliding her thumb over the damp tip, blowing my mind. I can't wait to carry her across the hall to my bed. I grasp her hips, lifting her off her feet, and push her back against the nearest wall.

"Oh, God!" she gasps as I lower her body, sinking my throbbing dick deep into her clenching heat.

We're instinctual and hungry. My hips thrust up as her thighs push against my pelvis. Her breasts bounce, and she moans, digging her fingers into my shoulders. I can't hold out any longer as the fierce orgasm spirals up my thighs, tightening my pelvis, and shooting out of me.

"Ember," I groan against her neck, pulsing deep.

In that moment, all uncertainty is gone. This is my future — us, here, together. It's the only thing I want.

Chapter 16

Ember

Having Jackson Cane in my life again is like waking from a ten-year sleep. It's like touching a match to the ashes lying dormant in my soul and suddenly being surrounded by light and warmth and protection. It's like stretching up to ride the wind or folding inward and becoming the fire.

Last night I lost the battle of resistance. I surrendered to the deep need I've been fighting since he returned. His touch awakened all that had gone quiet in my soul when I lost him...

Only, I didn't lose him.

Last night I was able to put these questions aside and luxuriate in the decadent satisfaction of reunion. Jackson touches me like no one ever has. He coaxes the sleeping goddess awake. When we touch, I remember all the first times. He's my teacher, my lover, my friend, my everything. When he says I'm his, my soul rings with assent.

I am his.

He is mine...

And he wants Coco.

He's not put off by her. My jaw tightens at the memory of the cruel words my mother spoke.

Lies, always lies.

The lies end now.

Wyatt is trimming the box hedge around the perimeter of his yard as I ride my bike toward my mother's house. I pass Kay Johnson on her knees in her front flowerbed, striking the stereotypical ass-in-the-air pose.

With each push of the pedals, an ache of satisfaction echoes deep in my core, and it makes me smile remembering making love last night, so many times. Nothing has changed between us. If anything, our passion is hotter than ever...

Now it's time for truth.

I'm rounding the corner toward the enormous house where I grew up when Betty Pepper comes racing down her walk to meet me.

"Emberly! Emberly Warren!" She's waving one hand over her head and clutching her bouncing bosom with the other. "I need to speak to you right this minute!"

Remembering what happened last night provokes a little growl in my chest, and I'm already on an angry errand. Still, I push the pedals backward and skid to a stop.

Stepping off Dixie, I walk her to the white picket fence surrounding BP's house. It's almost noon, and the blazing sun makes me squint and wish for sunglasses.

"Good morning, Miss B," I say without enthusiasm.

"Emberly!" She's gasping for breath and touching the beads of sweat off her upper lip. "I swear it's so hot today, I had to wear my Bermooda shorts!"

"Bermuda," I correct under my breath.

"Where is my Bucky? It's lunchtime, and he's still not home. Did he spend the night with you last night?"

"Good lord," I growl. "He did not spend the night with me. He tried to spend the night, and when I told him no, he tried to force me."

The older woman's hand is pressed to her chest as if she's on the verge of a heart attack. "My stars! I'm sure that was a misunderstanding. Bucky would never—"

"It was not a misunderstanding. Jackson was there. He got Bucky off me, and I called Chad Tucker. When Chad finally showed up, Bucky had run away!"

"What! I never... Well, that's just like you Emberly Warren!" Her face is indignant. "Bucky has a tender heart. He made you a special squirrel. I watched him spend hours getting it just right, and you stand here making up falsehoods about him! He's a good boy, and everyone knows the loose morals you have. Ever since you were a girl running around with Jackson Cane then getting pregnant out of *wedlock* by some stranger..."

White-hot anger flashes in my face and neck. "Don't you dare talk about my daughter."

"You're talking about my son," she shrieks. "Why, you probably tried to seduce him, and when he resisted, you told lies about him... like Joseph in the Bible. You're a Potiphar's wife!"

My hand twitches at my side, and I remember the stories Bucky said his mother has been spreading around town about me. I'd like nothing better than to slap Betty Pepper into next Tuesday.

Instead, I turn my bike, grumbling as I go, "Bucky smells like deviled eggs and he looks like Kip Dynamite. I'd rather seduce a pig!"

"Don't you walk away from me, Emberly Rose! You've got to help me find him! You were the last one with him."

"I'm not doing anything for you," I shout.

"You've always been this way, Emberly. You can't hear the truth about yourself. You never could."

Shoving my bike against my mother's fence, I spin around and storm across the street again, fire blazing in my eyes. "Don't tell me what I can't hear, Betty Pepper! You don't know me, and you clearly don't know your son."

"Oh, I know you. I know *all* about you and your family!" she hisses. My fists clench, and the old woman draws back, her elbows rising like a chicken. "What are you thinking? Don't you hit me!"

Her neck is pulled in, causing a double chin to form along her jawline, and her old blue eyes are bulging. I'm breathing so hard my chest rises and falls rapidly, and I realize how this must look. Last thing I need is everyone saying I hit an old woman.

Taking several deep breaths, I force myself to relax. "Tell your son to stay away from me. If you try to slander me, I know at least two other girls who will testify against him."

I turn and head back for my mother's house. My fight isn't with Betty Pepper, and I won't let her distract me from why I'm really here.

"Hypocritical busybody trying to hold me to some double standard to make herself feel important," I mutter.

I have a bigger fish to fry.

Pausing on the massive wrap-around front porch of my mother's house, I center my thoughts. I'm here for one very important reason. Inside, I don't see anyone on the first floor. Music comes from the second floor. It sounds like Coco is watching one of her children's shows. My brow furrows when I think about her hearing what I have to say. I almost back out when my mother rounds the corner from the kitchen into the foyer.

"Emberly?" She stops fast as if I've caught her in the act of doing something illegal. "What are you doing here?"

Several sheets of paper are in her hand, but I can't make out what's on them. "Is Coco here?" I ask, looking up the stairs.

"No, she had a play date today with Polly. I told you—"

"We need to talk." I sidestep her, going into the sitting room. "Would you mind?"

She hesitates, watching me. "What is this about?"

I'm not sure what to make of her defensiveness, but I don't have time to lose. "I talked to Jackson last night." *Among other things...*

"Jackson...?" She actually tries to pretend she doesn't understand.

"Jackson Cane?"

"Oh." She strides into the room and sits on the edge of her Edwardian loveseat. Her back is straight as a board. "Jack Lockwood."

"He never liked that name."

"It's his name." Her voice is flinty, and her eyes are cold. It's a side she likes to keep hidden, but I'm well acquainted with my mother the superbitch.

"After he left for college it seems he and I both got the same story." As I speak, my mother's eyebrow arches. "Why did you lie to keep us apart?"

"I don't know what you're talking about."

193

I take a deep breath and step toward the fireplace, putting my hand on the mantle. "You didn't like me with him. Why?"

"Emberly, your imagination is — "

"Why, Momma?"

Her eyes flash, and she speaks quickly. "He's a liar. He comes from a family of liars."

"Is lying genetic?" I sure hope not since Marjorie Warren is the queen.

She stands up in front of the small sofa. "He ruined you the same way his father ruined this town... the same way his mother ruined our family!"

A flash of fear hits my chest. My mother is speaking words I've never heard before. She's talking about deep secrets, things that have been buried a long time.

I'm ready with my shovel.

"How did his mother ruin our family?"

"I'm not discussing this with you." She starts for the door, but I dash across the room and cut her off. She tries to step around me, but I catch her wrist, accidentally knocking the papers from her hands.

"I'm sorry," I say, squatting down to gather them. She slaps my hands away, pulling the sheets fast to her chest, but I have one.

"Drunkenness, revelry, and the like are displeasing to the lord..." I read aloud.

"Give me that!" She snatches the page out of my hand. "That is none of your business."

I know exactly what she's holding, and I'm sick of the lies. "Whose business is it, Momma?"

"God's," she says, again attempting to leave.

My hand shoots out to grip the doorframe, my arm blocking her progress. "I know you write

Reverend Green's sermons. You can stop hiding it from me."

"I do not!" Her eyes blaze at me, but I'm not interested in that revelation. I want to get back to the bomb she almost dropped.

"How did Jackson's mom ruin our family?" I know how his dad did it—or how everyone thinks his dad did it, by developing Oceanside Beach and taking all the tourism dollars away.

I also know Jackson has never gotten along with his dad, which is why he prefers *Cane*, his mother's maiden name, to *Lockwood*.

"When Jack went to school, his father and I agreed your relationship should follow the normal course of high school relationships. It should end." She isn't answering my question about Jackson's mom, but I'm distracted enough by what she is saying to let it go.

"What did you do?" My insides are quaking. I'm not sure if my hands are shaking from fear or anger, but I have to know the answer to this question.

"We simply agreed to encourage you both to see other people."

"Jackson said his father showed him a picture of me with Mason Green. His father told him I'd been promised to Mason, and we were getting married as soon as I graduated and were heading to the mission field together."

My mother's eyes flutter and she looks to the ceiling. "If only the lord would grant me such a noble daughter. Instead I have you—willful and unworthy of my love."

The knot in my throat twists so tight it's physically painful. "Did you tell Jackson's dad I was engaged to Mason Green?"

Her eyes narrow, and she steps closer to me. "Randall Lockwood came to me with a proposition. If I wouldn't block his attempts in the city council to get approval for his new development, he would see to it Jackson never came back here for you again. He's a liar just like his son. He traded you for the right to destroy this town."

"And you gave it to him."

She glares at me a moment longer before striding from the room, Sunday's sermon clutched tight in her hand.

Idolatry.

Greed.

Lies.

I feel like the wind has been knocked out of me. I take two steps backwards before finding my footing and going to the front door. I'm having trouble breathing, and all I can think is I have to get to Coco. I want to find my daughter and take her home. I'm not leaving her in this house another second.

The wind swirls around the wooden structure, captured by the series of pillars, rails, and awnings. It's a natural wind tunnel. I look up the road at the unsuspecting people working in their yards like it's any other day and not the most significant day in almost eleven years.

For them it's not.

It's just another Saturday.

Looking across the street, I see Betty Pepper still huffing around her yard. She bends over and straightens a garden gnome. His pointed red cap extends past her shoulder as she grunts. *I know all about you and your family...*

I'm off the porch and hustling across the street again as the old woman stands and sees me.

"What do you want?" she grumbles, jerking her blouse down to cover the straining button on her Bermuda shorts.

"You've lived here, across the street from my parents' house since before I was born?"

"I've lived here for fifty-one years, Emberly Warren, and you'll do good to remember that." Her pale face is pink around the edges, and wisps of grey hair fly in the breeze.

"I was talking to my momma just now... she said something about Beverly Cane destroying my family the same way Randall destroyed the town."

"She did?" The old woman's eyes flash round, and I know I made the right decision coming here. "I can't believe she'd dredge up that old baggage."

"What did she mean?"

"You know very well what she meant. Randall Lockwood developed Oceanside Beach, and all the tourists left here. They all went to the strand, and our economy dried up." She walks along the inside of her picket fence.

I follow along the outside. "And Beverly Cane?"

She sniffs and lifts her chin. "I'm not one to go around spreading dirt about the dead. It's disrespectful."

"It's still my family." I give a little smile, hoping she'll soften.

"Speaking of disrespectful, you need to learn to respect your elders. Attacking me when I was simply asking if you'd seen Bucky..."

"You're right," I nod, doing my very best to look apologetic. "I had no right to speak to you that way.

I think the heat is making me tired." *Tired of the bullshit.*

"You could work on your temper." She jerks on her waistband. "Your father never acted that way. He was as helpful as he could be before... Well, he was helpful, and your mother — "

"Before what?" I smile and blink up at her.

She looks side to side, checking for eavesdroppers, and I know I've got her. Betty Pepper wouldn't be worth her weight in busybody gold if she could resist a blatant plea for gossip. "I can't believe you don't remember this, though I suppose you were only a child at the time."

"I barely remember my father at all," I say in a sad way I'm hoping she can't resist.

Strangely, I have no memories of my father, even though I was a little older than Coco when he and my sister died.

"You're old enough," she says as if giving herself permission. "It's only right you know the truth."

"The truth?"

"Beverly Cane was your mother's best friend... until she started sleeping with your father." My jaw drops, and even though the attachments are long gone, I still feel shock. "Your mother insisted they break it off, but that sort-of backfired on her. They decided to leave instead."

"My father was going to leave us?" I'm trying to decide if I'm devastated or if I blame him, especially after my last conversation with my mother.

The old woman's brow softens, and she touches my hand. "No, love. Your father would never leave you behind. He took you and your sister, and he and Beverly drove out of town. Or, they tried to."

Her voice moves away, becoming distant. The memory of my dream rushes in on me. Water is pouring in all around us, clear arcs coming in through the windows, black water rising up from the floor.

"It was a car wreck," I say in a whisper.

"Your father was driving when that car went off the   bridge.   You   were   the   only   survivor."

Chapter 17

Jack

"I'm not going back to the firm." Watching my father, I brace for the explosion.

It doesn't come.

He leans back in his chair and exhales deeply. "I had a feeling you might say this. I had a feeling it was coming when you bumped into that little girl again."

"Ember isn't a little girl."

"You realize you're making a mistake."

"The only mistake I ever made was not coming back here to verify your story." My words are angry, but my demeanor is calm.

I walk to the wall of windows in his penthouse office and look out over the vast stretch of ocean. Tiny sailboats are dotted throughout the expanse of blue. It's all so serene and beautiful, such a contrast to how I feel.

"So you're not going back to your firm." My father ignores my jab. "What will you do instead? Paint houses?"

The chuckle in his voice fuels my defiance. "Maybe." I continue looking out at the water, thinking about life with Ember, the life I've always wanted.

"Be serious, Jack."

I study him sitting behind the large mahogany desk. The gleaming wood and sturdy brass all project an image of importance. My father in his sleek charcoal business suit, his gray hair neatly trimmed along with his close-cut white beard. He's the picture of superiority.

I think about Brice Wagner and his façade of importance, his lies.

"I am being serious." My voice is quiet, contemplative. "I'm not interested in competing in the same way as Wagner and Bancroft."

"Bullshit," my father growls. "You can compete in any arena. You're a shark. You're built for speed, a natural born killer."

His assumptions actually make me laugh. "I'm not a killer, Dad. I never have been."

"Well, you've done a fine fucking imitation of it up to now."

With an exhale, I sit in the lower, quilt-stitched leather chair across from his desk. "I buried myself in the work, but I uncovered something. They're dishonest. They — "

"Ahh!" My dad holds up his hand in a stopping motion. "Don't tell me anything. You're not thinking clearly right now, and you might regret sharing it later."

Leaning forward, I prop my forearms on my thighs. I study my palms and think about how the only person who has ever seen me for who I am is Ember. She's the only person who has ever cared to know the real me, not the guy they want me to be.

"I'm thinking clearer than I have in a long time," I say, still studying the lines in my palm as if reading the future. "I'm moving back to Oceanside Village permanently. I'll paint. I'll consider taking on small cases, but only because I'm going to marry Ember Warren. I'm going to help her achieve her dreams, and we'll live our life. The life we dreamed of having together ten years ago."

He laughs and the derision is like sandpaper against my skin. "Ten years ago, you dreamed something you never would have had if you'd stayed there." He pushes out of his chair, and walks around the desk, leaning against it. "So you'll do what? Wills and estates? You'll paint and marry the town baker? What about her kid?"

My jaw clenches, and I cut angry eyes at him. "I'm warning you. You interfered in our lives once. Don't do it again."

Both hands go up this time. "I have no interest in interfering. I'm only asking the obvious questions."

"Her daughter is a beautiful little girl. I want her to like me and think of me as a father." Rising from the chair, I start toward the door. "I'd like to give her brothers and sisters as well."

"Jack," his voice changes, becomes placating. "Stop... don't leave angry. You haven't been home in years. Let's get lunch."

My throat is tight, and I'm frustrated with his attitude toward my plans and Emberly, but at the same time, it's been just Dad and me ever since the accident.

"I came to you for advice. You're in the business world. I'm facing a serious decision, and I need to do the right thing. I'm not sure how."

"You always do the right thing, Jack. It's who you are." He pats me on the shoulder. "Come, let's have lunch."

* * *

The task ahead of me weighs on my mind the entire drive back to Oceanside. Perhaps Dad was right about not telling anyone yet. Perhaps I should wait on telling Ember what I've planned to do.

In his mind, waiting means not burning bridges for when I "wake up" and return to my life in the city, return to the firm. In my mind, I simply don't want Ember to worry. I shouldn't be implicated in what happened, but it's possible I might have some liability if I can't prove I didn't know about the hidden files.

Also, there are the circumstances of the case. I don't want to dredge up painful memories for her. We've never talked about her sister and how she died. Ember was so young, I'm not even sure if she remembers. She was about the same age as her daughter when it happened...

Her bike is parked outside the bakery, so I stop there first. It makes me laugh she doesn't own a car.

"Did you even learn how to drive?" I ask, pushing through the old door.

She's across the room at that massive wooden table in front of her shelves of ingredients, and I swear, every time I see her, I forget everything clouding my mind.

A spot of flour is on her cheek — at least I think it's flour. Her long dark hair is swept up on top of her head, and she's dressed in those cut-offs again, which reveal her sexy legs. Ember isn't tall, but she has great legs and of course, those curves.

I want to lift her onto that table and taste everything she's hiding in those shorts then sink my cock...

"What?" She's pouring something white into a bowl of more white, and when she looks up, I see she's troubled.

Shaking away my dirty thoughts, I go straight to where she's standing and lean beside her. "What's wrong?"

She'd planned to confront her mother today, and her mother is one powerful force. My girl is pretty powerful, but locking horns with someone like that still takes the wind out of your sails.

She shakes her head and continues pouring. "I'm just... thinking about this recipe."

I'm not convinced it's the whole truth, but I'll let it go for now. "What is it?"

"Tabby called about an hour ago. A couple in Oceanside Beach need a gluten-free birthday cake. I saw this on a TV show — it's called a Hazelnut Dacquoise."

My eyebrows rise, and I look down at the bubbly white foam rising in the bowl as the silver beater turns. "What's in it?"

"Hazelnuts, of course." She quickly switches off the mixer, and I stand back as she removes the bowl and steps down to where a clear blue plastic bag with a large, cone-shaped tip waits beside three white mats. "I'll alternate three meringue layers with a coffee-flavored mousse between them..."

"Sounds delicious."

She scrapes the white mixture into the bag. "I hope so." Her brow lines as she begins squeezing the white stuff into a spiral the size of a dinner plate.

"You're really good at this. Is that like divinity?"

"Sort of, but crisper." Her eyes never leave her work. She keeps going until the large spiral is finished. "Once it's all together, I'll pipe chocolate ganache peaks around the edges then top them with hazelnut pralines."

"Damn..." It's the best I got. "I want one."

Her lips press into a smile, but whatever is bothering her doesn't allow her to laugh. I don't like it, but I'm still pretty fascinated by her new talent. I imagine piping chocolate ganache on Ember's naked body and licking it off.

"You can have this one if it doesn't come out right." She moves to the next white sheet and starts the second plate-sized spiral.

"What would make it 'not right'?"

She proceeds to spiral number three without looking up. "If the meringue is chewy instead of crisp..." She turns and opens the large oven. "If the custard is runny. If I overcook the hazelnuts and the praline is bitter."

"Wow. I just thought you meant if it was lopsided."

Her brown eyes meet mine. "It can't be lopsided either! I'm charging money for this."

Catching her around the waist, I pull her to me. "When did you learn to make these amazing desserts?"

She rests her hands on my chest, playing with the lapel of my shirt. "I took a few classes, but mostly by watching videos, TV shows. Then just practice, practice, practice."

Reaching beside us, I swipe a bit of meringue off the side of the empty bowl and touch it to her bottom lip.

"Jackson!" She pulls her head back, but I lean forward and lick it away, pulling her lip into my mouth.

She immediately relaxes in my arms. I dip my chin and kiss her deeper, sweeping my tongue inside to find hers. Her soft lips part, melting against mine as she kisses me back.

Just as fast, she pulls out of my arms. "I've got to start the custard. Tabby said they need this for tonight. It's going to take at least another hour."

Looking around the bakery, I see the plastic bucket and little pots of play-dough abandoned on the other end of the table. "Where's Coco?"

"Tabby took her." Ember pours cream and breaks eggs into a medium-sized pan. She exhales a little laugh. "Now that I'm paying her, she's pimping out my child to sell fine baked goods."

I smile and watch her work in silence several minutes longer. I've waited as long as I can, so I just ask.

"How did it go with your mom today?"

Her dark brow clutches. "It was... interesting. It was what I expected, but I learned some things I never knew."

"What kind of things?"

She shakes her head. "I'm still sorting it out, but I know one thing. I'm not leaving Coco with her again. She'll stay here with me."

"It's too hot here." I go to her, sliding my hand down her back. "You'll both stay with me at the cottage."

Her eyes flicker to mine and just as quickly return to the pot she's stirring. "Is that a good idea?"

"Have you changed your mind about us?" My throat tightens at the possibility she could say yes.

Her chin is still down, but she says what I want to hear. "I haven't changed my mind."

I have an idea. "I need to take care of some things before tonight. Bring Coco home when you're done."

Brown eyes flecked with caramel flash to mine, and relief floods my veins when I see happiness shining in them. "Home?"

"Yes." It's settled, no discussion.

"Okay," she replies, and it's all I need for now.

Chapter 18

Ember

Tabby returns and exchanges the Hazelnut Dacquoise for Coco and six more orders.

"She's a born salesperson," my best friend announces as my pixie takes off to the back of the store and up the stairs to my apartment.

"She's four," I say, placing the elegant dessert in a box on the counter.

Before I close it, we both stand back in wonder at how beautiful it is.

"You're really fucking good," Tabby says, her voice hushed.

"It turned out well," I say, my voice equally hushed. Then I start to laugh. "Aren't we supposed to have faith in my abilities?"

"Yeah, but… wow. This leaves those penis cakes in the dirt."

"Ugh—where I'm happy for them to stay." I roll my eyes, annoyed at the memory of Betty Pepper using her cake orders against me. "I want to be known for bakes I can actually be known for."

"I don't know." Tabby shrugs. "Nothing wrong with being the perverted Peggy Porschen."

"Only if it's very small and on the side." I say, closing the lid and wrapping a wide, iridescent bow around the box.

"My worst nightmare — small and on the side." She starts to giggle. "That is *not* what she said… Or if that's what she said, she said it and ran."

I snort and roll my eyes as Tabby lifts the box in both hands. Coco comes dancing back into the room. "I'm locking up when we leave," I say, scooping my daughter onto my hip. "We're spending the night at Jackson's."

Tabby spins back around her velvet lips parted, eyes sparkling. "What does that mean?"

"It means it's too hot to stay here, and Coco's not going back to my mother's."

Black-rimmed eyes blink back and forth from my daughter to me. "You wouldn't do this if you weren't serious. I know you too well."

I only shrug. The decision was made last night in Jackson's arms. It was reinforced today when I learned the truth about our past, and it was set in stone when he looked in my eyes and told me to bring Coco *home*.

"It's serious."

My friend's face goes dreamy, and she sighs as she walks to the door. "It's like a fairytale. Happy endings do happen in real life."

"I'll see you tomorrow — I've got work to do."

* * *

Coco sits at Jackson's kitchen table, her collection of play-dough toys neatly assembled around her. She's humming her made-up tune as she rolls out red dough, and I return to staring at my weathered notebook. Almond cake with strawberry preserves and buttercream lattice icing, fresh flower decorations, daisies and lilies.

Not lilies — those are funeral flowers.

Funeral...

I'm trying to plan Donna's wedding cake, but my stubborn brain keeps circling back to Betty Pepper's story.

My father was leaving my mother.

He was leaving with Jackson's mother.

She was my mother's best friend.

I was in the car.

Minnie was in the car.

Jackson's mother was in the car.

I was the only survivor.

He lies just like his family lies...

Anger rises in my chest. It's another attempt at keeping Jackson and me apart, and it won't work. I left my mother's home furious, but I got the answers I needed. I know the root of her hatred for Jackson and me.

Before today, I'd thought my father and sister died in a car crash, plain and simple. It was terrible, but I'd dealt with the pain and moved on...

Or so I'd thought.

I was in the car.

In the past, when I'd researched "recurring dreams of drowning," I found explanations ranging from being obsessed with an idea to losing oneself too deeply in a relationship. I assumed it had to do with Jackson leaving, since my dreams stopped when we were together. I never had a single nightmare when I was with him... Jackson was my comfort, my strength. He took away all the fear and pain.

But they'd started before we did...

"Red monster number five!" Coco says, scampering up to me and breaking my thoughts.

211

"Cinco!"

In her hand is a red play-dough sausage she's shaped into a number five.

"Cinco!" I say, forcing a smile. "It's Spanish for five."

"Cinco de Mayo!" she shouts, and I laugh, pushing a curl off her cheek.

"Who says that?"

"Polly's dad said it when we were playing monsters."

"Let's see..." I do a little grunt when I lift her onto the counter. "Who are all the monsters again?"

She rocks back and forth as she rattles them off. "Green monster number one..." She holds up her chubby index finger. "White monster number two..." two fingers. "Purple monster number three..." three fingers. "Yellow monster number four..." four fingers. "And now..."

We say it together. "Red monster number five!"

I add the numbers in Spanish, "Uno, dos, tres, cuatro, cinco!"

"Cinco de Mayo?" The familiar male voice draws our attention to the door, and I look up and smile as Jackson enters the room. "It's all ready."

His blue eyes warm when they meet mine, and a rush of comfort soothes my aching chest. Walking quickly to where we stand, he leans forward and kisses me, and I feel the little body in my arms stiffen.

"You paint," Coco says, pushing on his shoulder.

Jackson leans back and looks down at her, and the warmth that remains in his eyes makes me fall in love with him even more.

"That's right," he says. "I paint."

212

"You kissed mama." Coco's dark brow is clenched, and she's glaring as only a four-year-old can.

"I love your mama."

"Oh," I whisper as emotion hits my chest like a wave, sweeping all my fears away in its wake.

It's the first time he's said it since he returned. All through last night, the words rose in my mind, loud and insistent, but for whatever reason, they never made it to my lips. Now he stands here declaring it to my daughter, and I'm blinking fast, trying not to cry.

Coco's frown softens, but she's still watching him. "I love my mama."

He looks up at me, and when he sees my expression, his smile grows a little wider. "Can we both love your mama?"

Her rosebud lips press together, and she looks at me. I can't help smiling at her careful consideration of the question. She looks over at Jackson again, and after a few more seconds, she answers. "Tommy Johnson said he loved me at school..."

That catches my attention. "He did? When did that happen?"

She nods, looking up at me, her brown eyes round and serious. "Granny said he's naughty. He isn't allowed to say that."

I'm immediately suspicious, but my daughter continues her preschool logic. "Are you naughty?"

"I try not to be," Jackson says, and I can see he's also trying not to laugh. "Would you like to see the room I made for you?"

Coco's entire demeanor changes so fast, it's my turn to swallow a laugh. "Is it a princess room?" she asks.

"Better." He holds out his hands, and she reaches for him.

I stand back and watch as the man of my dreams carries my baby girl on his hip away from the kitchen and toward his small art studio. I follow behind them, curious as well. Jackson wouldn't even let me see what he'd done after he left me this afternoon.

When they get to the door, he stops. "It's an entire kingdom."

She hops out of his arms and dashes inside squealing. I step up behind him, and my jaw drops. A twin bed is centered against the wall, and a loop is attached to the ceiling above, allowing cascades of sparkly aqua chiffon to float around the edges. Mermaid decals are on the walls, and the existing beachy décor has been incorporated into an underwater scene perfect for a little girl.

"I'm a mermaid!" She climbs onto the bed and lifts her arms under the netting. "I'm Ariel."

Jackson goes to where she's standing, surrounded by aqua chiffon. "You're better than Ariel. You'd never trade your voice for a boy."

"She traded her voice for legs!" Coco argues. "She wanted to run all day in the sun."

"Well, you're Coco the Princess of Atlantia, and all the sea creatures do whatever you say."

She stops bouncing, eyes wide. "Atlantia?"

"It's your underwater world," he continues. "You can sleep all night here, and you'll be safe and protected by your magical creatures."

"What are my magical creatures?" she whispers, and I lean against the doorjamb completely captivated.

"What are your favorite kinds?"

214

"Mermaids..." Her little eyes move around the room. "Goldfish and seahorses."

"They'll all keep you safe and warm while you sleep."

"I want to sleep now."

"Have you brushed your teeth?"

She dashes out of the room to the hall bathroom where a little cup sits with her toddler-sized toothbrush.

I give him an amazed grin. "How?"

"André's wife had it all in boxes. It was left over from their daughter's room when she was a little girl."

"I'll have to thank him." Stepping forward, I catch the front of his shirt and kiss him softly. "And once the princess is asleep, I'll give you a special thank you."

His eyebrows shoot up. "Coco, your seahorses need to sleep now!"

Laughter bursts through my lips.

* * *

My little girl is settled and sleeping in her underwater kingdom—complete with a nightlight that projects fish swimming around her walls. Once again, Jackson has disappeared on another mysterious errand, and I've run a hot bath in the large, claw-footed tub in the master bedroom.

Leaning back, I close my eyes as the relaxing scent of lavender bath salts drifts higher on pillows of steam. My emotions have been on a rollercoaster the past two days, from happiness to anger to surprise and now here, in this house, with Jackson saying he loves me and treating my daughter like a princess.

It's all happening so fast, but the happiness ringing deep in my soul tells me it's right. It's everything we've always wanted.

When we were teenagers, this cottage had been one of our many hiding places, one of the places we ran to be together. It's where he painted me the first time.

Now it's completely new, but still as beautiful.

Jackson calls it our home.

Home...

It's a word I haven't associated with anything in so long, it sounds foreign. Yet when spoken here, it feels right to me. I know I can trust him. I always have.

I don't even realize I'm asleep until warm lips press against my temple to wake me. My eyes blink open to meet ocean blue ones, and I rise up to kiss him. I hold his face as his hand slips into the water, cupping my breast, sliding his thumb over my tightening nipple.

"I want you," I whisper.

With precision speed, the door is locked, his clothes are quickly discarded, and he lowers into the warm water behind me, pulling my slippery body against his chest. I turn to face him, so our lips can meet, and his hands are on my waist, sliding down to my ass.

"You love me?" I say softly, kissing him again.

"I've always loved you, Ember Rose." His deep voice vibrates against my skin, making me smile.

"I love you," I say, and my words change into a moan as he slips inside, stretching and filling me.

216

Our mouths collide and we move together, rocking, chasing that irresistible bliss. He's holding me, moving me, and I grip his shoulders, molding my mouth to his, getting lost in the warmth of his kisses, the feel of his tongue, the heat of his body against mine.

Our flavors and textures are lavender and cedar. Hard and soft colliding and rising, growing thicker and stronger, deeper and more insistent. My mind takes flight as his mouth moves to my ear, and he whispers words of longing and desire as I come apart, clenching and pulling him deeper into me, feeling him come apart with pulses and heartbeats and groans.

Sparkling light is behind my eyes, and our lips unite again and again. It's lush and decadent and sprinkled with *I love yous* — a healing agent. Three words we've never had the chance to say enough, now filling the cracks, mending the old wounds, binding us together.

As my senses come down and my brain finds its way through the haze, I blink into his eyes. His dark hair is damp and lovely, his lips curve into a smile, and mine echo the movement.

He reaches up and moves a lock of hair away from my face. "I want you and Coco to be happy here. I want you to think of this as your place, as your home."

"Is it your place now?" The thought had only briefly crossed my mind earlier. "I thought it belonged to your father."

"It actually belonged to my mother," he says with another kiss. "He and I discussed it when I came back and again today at lunch. The cottage became mine when she died, but he didn't think I'd ever come back here."

"No one did," I say quietly.

"Not even me." His voice changes from gentle to serious, and despite our renewed bond, a touch of anxiety trickles through my chest.

He moves us up in the now-cool water and holds my hand as I step out of the tub. Handing me a thick white towel, I watch as he quickly moves his own down his perfectly lined body. He's so much the same.

Once I'm dry, I drop the sundress from last night over my head. He pulls on a faded pair of jeans, and I see champagne on the small table in the center of the room.

"I wanted to celebrate this night." He hands me a glass and we clink the delicate crystal. "Having Coco here changes everything."

My throat tightens. "In what way?"

Stepping to me, he puts his hand around my waist. "Earlier today I was afraid you were having second thoughts. By bringing her here, you proved me wrong."

I set my glass aside and wrap my arms around his waist. "I'm sorry."

The story I got today might be new to me, but Jackson is three years older.

"I never knew our parents were together when my dad and Minnie died."

He moves slightly and puts his own glass aside. Strong arms go around me, and he carries me to the bed where he sits and holds me against his bare chest.

"I always thought you knew. You were old enough to remember what happened."

Nodding, I try to remember that night, but all I remember is my dream... water filtering in through the windows, coming up from the floor...

My whole body is tight, and fear echoes through my chest. "You were there?"

"I was in the car with my dad chasing after them." Jackson's voice is grave, like he's speaking memories of pain. "She told me goodbye when she tucked me into bed."

Pushing out of his arms, I move so I can see his face. "She left you behind?"

"She said boys needed their fathers more than their mothers. She said I'd see her again one day."

Tears heat my eyes, and I reach up to place my palm against his cheek. "I'm so sorry."

He turns his face and kisses my palm. "It was a long time ago. It's in the past." Wrapping his arms around me, he pulls me to him, smoothing my hair with his hands. "We're here now. We're together." I feel him kiss my head. "That's what matters."

Snuggling down against him, I let his scent of warm woods and citrus calm my fears. I listen to him breathe and allow my heart to slow in time with his. My mother wants to cling to the past, but my present is here.

We're moving forward together.

* * *

The scent of bacon and eggs wakes me the next morning. I open my eyes in a sunlight-filled bedroom with the warm indentation of Jackson still beside me in the bed. Rolling forward onto my stomach, I bury my face in his scent on the pillow, cedar and citrus. My thoughts return to last night, making love in the tub, making love in the bed…

Early this morning, making love again.

Voices in the kitchen pull me from my daydreaming and I hop up to investigate. I round the corner and quickly step back before they see me. Jackson stands in front of his stove in those sexy faded jeans and a white tee. Sitting in the crook of his arm is Coco.

"I don't like tomatoes in my eggs," she says quietly. "Or onjions."

My hand covers my smile at her mispronunciation.

"These can be for mommy and me." His voice is gentle, patient. "What do you want in your eggs?"

"Cheese."

He waits a beat. "That's it?"

"Uh-huh."

She wipes her cheek against his shoulder then rests her head there, a golden-highlighted curl, dropping down. Her small hand is on his back, her bare feet dangle past his waist, and when he leans his head against hers, my insides melt.

His voice is a little quieter. "Do you like bacon?"

She nods. "And toast and chocolate milk."

He gives her a little boost, and I know he'll need help if he's going to fill that order.

"How was Atlantia?" I say, going to where they stand and holding my hands out to my daughter.

"Good," she says, looking down at me and not making any moves to enter my arms.

I really laugh then, catching her waist and pulling her to me. "Come here and let Jackson finish your breakfast."

220

She makes a little complaining noise, and he smiles down at us. I rise on my toes and kiss his lips before carrying my daughter to the table. A knocking on the side door makes me frown.

"Who's here at this hour on a Sunday?"

I put my daughter in front of her bake set, and when I open the door, my stomach drops. Outside stands my mother in one of her Sunday suits. Her hand is on her hip, and she isn't smiling.

"Emberly. I thought I'd find you here."

I quickly step outside and pull the door shut behind me. "What do you want, Momma?" Welcome is not in my tone.

Her lips pinch. "I see you're following in your father's footsteps."

"I don't know what you're talking about. I'm not cheating on anyone."

"Your father was determined to bring your sister and you into his den of iniquity. You're doing the same with Coco."

"It's not a den of iniquity," I hiss. "Jackson is making her breakfast."

"Did you spend the night here?" Her eyes are cold, but I'm not lying or hiding. I never have.

"Yes." My chin lifts.

"Where did Coco sleep?"

"Jackson fixed up the smaller room with a twin bed and a canopy and mermaids and goldfish and seahorses. She loves it."

The door behind me cracks open and Coco steps out. "Granny!" She runs forward and hugs my mother's legs.

Instinctively, I want to snatch my daughter back. My fists clench, and I resist the impulse, allowing her to hug her grandmother. I don't want to teach her to hate this woman. I want her to make her own decision when she's old enough.

"Coco, you're coming home with me," my mother says.

That, however, is not going to happen. "She is not—" I start.

My daughter cuts me off, "No, Granny! I have to stay in Atlantia!"

"What's...?" My mother's eyes flash, but I'm done with this conversation.

"No, Momma. She is not staying with you anymore."

The door opens a bit wider, and I feel warmth at my back. From the change in my mother's expression, I know Jackson is behind me.

"Good morning, Marjorie. Everything okay out here?" He puts his hand in mine, and I feel stronger.

Her lips press into a line, and her eyes flash from him to me to Coco. My daughter tugs on Jackson's arm, and he quickly lifts her onto his hip. I don't take my eyes off my mother.

"I won't stand for this, Emberly. I will protect my granddaughter."

"Are you threatening me, Momma?"

Jackson's hand covers my shoulder. "She wouldn't do that. Would you, Marjorie?"

Fury blazes in her eyes, but mine are equally hot. "It's advice."

"Take Coco in the house," I say quietly.

He hesitates, and it's the first time my eyes leave my mother's. They meet his, and his brows quirk. Still, he does as I ask. The door closes, and for a moment we observe each other in silence.

My mother speaks first. "When you needed me, I was there for you. I raised that child the right way, and I'm not letting you take her from the path."

"You lied to me. Now that I know the truth, I'm not letting you do any more damage."

Her hand goes to her hip. "The Lord brought her into my life, it's my responsibility to protect her."

It's an old argument I know I'll never win, so I don't even try. "You said you gave me a bit of advice earlier? Well, I have some advice for you: butt out. I'm not Pastor Green. Your dictations aren't welcome here."

Her back stiffens and she turns to go. "This matter isn't over."

I don't respond. She's said those words to me before, and they've meant nothing. This time, I'm a bit more concerned about her level of commitment.

I stand firm, not backing down until I know she's gone.

Chapter 19

Jack

I'm on the other side of the door, holding the handle in case I need to go out there again. Once we're inside, Coco wiggles out of my arms and runs to the table where her breakfast waits.

Naming her Princess of Atlantia won me major brownie points with the sassy preschooler. That, or it won me the title of Royal Packhorse, or bodyguard.

Two positions I'm more than happy to fill.

Outside, neither Ember nor her mother's voice is raised, but I can hear the tension through the door. I saw it in their eyes, and it radiates off Ember's body. I know their history is rocky, and I know Ember wants me to let her handle it.

Still, Marjorie Warren has already gone to great lengths to keep us apart, and I won't let her get away with it again. I won't let her get away with threatening my girl. I am still a lawyer, and I can stop her.

Finally, I see her mother leaving. Ember waits a few seconds longer before slowly reentering the cottage. She looks wounded, and I hate she's dealing with this — especially in view of what I have to do.

Going to her, I put my hands on her waist. "You okay?"

She shrugs. "I don't like fighting with her. But it's the only thing she understands."

"Control is the only thing she understands," I say. "Anything out of her control is a threat." Dark eyes blink up to mine, and I place my palm against her cheek. "You're safe with me."

She smiles, and I lean forward to kiss the tip of her nose. Her hands are around my waist, and she's looking at me with that expression she used to have. Like I was the most important guy in the world. It gives me so much confidence.

"What shall we do today?"

I glance over to the clock then down to the table where our breakfast sits. "Let's finish up here then head to the beach. We can spend the afternoon at our place."

* * *

"Your truck is loud!" Coco shouts, sitting between us in her seatbelt on a mermaid booster chair, also courtesy of Thelma.

Her hands are clasped over her ears. The windows are down, and my arm is propped on the door as I drive. Emberly looks out the open passenger's window, catching her long dark spirals as they wind around her neck and face.

"It's an old truck, but it's good for hauling," I explain.

"What's hauling?" Coco frowns up at me.

"Carrying stuff."

Soon I'm slowing us down, pulling off to park in the copse just beside the road. Coco bounces in her seat, quickly unfastening her seatbelt and hopping out after her mother. Ember grabs the enormous tote bag she packed with more shit than I've ever taken to the beach.

"Taking Coco requires more supplies," she explains.

I'm still not convinced.

I grab the umbrella and towels, and I'm following behind the two of them. Coco runs full-speed, clearly familiar with this private beach spot. I watch Ember's cute little ass sway in her cutoffs. Her dark hair hangs in spiral curls to her waist, and my thoughts go to the last time we were here.

I wonder if Coco naps at the beach...

The trees open, and pale brown sand extends to dark blue waters. The little girl drops everything she's carrying on the spot and runs straight into the water squealing with glee. Ember looks over her shoulder and smiles at me. I wink back. I can relate to that expression of unbridled joy pretty well.

The little girl runs up and down the surf as we set up camp. "She's been coming here since before she could walk," Ember says, sitting on a towel and watching her daughter. "I'm so happy she loves it as much as me."

"I've missed it," I say, dropping beside her. "It's the only thing I missed as much as you."

She smiles and scoots closer, resting her back against my chest. The warmth of her skin on mine is the best thing in the world.

"Tell me about what you did when you left," she says softly. "I only had the one letter."

My brows pull together. "I'd forgotten about that. What did it say?"

"Not enough to live on for ten years." She lets out a sad little laugh. "You were getting settled in. You missed me. You wouldn't be home until fall break in October. You never came home."

An old ache twists in my chest, and I kiss the side of her head. "I'm home now. We're all home."

"Home..." She turns to the side and wraps an arm around my waist, pressing her lips to my skin before placing her cheek against my chest. "Let's don't be sad. Tell me what it was like."

"It was the normal college experience, I guess. Books, studying, exams, more exams. It was pretty boring compared to all the interesting things you were doing back here."

That makes her laugh for real. "Flailing around, trying to grab onto anything that would anchor me? Yeah, that was awesome."

Coco charges up then. "Mama!"

Ember sits up and holds out her hands to catch her daughter's sandy ones. "What?"

"Is today a holiday?"

Ember smiles and holds her. "No, sweets. What makes you think it's a holiday?"

"We didn't go to church!" Her little brow clenches. "Are we in trouble?"

That makes her mother laugh. "Why would we be in trouble?"

"Pastor Green yells so loud!" Her voice goes loud and she holds both hands up beside her face. "He's going to shout at us for not being in church."

"It's okay, honey." She leans forward and hugs her daughter. "Not everybody goes to church every single Sunday."

"Bad people," she says, nodding. "People who sit in the naughty chair. When we get home will we sit in the naughty chair?"

"Nope!" Ember says, with a big smile. "We're going to play, and when we get home, you'll take a bath, and you can have a red monster number five cupcake."

That does it. Coco throws both hands over her head and does a little dance in a circle. She stops quickly and reaches around.

"Ouch," she says, and Ember pulls her close.

"What's the matter Coco bean?"

A quick examination shows the tag is chafing her tender skin, and Ember takes it off. "Run like the mermaid babies!" she cries, and Coco does another dance, running into the surf in only her bikini bottoms.

Watching the interaction start to finish, I'm so solidly in love. "She's adorable. I want to paint you with her. Mermaid mother and child."

"I'd love that." Ember tosses the offending top aside and leans against my chest again. "She'd love it, too. She really likes you, and that makes me happy."

My hands slide up and down her arms. She never finished telling me about Coco's father, and I decide in this moment I don't need to know about him.

Still, I can't understand one thing. "I don't know how he could give her up. I don't know how he could give you up."

She squints one eye at me, and does a little smile. "Are you sorry he did?"

"Hell, no. I'm the luckiest guy in the world." Catching her face, I kiss her solidly, pushing her lips apart with mine and sliding my tongue against hers. I do it again, once more just to be sure she's feeling it.

I let her go, and when our eyes meet, the heat is palpable. "Hmm..." she says, a sly smile on her lips.

"What's that about?" I ask, sliding my thumb over the faint cleft in her chin.

"I've always loved being here with my daughter…" As her voice trails off, she starts to giggle, eyes twinkling.

The little girl squeals, and we both look over to see her in her pink inflatable ring, riding in and out on the surf.

"She's having a great time," I say quietly.

"She'll sleep well tonight."

I hear the suggestion in her tone, and I know it's time. I have to tell her the truth. "I have to leave Oceanside." Her expression changes to confusion, and my hands tighten on her sides. "I left some unfinished business. I've got to go back and finish it."

Ember is so strong, but in that moment, I see a flicker of fear in her eyes. "How long will you be gone?"

"I'm not sure," I answer truthfully. "I hope only a few days, but it might take me a week."

She sits up, moving away from me, and the cool breeze underlines the fact she's no longer in my arms. Her chin drops, and long hair ripples across her face.

"Are you crying?" I place my hand on her calf.

A little sniff, and she touches the back of her hand to her eye. "I just had the most painful feeling… like I could lose you again, that you won't come back. That you'll disappear."

My arms surround her so fast, she exhales a little noise. "Look at me." She's on my lap, and her dark eyes flicker up to mine as she obeys me. "I will come back." My voice is stern. "I am coming back, and after that, I won't leave here again. Unless I take you with me."

She drops her head to my chest, and I tuck it under my chin. My heart thuds painfully in my chest, and I understand her panic when I say I'm leaving. It's a whisper in the back of my mind. Too many echoes of the past are bound up in those words.

"We won't say goodbye," I speak against her silky hair, kissing her head, inhaling lavender and sugar. "We'll never say goodbye again."

Her head moves in a nod, and her hand is flat against my chest. Pushing gently, she leans back, and while her eyes are glistening, I see resolve in them. Things are not the same as last time.

"We're not children anymore."

"We also have modern tech." I give her a wink, and she does a little half-smile. "I'll text you constantly, and when my thumbs fall off, I'll call you."

"I have to wait for your thumbs to fall off?" A dark eyebrow arches.

"I'll call you every minute of every day. Every time I think of you, your phone will ring."

"Okay," she laughs. "Now you're being ridiculous. I have to work."

That makes me smile. "Only if you promise not to worry otherwise."

Dark eyes soften, and she kisses my lips. "I promise."

* * *

Ember and Coco are safe and secure in the cottage when I leave. Coco demands a detailed explanation

231

of where I'm going and when I'll be back. I can't tell her everything, but she's satisfied with my promise to call and hear her decrees for Atlantia every night. She's as adorably bossy as her mother, who stands back quietly smiling, her eyes glistening with unshed tears.

Pain twists in my gut, and I pull her to my chest, holding her small body molded perfectly into mine.

"I'll be back in a few days," I say against her head.

Her slim arms are around my waist, and she nods against my chest.

"Nonstop calling, texts until my thumbs fall off," I continue.

She only nods again.

"We're in control of what's happening now." My hands travel up her arms to her shoulders, and I move her back to see my eyes. Hers are still gleaming, so I kiss one, then the other. "Tabby has instructions to keep an eye on you. Chad is still searching for Bucky, who I owe an ass-kicking…"

Her nose wrinkles, and she shakes her head. "I'm pretty sure he's running scared."

"Still." I touch her chin with my thumb. "While I'm away, I've made sure you're protected."

"Who's protecting you?"

My palm cups her cheek, and I kiss her deeply, pushing her lips apart, tongues colliding. She moves in closer, and heat rises below my belt.

I could kiss her forever, but I take a breath, lifting my chin with a groan. "Fucking unfinished business."

"I'll be waiting for you," she says, and I kiss her hand before getting in my truck.

* * *

Driving The Beast into the city, I rehearse the plan in my mind. I'll schedule a meeting with Brice first thing this morning, tell him what he has to do, and give him two days to come clean.

When I'd gone to his estate, I was shocked and reeling and trying to figure out how and if I was implicated in his deception. I hadn't made an ultimatum.

Leaving, going to Oceanside, finding Emberly and Coco and knowing what I want for my life has put everything into perspective. I won't be the guy who knows about something like this and lets it go without a word. Even if it's career suicide, I'm not covering it up. The stakes are too high.

Standing in the lobby of the twenty-story high-rise, I smooth my hand down the front of my custom tailored suit. It's dark grey with only the faintest pinstripes. It fits my body like a glove, no bagging or extra fabric. I remember being angry before if such things weren't right. My image was all I had.

It's been weeks since I've worn a suit, and while I still like the feel of it, the attraction of being in this place has faded. Using my card, I'm able to enter the building before business hours. I've come early to beat the crowd, to avoid the surprised questions of where I've been and why I'm back. I have one purpose in being here — to confront Brice and resign.

Polished steel doors open, and I step inside the glossy wood-lined box. I hit the button labeled 21 and the doors close. Riding up in silence, I reflect on the decade I buried myself in paper and books and cases hoping to forget her.

I'm not even angry about it. Knowledge is never wasted. I'm glad for the experience. I just have a different life waiting for me back home. My priorities have changed.

With a ding, the doors slide open, and I step out onto pale marble tiles. The gleaming glass doors etched with the words Wagner & Bancroft greet me. A new receptionist is behind the desk, and I'm glad I don't have to see Tiffany again. This one is short with dyed red hair cut in a classic bob, bangs and all.

"I'm sorry." She stands quickly, hitching her navy skirt up at the waist of her pinstripe oxford shirt. She briefly reminds me of Tabby with her winged eyeliner and red lips. "Do you have an appointment?"

"Hello…" Leaning forward, I read her name off the plate. "Erica. I'm Jack Lockwood, one of the partners here."

"Oh!" A perfectly outlined brow arches, and green eyes quickly scan the cut of my suit. "Mr. Lockwood. I thought you were… on leave."

Figures they'd make up some bullshit story about why I disappeared so abruptly. "I've been out of town," I say. "I have a meeting this morning with Mr. Wagner."

A few mouse clicks and green eyes move to mine. "Mr. Wagner doesn't have you on his schedule for today."

I'm frustrated by the possible delay in my plans. "Will he be in this morning? Is his schedule open?"

Erica's eyes slide over my suit, down my arm, and straight to my left hand, third finger. "He will. His schedule is clear, but I'll enter your name for…"

"Nine."

"Oh, I have a bit of your mail here." She bends forward slowly, extending her derriere in my direction. When she straightens, she's holding the latest issue of the bar association journal. "They have a very interesting article just inside..." Her finger holds the flap, and I take it.

"Thanks." As I head down the hall leading to my office, I look inside the magazine cover. A card drops out, and I have to stop and retrieve it.

It's one of Erica's business cards. Flipping it over, I see on the back in a hasty script is written, *Call me anytime.*

My eyes narrow, and I wonder what exactly we're putting in our want ads for receptionists these days. Tossing the magazine and the card onto my empty desk, I boot up my computer. While I wait for it to load, I glance around the room. It appears all my files have been removed. I open one of my desk drawers, and it's clean as well. I guess Brice took me at my word when I said I was leaving.

Once my desktop is online, I access the office intranet, searching for the files I'd uncovered the night of our win. I'm not surprised to find everything has been wiped clean.

I slip my hand in the my pocket of my blazer and take out the thumb drive I'd used to download everything that night — while I sat and polished off a fifth of scotch... before I left here with Tiffany.

"What an asshole," I grumble, thinking of my former state.

At the same time, I'm not so quick to judge. I'd thought this firm, this status and position were my life, and I thought it was all crumbling to bits around me. I'd thought Ember was gone forever, and I was losing everything all over again. I had no idea I was so close to getting it all back... with benefits.

Being alone really fucks with your head.

Being alone and trapped in a life you hate is even worse. Passing a hand over my mouth, I hope I never find myself in that state again. Leaving this place and returning to Oceanside, even if I hadn't found Ember waiting for me there, even if I'd only returned to a simple life of painting houses and being friends with André and being a part of that small community — it was the best decision I ever made.

Pulling out my phone, I send a quick text.

In the old corner office — couldn't be more ready to leave.

A few moments pass, and I wonder what she's doing now. She's taking Coco to school and working on the new orders Tabby brought in on Saturday. She has Donna's wedding cake to plan. I imagine my girl will be so busy this week, she might not even have time to miss me.

Although, I selfishly hope she does.

Hate sleeping alone now. CC wants cheesy eggs, #amgrumpy and all the coffee in the world isn't making you here.

I laugh at her words.

Miss you, too. I love you.

Seeing it there, knowing she's reading how I feel causes my chest to rise. It's nothing compared to her words in response.

236

I love you, Jackson Cane.

The small clock on my desk chimes gently, letting me know it's nine. I glance up at the square, brass device my dad had given me when I'd joined the firm. Nostalgia aside, I know what it means — here come the minions.

I slip the thumb drive into my pocket, knowing what I suspected is true. Brice didn't waste time waiting to see what I'd do with the information I uncovered. He started deleting files and burying evidence the moment I left his mansion.

Tension tightens in my stomach. I wonder what else he's done to protect himself and this firm. I have to be careful — I've been off the grid for almost two weeks. A lot can happen in that time.

My phone buzzes, and I snap into shark mode. Fuck what I said to my dad, I am a natural-born killer when it comes to this game, and I'm not letting these assholes get away with anything.

"Mr. Lockwood?" Erica's voice purrs through the line.

"Yes, Erica," I say coolly.

"Mr. Wagner will see you now."

Standing, I have only the thumb drive in my pocket. My hands are empty when I stride toward the door. I want it that way. I want him to think I have nothing and he's won. It actually tilts the balance of power in my favor.

"Jack." Brice leans back before rising from his buttery leather chair. "What an interesting surprise."

His office is the largest corner in the building. It faces southwest. Alex Bancroft is on the northeast corner in the mirror office to this one. I've only had limited dealings with Alex in the eighteen months

I've been here. We never worked together on a case, so I don't know if he's as shady as his partner. Still, I have to believe if they've come this far together, they support each other's decisions.

"Is it?" I watch him for any indication of what's to come.

He holds out his hand, and I sit in the low leather chair. It's the same setup as my dad's office — it's the same as every office I've ever been in where the balance of power is determined by whoever has the higher ground.

He returns to his chair. "What brings you in today?"

It's been less than a month. The ink isn't dry on the court papers. "My name is attached to a situation where fraud and dishonesty were used to cover up evidence. I'm here to make matters right."

Brice's thin lips curve into a smile. "Is that so? And to what situation are you referring?"

He knows damn well what situation, but I'll play along. "Our last case together."

He has the nerve to act confused. "You mean the case where we successfully defended Big Traxx against a multi-million dollar lawsuit that would have put them out of business?"

"The one where I found suppressed evidence the driver took medications provided by his employers. Amphetamines that allowed him to drive longer than is legally permissible, which resulted in the death of a child." Coco's little head on my shoulder, her hand on my back flashes through my mind. "I'm here to make it right, to be sure the family receives restitution, and yes, if it means Big Traxx has to go out of business, then that's what it means. At least no other children will be killed."

The room falls silent after my speech. The only sound is the ticking of the clock facing me on Brice's desk, the squeak of his chair as he moves in it.

"I don't know what you're talking about, Jack. I've already told you such evidence doesn't exist."

My jaw clenches. I see clearly where he's headed with this. "I saw everything."

Rising out of his chair again, he walks over to the window facing the city skyline. "Jack, you're exhausted. You worked so hard to earn your place at this firm. You worked so hard straight out of law school." He clasps his pale, meaty hands. "Tiffany came to me quite upset. She told me about the little drive you two made down to the lake, how you forced fellatio—"

"Tiffany? What?" My throat tightens. *What the fuck?*

"Oh! Not that I blame you." He holds out a pale meaty hand. "Tiffany Rogers is one heck of a pretty girl, but still, we can't condone such behavior among our partners. Times have changed."

Panic rises in my chest. *Emberly...* "I never touched Tiffany. We had a few drinks. We went for a drive—"

"Drinking and driving?" His eyebrow cocks. "Not a good combination. But I know, I know. We were celebrating a big win... you'd been celebrating quite a bit. When I heard Tiffany filed a sexual assault complaint with the police, it was all I could do to keep them from putting out a warrant for your arrest—"

"That's a lie!" I'm out of my chair now. "You have no proof of any sexual misconduct on my part with her because there is none."

His congested laugh makes me nauseated. "And you have no proof of any wrongdoing on the part of our client. Because there is none."

Blood runs cold from my face down my neck into my arms. My hand goes into my coat pocket, and my fingers tighten around the thumb drive as Brice continues.

"We're prepared to make this entire matter about you and your inability to conduct yourself in a professional manner, start to finish. Sexual assault, driving under the influence, making slanderous accusations of suppressed evidence..." He pauses, and levels his cold blue eyes on mine. "Or you can tender your resignation and admit you were suffering from exhaustion. We'll chalk it up to a misunderstanding, get the charges dropped, and you can crawl back into whatever hole you've been hiding in for the past few weeks."

These guys don't just want to end my career, they want to end me. They want to send me to prison.

"I guess you've got me," I say quietly.

"We've got you." Brice smirks. "It's possible a lenient judge might drop the other charges, but sexual assault means you'll have to register as a sex offender."

I'm having difficulty swallowing. *Coco...* A pain in my temple tells me I have to fight. If I back down now, they'll destroy me. The wheels have already been set in motion, and I had no idea.

"Sounds like I have some packing to do," I say giving what I hope is a defeated smile.

His brow relaxes, and he thinks he's won. "I'm glad you're seeing reason."

"I'll be in touch."

* * *

"Jack Lockwood, the enemy!" Homicide detective Ian Carney is one of my oldest friends in the business. He's also oddly cheerful. "What's new in running from justice?"

"What happened to innocent until proven guilty?" I ask with an equal dose of sarcastic cheer. "Nice to know some things never change."

"Call me paranoid, but I'm naturally suspicious when a high-powered defense attorney calls me out of the blue. Especially one who's trying to dodge a sexual assault charge."

My lips tighten. As much as I like bantering with Ian, this situation has become darker than I expected. "Actually, I'm calling to see if you can meet me for coffee. I need your help."

I've met angry truckers, private detectives, and nervous doctors at Grinder's. It's the first time I've been the one on the ropes meeting with a man I hope can help me out of a jam.

"What'll you have today, sugar?" Meg, my usual waitress, stands beside the booth chewing gum and pulling a pencil from behind her ear.

I glance over to the case and see a couple of pies circling. It makes me think of Emberly and how I've got to fix this and get back in her arms.

"Coffee with cream."

Her eyes move to Ian, and he nods. "Same."

Waving her hands she does a little "Fine" and heads back toward the bar. I'll still leave her a decent tip, but I'm not in the mood for anything else.

"So you have proof evidence was hidden, but you don't have proof you weren't involved." Ian leans forward on the table. "And the sexual assault claims?"

I've told him everything, given him the thumb drive, of which I made a copy before leaving my office.

"It's our former receptionist, who they replaced while I was gone. We were always friendly..." *Why would Tiffany lie for them?*

Meg puts two coffee cups between us with one hand then fills them from a glass carafe in her other. "Anything else?"

"Not now," I say quickly. "Thanks, Meg."

She saunters off, and Ian takes a sip of black coffee, equally black eyes never leaving my face.

"Well?" he says.

"Well what?" I reply, pouring one cream into my cup and giving it a stir.

"Did you sexually assault the receptionist?"

I nearly spit the sip of coffee back into my cup. "No! I never. We went for a drive my last night here. She wanted to go skinny dipping..."

I'm not even going to say what all Tiffany wanted to do.

His eyebrow cocks, and he leans back against the red vinyl booth. "So you fucked her?"

"No." I set the cup down hard. "I never touched her — except to put her in a Lyft and send her back to her apartment."

"Look, Jack, I've been to your office. I've seen Tiffany." He holds his hands like he's gripping melons in front of his chest. "I mean, I've seen her."

"I never touched her." My voice is seething. "I was furious about what I'd uncovered and trying to decide what to do about it. I knew if I said anything, they'd deny it. I didn't know they'd pin it all on me with a side of sexual assault." Leaning back, I exhale a groan. "They're trying to destroy me."

He's quiet a moment, staring at his cup. Then his dark eyes cut up to mine. "How do you know she's on their side?"

My head jerks back. "What's that?"

"Brice told you she's on their side, but have you talked to her? Why would they replace her if she's threatening a lawsuit against a lawyer they want to control?"

"They don't want that kind of publicity. They're one of the oldest firms on the eastern seaboard. Sexual misconduct kills female business and pisses off female judges faster than anything else."

He's shaking his sandy brown head. "Nope. They let her go to hide her. How long had she worked there?"

"She'd been with us about a year."

"Now set that aside. It's a separate issue, a smokescreen—"

"A smokescreen they can use to destroy my life and make it look like I invented suppression of evidence to save my hide."

He scoots forward in the booth. "Mind if I take this with me?" He holds up the duplicate thumb drive.

I do a little wave. "Take it. It's half the reason I asked you to meet me."

He studies the small black drive in his hand. "I'll go through it and see if I spot anything that absolves you while implicating Wagner and Bancroft."

"In the meantime?" I know what I want to do, but I want him to give me permission first.

"Lay low. Act like you're playing their game."

I make a disgusted face. "For how long?"

"It'll take me a day or two to go through this, but I'll see what I can find. Time is our enemy now."

Leaning forward, I dig out my wallet and take out a twenty. "What if we talk to the driver?"

We stand together, and Ian scrunches up his face. "Dirk Underwood?"

"That's right." Reaching out, I hold the glass door for him to exit. "If he grows a conscience and confesses, that's how I'll get justice here."

"Won't happen." My friend puts a toothpick in the side of his mouth. "Those guys have too much to lose to turn whistle blower. If he doesn't own his own truck, if he's completely in their pocket, which it sounds like he must be for them to be able to push him into jeopardizing his license, I'd stay far away from him. You'll only tip them off."

"Shit," I mutter, stopping in front of The Beast.

Ian starts to laugh. "I'd say the same if I were driving that thing. What happened to your Audi?"

Looking up, I smile in spite of myself. "This old heap feels more like home."

"Take it easy, Jack. Work on something else for a few days. I'll have something for you this week one way or the other."

Driving back to my condo, Ember is heavy on my mind. This sexual assault thing would kill her. Even if we weren't together at the time, I never want her to think of me that way. Sexual assault… My insides go cold. An accusation of that magnitude threatens my ability to be around Coco.

"We have to get to the truth," I say to myself.

Running back through everything we said at the coffee shop, I decide to track down Tiffany. I don't know how they convinced her to lie, but she and I were friends. I've got to appeal to her better nature.

The sun is dipping low when I arrive at my former home. I pull into the parking garage right next to my Audi. It's locked and secured, but I put The Beast's keys in the visor before heading for the elevator. Memories of living here, of keeping up with the single life, dating women whose names I don't even remember... Tiffany on her knees in front of me in the dark, giggling as she unfastened my belt...

All of the lies and the pretension, the fakery and pretending to be something you're not—it all disgusts me now and has me reaching in my pocket for my phone. I need to tell Ember what's happening, just on the remote chance it somehow gets back to her.

I swipe my card and hit the button for the top floor. My phone is in my hand, and I watch for the bars saying I have reception. A soft ding, and the doors slide open at the penthouse suite. I step into the open lobby ready to hit the call button when my phone starts going off in my hand.

The lights are out. I'm in total darkness as I read the face. Two missed calls from Emberly followed by a brief text.

My pulse spikes, and I fly back into the small box rapidly pressing the button for the garage as I read her words.

I need you! It's Coco! Please come home now—hurry!

Chapter 20

Ember

Saying goodbye to Jackson filled me with such indescribable dread. I'm like a trauma survivor being hit with my worst fear all over again. My stomach is sick, my hands are clammy, breathing is labored…

But true to his word, Jackson calls and gets his update from Coco on Atlantia, and when I finally get the phone, his voice calms my fears.

"I've created a monster." He laughs, warming me head to toe. "Who knew she'd take it so seriously!"

"She's four. Everything is real to her—even fantasy."

We're quiet a moment, listening to the sounds of each other breathing. It feels too soon for him to be gone again, even if only for a few days.

"I had such a good time at the beach this afternoon," I say softly, remembering holding him in my arms in the waves, lying on the sand and watching Coco.

"It'll be our Sunday afternoon tradition."

"I love it."

Even after saying goodnight and disconnecting, I send one more text telling him I love him. It's a luxury we never had when we were young. It's a luxury that might have saved us.

I love making plans. I love that every time we talk, we're moving forward with the life I thought I'd lost.

My argument with my mother lurks in the back of my mind, and I hate that she still has the power to scare me. Yes, she helped me when Coco was born. I'm grateful, and it's a debt I can never repay. She says Coco is her granddaughter, and it's her duty to help care for her, still, it feels like Coco is turning into another pawn in her game of control.

Pulling out my baking pans, I run down my new list of cake orders from the weekend. Most of them are simple two-tiered rounds, but a few want piping and more elaborate decorations.

Not a single one is a penis.

"Well, hallelujah," I say with a laugh.

"The package is delivered!" The little bell over the door dings, and my best friend enters with a flourish. "I swear, they are such Nazis about that preschool carline."

"Enter from the left," I say, without looking up from my book of decorator tips.

"That doesn't even make sense," she complains, crossing to where I stand. "Entering from the left means you have to pass the school and then loop back around. It would make more sense to enter from the right..." She looks at me. "Right turn? Get it?"

My eyes flicker up to hers then, and I just give her a look. "You're fighting years of preschool traffic patterns. That flow was established when we were kids."

"Doing something the way it's always been done is no excuse to keep doing something wrong."

Blinking fast, I try to sort out what the hell she just said. "Your logic is dizzying." I go to the wall of ingredients. "Thanks for taking her in."

The table makes a squeak when she hops on it. "Now! I've got gossip. Bucky Pepper has reappeared!"

"What!" I almost drop the big bowl holding the flour, baking soda, and vanilla extract I'm cradling as I climb down. "What happened to him?"

"Chad said he ran because he feared for his life."

"He'd better fear for his life," I grouse, placing the ingredients out on the table. "If Jackson gets a hold of him... Wait. Does this mean you're talking to Chad?"

"I always talk to Chad." She looks down at her nails, and I shake my head.

"You do not. You push him away, and Chad is smoking hot. You need to get over yourself and nail his ass."

Red velvet lips part. "Such language! What would Marjorie say?"

"I don't give a shit." I measure out four scoops of flour for the banana sponges. "What else did Chad say about Stinky Pepper?"

"He said if you want to press charges, let him know." She leans forward to catch my eye. "You never told me the whole story. It was you and Bucky, then Wham! You and Jackson. Not that I'm complaining..."

I pause and glance at the ceiling. "It was strange... and very creepy. He didn't exactly attack me... He was very pushy and wouldn't take no for an answer." Returning to my bakes, a little flush of warmth hits me when I remember Jackson rushing in to save me. "Jackson pretty much threw him out the door."

"Holy shit!" Tabby hops off the table, and my water spills.

"Tabs!" I cry.

"What the hell is this?" She holds up the two-bodied squirrel I'd tossed in the trash. Tilting it side to side, she turns it around in her hands. "Is it a Siamese twin?"

Lowering the beater into the bowl, I switch on my mixer. "That's what I thought! One set of feet, but two torsos…"

We look at each other, noses curled. Tabby breaks first.

"You are not throwing this away." She marches over to the corner and climbs a stool, placing the monstrosity on a ledge above the windows.

"Tabby, take that down. It clashes with my vibe."

"It's a freak of nature!"

"Bucky is a freak of nature." I go to the fridge and pull out my natural peanut butter and a brick of cream cheese.

"Oh!" She hops down and runs to where I'm working. "You're making the banana cake with peanut butter cream cheese frosting!"

Looking at the list, I nod. "The Schlotskys didn't specify. They just said something beachy. Bananas are beachy, right?"

"Sure!" She picks up the list of orders, but her eyes wander to me. "So… you and Jackson?"

My eyes are fixed on the glass bowl where I'm blending the frosting, but I can't stop my smile. She squeals, and a laugh bursts through my lips. I feel my cheeks getting hot and my eyes water.

"Oh, crap, you're really back together." Her voice is quiet, almost reverent. "You're crying."

"I am not!" Using the back of my hand, I touch my eyes. "I'm... happy."

"Ember!" She dives forward, hugging me so hard the bowl tips. "I knew it would be this way. I'm so glad I gave him your number!"

Lifting my arms, I shrug her off me. "Yeah, about that..." I narrow my eyes and pretend to be angry.

"Are you mad? But it all worked out!"

Shaking my head, I look down at the mixture. "I'm not mad." I inhale a deep breath and just let it out. "He moved us into the cottage—he said he wants us home with him." Tabby swoons. "He says he loves me... he says he loves Coco. He made this whole sea-themed room for her they're calling Atlantia, which is silly, but she's completely into it. Yesterday afternoon we went to the beach, and we spent the day together just like..." I hesitate to say it loud, but the words light up the front of my mind like a neon sign.

Just like a family.

"Oh!" My best friend's eyes sparkle. "I love Jackson, too."

"My momma is pissed," I announce, bringing us back to reality. "He's out of town for the week wrapping up whatever he left in the city..."

"But you're together!" Her head rests on her hand, a dreamy look in her eye. "All that shit'll sort itself out." She presses her lips into a smile and her eyes roam around my face.

"What?"

"You look like you used to look... Happy."

"I am happy... And I'm happy to be working! Now help me sort these orders."

* * *

I choose my signature spice cake with apple butter filling and cinnamon buttercream frosting for another unspecified order. One simply says "dark chocolate." Tabby notes it's for an anniversary, so I make my dark chocolate cake with purple passion fruit curd and chocolate mirror frosting with little peaks of salted chocolate ganache. My best friend holds her heart and falls against the counter in ecstasy. I only laugh and keep going.

By afternoon I've plotted out all the orders for the week. Tabby returns with bags from André's. "I had the most amazing idea!" she announces, holding up the two bags. "You and André — joint restaurant owners!"

"What did you bring me?" I drop the plastic piping bag of chocolate ganache on the table. "I'm starving."

"He sent you his signature chicken salad with purple grapes, hand-pulled rotisserie chicken, and walnuts."

"Ahh! He knows me so well." I hold out my grabby hands.

"I stuck with the grilled turkey, Brie, and apple butter."

My nose wrinkles and she rolls her eyes. "You seem so sophisticated with the cake flavors you invent, yet you can't appreciate turkey, Brie, and apple butter?"

"Not a fan of the Brie." I quickly unwrap my late lunch. "It's too rich."

"Wrong," she gripes.

We each take a bite and emit our own groans of delight. Sweet grapes gentle the smoky chicken, and the walnuts cut the tang perfectly, keeping it all from being too overwhelming.

"André is a savory genius," I say.

The texture is perfect, with just the right amount of crunch. Bits of celery add a zing of freshness.

"Oh no!" I'm out of my chair the second my eyes hit the clock. "I'm going to be late getting Coco!"

Running to the door, Tabby calls behind me. "I'll deliver these three cakes and head home. See you tomorrow?"

"Sure—I can't believe how fast this day went!"

I'm out the door and on Dixie standing in the pedals and pushing hard. Coco's teacher Miss Pat gives me the stink-eye whenever I'm late, and even though it's just a look, I always feel terrible.

A giggle bubbles in my stomach when I think about the day. I was so swamped with new business, I lost track of time. New business! The words make me smile so hard. They mean success and potential and my dream coming true. I've got it all—my baby, my man... And I was too busy to miss Jackson!

At school I hastily shove my front tire in the bike rack, and race up the stairs. I'm greeted by the usual preschool scents—paste, cardboard, and play-dough, with a backdrop of Lysol.

Up ahead I see Miss Pat stepping out her door. The light is off, and her face is neutral. I frown when I see her slipping the key in the lock.

"Pat?" I jog to where she stands, my heart beating faster. "Hey! I'm here. Where's Coco?"

"Oh!" She clutches her chest. "Emberly, you startled me."

"I'm sorry, but—"

She does a little laugh. "You must've had a miscommunication. Your mother picked up Coco half an hour ago!"

"My…" A fist tightens in my chest, and I turn on my heel. "Thanks, Pat!"

I'm running for the door, hopping down the stairs, and pulling Dixie out of the bike rack in a blur. It didn't even occur to me to update the pickup list at Coco's school. Like an idiot, I thought my wishes would be honored. Anger fuels my speed, and I stand in the pedals, pushing hard. *She won't do this. I won't be ignored.*

Pushing harder, I take the left away from our small business district into the old, familiar neighborhood where I grew up. It's all the same with the low-hanging branches and shadows falling across narrow roads. The nights here are so dark.

As I get closer to my mother's house, I see something I don't recognize. A state trooper vehicle is parked in the front, and panic seizes my limbs. The front tire of my bike wobbles, and I jump off, letting it fall to the sidewalk as I run the rest of the way.

Something's wrong.

My hand is on the gate, and I'm flushed with panic. The last time I remember seeing a state trooper vehicle was the day my life changed…

The day my father died.

Minnie…

"Momma?" The door is locked, and I start beating on it with my fist. "Momma!" My voice is breaking, tears are in my eyes, and I'm shaking with fear.

I'm about to scream again when I see a dark shadow approaching through the lace curtain. The door opens, and I push to go through it, but a strong arm stops me. The door is held in place against me.

"Miss Warren, I'm sorry but you're not allowed in the house."

"What?" I'm having trouble catching my breath. "This is my house. Where is my daughter? Is she okay? Where is Coco?"

"Your daughter is upstairs with your mother —"

Red floods my vision. "Momma!" I shout, pushing against the large officer. "*Momma!*"

"Miss," the man grunts, holding me back. "If you continue with this, I'll have to arrest you."

"Arrest me?!" I'm so angry, I'm shaking. "What is happening here? I want my daughter. Let me go!"

Tears drop onto my cheeks as I continue to struggle. The man is big as a house and equally strong.

"Your daughter is fine. She's not hurt."

"*Momma!*" I yell again, gripping the doorjamb for leverage.

A little voice from above pierces my heart. "Mommy!"

"*Coco!*" I scream as a new surge of tears coats my cheeks. "Coco! Mommy's here!"

"Mommy!" I hear her little voice again, and it rips my heart in two.

"Let me go," I struggle. "Please!"

"Stop this at once!" The rapid clatter of heels on wood accompanies my mother down the stairs to the door. "Emberly Rose! Stop!"

"Give me Coco, Momma!" It's more of a snarl.

"Calm yourself, Emberly." Her eyes are blazing. "Colette's father has asked me to keep her here with me. He has an emergency court order placing her in protective custody with me until he's able to come to Oceanside."

"Her father..." My body goes limp as the air leaves my lungs. "Brandon? Why would Brandon—"

"I told you yesterday I will not allow Colette to be subjected to your lifestyle—"

"My lifestyle! What the hell is that supposed to mean?"

"She is being kept here for her safety. You are not allowed to see her at this time."

I'm shaking hard, and my emotions are so tied up, I feel like I'm going to be sick. "Do not do this, Momma. Do not—"

"I only thought you were living in sin. I had no idea the situation was so dire."

"What are you talking about? Coco is not in danger. She is perfectly safe with me. Jackson loves her. We're going to be a family."

She leans closer. "That will never happen." Stepping back, she waves to the trooper. "Please remove her from the premises."

"Momma!" I shout, jumping up as the man tries to drag me out. "Do not do this!"

"Mommy!" Coco's little voice echoes from above. "I'm upstairs, Mommy!"

My heart breaks as the door slams in my face. I stare at the painted wood, shaking and crying. All the questions flooding my mind...

The situation is dire?

Brandon is coming?

Where is my phone...

Chapter 21

Jack

"You didn't answer your phone..." Ember is curled in a ball in the center of her bed sobbing when I find her in her apartment. "I drove as fast as I could. I went to the cottage—"

"Jackson, help me..." She sits up, reaching out her slim hand.

I can't bear seeing her cry. I drop my keys, everything at the door and climb to the center of her bed. She's on my lap in a sweep, holding the lapels of my blazer, burying her face in my shirt.

My stomach is in knots, and I'm seriously panicking. "Is Coco okay?"

She nods against my chest. "I think so. Momma has her... She won't let me see her! Oh, God, Jackson."

Holding her on my lap, my arms are around her. "Shh... now. I'm here. I'll fix this."

"She has this strange cop at the house, and he wouldn't let me in... " Ember's voice goes high. "Coco was upstairs calling me, and he wouldn't let me in!"

She covers her face with her hands, and my insides twist. Rocking her in my arms, I smooth my hand down the back of her head. "Tell me exactly what happened."

A sniff, and she lifts her chin. "I went to pick her up from school, and her teacher said Momma had already picked her up. So I went to the house. She kept saying it was for Coco's safety... she said the situation was dire. I don't even know what that means! She's taking her away from me..."

Her whole body shakes, and I hold her tighter. "Listen to me," I say gently. "Your momma might have power here in Oceanside Village, but you are Coco's mother. She can't take her away from you without proof of some sort of imminent threat." Another tremble moves through her. "You've done nothing wrong."

"She said it was because we were living together."

"Impossible." My mind is racing through all the potential solutions. "Judges don't take children from their mothers over living arrangements. Unmarried people live together all the time and raise children."

"She said Brandon got a court order placing Coco in her custody..." Her voice is small, and my brow tightens.

"Brandon is the father?"

"Yes." She nods against my chest again.

I'm quiet a moment, thinking of who I know in family law. She shudders with another sob, and I hug her tighter. "Okay, but you're still the only parent Coco has ever known. Judges care about that. Brandon forfeited his custodial rights years ago."

"I said we were going to be a family, and she said that would never happen." She buries her face in my chest. "Oh, Jackson—she can't do this to us again."

My fingers thread in the back of her hair. "Hush now, she's not doing anything to us. I told you I'm going to fix this. I am." The panic of Coco being hurt or worse has subsided and anger is driving me now. "I want to see that order."

I'm just pulling out my phone when the door bursts open and Tabby runs in followed by Chad Tucker.

"Sorry I was gone longer than I expected." Tabby's voice is sharp with the same anger flooding my chest. "Jackson! Thank God."

I give Ember another hug, speaking right at her ear. "Sit tight. I'm going to see what I can find out." Her small hands tighten on my shoulder blades, and I hate letting her go, even to make a phone call. "Tabby's here. I won't be far."

I give her best friend a nod and slip out of Ember's arms. I immediately hate the cool absence of her body sheltered by mine, but I'm determined to get Coco back with her mother tonight.

Chad meets me as I go to the balcony. "I talked to the trooper. He said it's a judge Anniston who signed the order."

"I don't know him, but I'm not familiar with all the judges in this area."

"I had no idea this was happening." His voice is laced with frustration. "I would never have let this happen."

"There's not much you could have done. I'm going to see if I can find another judge to issue a temporary restraining order. Worst case, Marjorie can't hold her longer than seventy-two hours without just cause."

"This is bullshit." Chad's fists flex, and I like this guy.

"I agree." I'm scrolling through my contacts, looking for a number.

We're standing on the balcony when I hear the voices rising inside. "How dare you come here?" Ember shouts, and I hop back into her apartment.

Her mother stands in the doorway with her hands on her hips. I'm frozen in place when her eyes lock on me like lasers.

"I see you're back," she says in a low tone.

"I see you're up to your same old tricks." My voice is equally low and furious.

She shakes her head and dares to laugh. "You can't make me the bad guy in this scenario, Jack Lockwood. I called my detective the night you came back. Phillip is very good at his job."

My brow lowers. I guess she thinks she's intimidating me. "I'm sure he is."

"Why, Momma?" Ember's voice is strong, but I hear her waver. "How can you do this? You want Brandon to take Coco away from us?"

Turning on her heel, she looks straight at Ember. "I would rather see her with him than here in this toxic environment."

Ember clutches her head and does a little growl. "What toxic environment? Love? A real home? Are you afraid Jackson's going to take your place?"

"If only it were that innocent." Marjorie's voice crackles, and she turns to face me as she addresses her daughter. "Did you ask him why he came here? Did he tell you the truth or did he lie like I said he would?"

Rage filters through my blood. My fists clench— I've never wanted to hit a woman before...

"He came back for me..." another waver in Ember's voice, "He came back to find me."

"He didn't even know you were here." Marjorie's brow lowers, and my heart beats faster.

"He came here because he was running away. Tell her the truth, Jack Lockwood."

My eyes flicker to Ember, and she's looking at me with round eyes. She's still mine, I can see it in her posture, but her mother has successfully thrown her off balance.

"You're right, I didn't know Ember was still here," I say, controlling my tone, restating the truth I believe in my heart. "The moment I saw her, I knew I'd come back for her."

"Liar." Marjorie's voice is even. "He came back because he's running from sexual assault charges. His law firm put him on professional leave for forcing a young woman named Tiffany Rogers, the receptionist at his office, to perform despicable acts against her will. She filed a police report—"

"That is *not true!*" Emberly screams at the woman. "How dare you?"

"How did you..." I can only whisper.

Phillip is very good at his job...

"It is absolutely true," Marjorie continues, watching me.

"What the hell?" Tabby shouts at me.

"For that reason," Marjorie continues. "I will allow Ember to come home with me tonight and be with Coco. I don't agree with her choices, but I know she is not a threat to my granddaughter."

Tabby's arms are tight around her friend, and Ember looks up at me through damp lashes and a deeply furrowed brow.

"Jackson?" The fear and confusion in her voice shoots ice through my stomach. My eyes meet hers, and they're flooded with tears. "Is what she's saying true?"

"Yes, but—"

261

"Oh, God," she gasps, holding out a hand and shaking her head. All signs she's still mine are gone. She's backing up on her bed, defensively holding onto her friend. "What does that mean?"

"It means you're coming home with me now." Her mother holds out a hand to her daughter. "Jack Lockwood is a sex offender. I will not have my daughter or my granddaughter anywhere near him."

"Jackson?" Chad's deep voice cuts through the panic paralyzing my mind. "What's this about?"

"It's a smokescreen. That's not why they're after me—it's about a case. They're doing this because I found evidence—"

"Come, Ember." Her mother stands at the door, holding it open.

None of my words are making it through to my girl. I can tell by her body language she's completely shut down. She's shaking and crying. Tabby helps her to stand, still keeping her arms around her shoulders. I take a step forward, and I'm cut off at the knees by her icy green glare.

"Step back, Lockwood," Tabby snaps. "You've done enough."

Fuck this. Fuck all of this! I was searching for Tiffany to fix it. I dropped everything to race back here when I got Ember's call.

My fists clench and unclench. I want to shout my innocence at all of them. I want to snatch Marjorie Warren by the shoulders and shake her until her teeth rattle. I want to take Ember in my arms and carry her with me to the cottage and convince her this is a sinister lie...

But even in the fury and absolute violence blanketing my thoughts, I heard the most important thing—the only thing that matters right now.

Marjorie is letting Ember be with Coco tonight.

Nothing I could do would make that happen. Her detective found Brice's lie, and she's using it to reinforce her own controlling agenda, whether she knows it's a lie or not.

Ember hesitates at the door and looks at me, her broken heart in her eyes.

Marjorie's voice snaps from the stairwell. "Make your choice, Emberly Rose. Come with me now or stay here with this monster."

I'm breathing hard, fighting every instinct in me to stop her, but I don't.

Coco needs her mother.

Emberly needs Coco.

"Go." My voice is ragged, and my heart dies when two crystal tears hit her cheeks.

A soft noise like a sob follows her down, and I collapse against the wall, holding my cramping stomach. Emberly is devastated, we're apart, Marjorie is wielding Coco like a sword to cut us in two...

"Fuck," I groan.

"You'd better tell me what's going on." Chad stands over me like a brick wall.

"How much time do you have?"

Chapter 22

Ember

My muscles are weak following that surge of adrenaline. I feel the cold recession of all strength from my limbs.

Dixie is abandoned at the apartment, and I'm in my mother's town car, riding the very short distance to the house where I grew up. The lonely prison I stayed in for three years after Jackson left—until I was old enough to move into Aunt Agnes's abandoned store.

"You rushed straight into his arms. No questions. No regard for your daughter's safety..." My mother is relentless in her berating.

Thankfully, the car stops in the driveway, and I get out before she's even finished speaking. Numb, I go slowly through the side entrance not even acknowledging the mountain of a storm trooper standing in the foyer, confusion lining his face.

Yes, I'm the same one you threw out of here four hours ago, asshole...

I continue straight up the familiar staircase down the creaky wooden floors of the hall to my daughter's room. The room that once was mine. The room where I would lie in bed and stare at the ceiling dreaming of the boy who would sit outside in his car beckoning me with the noise of an engine.

Coco is curled in a little ball in the center of the queen-sized bed. She's breathing just loud enough for me to hear, and I don't even take off my dress. I slip between the sheets and slide across the cool mattress to curl my body around hers.

She makes a noise and moves toward me. I pull her closer against the twisting ache in my chest. Her sweet scent, her chubby hands, her soft hair, all these things soothe the pain and confusion. The words replay in my mind...

Is what she's saying true?

Yes.

Go...

My eyes squeeze shut against the tears. It doesn't make any sense—none of this makes sense. I'm hurt and exhausted. I've been from panic to anger to relief to devastation in the last eight hours, and I'm pretty sure I can't take another thing. I sure as hell know I'm not up for another round with my mother.

Holding my phone, I stare at the face trying to decide if I even want to try. Of course, I want to try.

I don't understand.

It doesn't take long for his reply.

I'm working on it. Stay with Coco.

My arm drops and I thread my fingers through her silky hair.

"Mommy?" Her soft voice is full of sleep, and I'm not convinced she's entirely awake.

"I'm here, baby."

"What about Atlantia?"

My heart aches at how perfect our life was for one brief moment. One magical night I got a glimpse of what my life could be. If only…

"Don't worry, baby. Jackson is watching over Atlantia. Everything is going to be okay. Sleep now."

Her arm goes around my waist, and I kiss her head. She's little, but she's a powerful weapon.

* * *

"I can't raise a child right now, Emberly." Brandon Lancaster stands on my mother's front porch in a light grey Armani suit with sky blue pinstripes.

His blue eyes are stern, and his blond hair is short — shaved around his head and just a little spikey where it fights against the product forcing it to behave.

For a second, I'm relieved. Five years later, and he's just as handsome as he ever was. I feel less of a total slut for hooking up with him after only five hours of conversation.

The only problem is he's the same self-centered asshole.

"I don't want you to raise her!" I pace the painted wood porch in my bare feet.

I hadn't expected him to arrive so early this morning. I'd been standing in the kitchen in cutoffs and a white tee, my dark hair swept up in a ponytail when the knocking started.

Thankfully, my mother is driving Coco to preschool — I'm not allowed to take my own daughter anywhere. I'm a flight risk.

"Well, what the fuck is going on?" The light beard on his chin doesn't hide the lines around his mouth, making him appear even more impatient.

"Your mother said you're dating a sex offender? I'm not prepared to raise her, I'm sure as hell not going to let my daughter get hurt."

Nice to know he has some shred of paternal feeling.

Anger rises in my chest. "Is that really what you think of me, Brandon? You think I'd let someone hurt my daughter?"

His voice rises to match mine. "I don't know! You might recall we haven't spent a lot of time together outside a bar."

He's got me there. The last time we spoke I'd given him a courtesy call to tell him I was pregnant. He'd held his breath waiting for me to say what I wanted to do about it... (His question.)

When I'd said I was keeping her, he exhaled heavily and asked if I expected him to marry me. I almost laughed in his face. (Or ear.)

I did not expect him to marry me.

"So who is this guy? What's his story?"

"He's..."

He's my first love.

My last love.

My only love.

"He's a guy I've grew up with. He used to live here."

"Is what your mother said true? Is he a rapist?"

"No!" I hate this. "I don't know what happened..."

Brandon exhales a groan, shoving his hand along the side of his neck. Lowering it, he inspects the chunky stainless-steel watch on his wrist. "I don't have time for this. I've got to be back in the city by noon."

"I just need a little more time."

"The judge says you've got two more days." He walks past me to the steps, to the grey Land Rover in the driveway. Just before he gets inside, he pauses, blue eyes running up and down my body. "Don't make me do this, Ember."

A knot twists in my throat, and I can't speak. He gets inside, closes the door with a tight thump, and backs out, disappearing down the street as my mother pulls up in her large vehicle.

"Was that Brandon?" She gets out and hurries over to where I stand at the edge of the porch. "Why didn't he wait for me?"

"He doesn't want to talk to you, Momma. He doesn't want to deal with this." I'm so angry with her, I have to clench my fists to avoid throwing things. "I can't believe you'd give her to him, send her away, just to keep Jackson and me apart."

Her back stiffens, and her face turns pious. "Sometimes God asks us to make sacrifices. He asked Abraham to kill Isaac—"

"We're not living in the Bible!" I shout, turning and storming away from her, stopping at the porch swing. "What do you expect to happen, Momma?"

"Brandon Lancaster has no intention of raising that child," she says, and I hate her superior tone. "I'll talk to him, and we'll work it out so that Coco lives here with me. Permanently."

It's now my turn to throw her words back in her face. "That will never happen."

I'm off the steps walking fast into town. Pain twists in my chest, and with every step, I feel the fear rising. I believe Jackson when he says it's a smokescreen, although I'm not sure what that means.

I wish my faith were stronger.

It's so hard.

We haven't had enough time...

André steps out the door as I pass the poboy shop. "Emberly!"

I stop and look up. A white apron is tied around his waist, and his dark face is lined with a frown. "I heard about what happened."

"Of course," I say quietly. "I'm sure Betty's told everyone by now."

What a perfect way for her to clear her grabber-son's name.

"Nope." He shakes his head. "Heard it from Jackson—just before he left town."

"Oh..." I look down the lane toward the cottage.

He's gone again.

My stomach sinks.

"I haven't known Jackson very long. Not nearly as long as you have." He looks at me, dark eyes serious. "He's a little reckless, playful. Still, it's hard for me to believe he'd intentionally hurt someone who wasn't asking for it."

I take a deep breath, trying to ease the tension. "It's hard for me to believe."

"Then don't." His gaze moves from me up the lane, toward the old neighborhood where my mother's house is located. "People see what they're looking for. We don't have the whole story. The truth might be real simple."

Looking back the way I came, I don't answer. I only nod.

He starts to go back inside the store, but he pauses. "I've been talking to Tabby. She's got some good ideas for marketing—you and me working together, cross-promoting..."

I squint up at him. "I finally started paying her."

That makes him chuckle. "I like her ideas. I think if we put our heads together we could bring more tourists up this way. Daisy has the antique shop. Count me in."

"Okay," I say, managing a small smile.

The ugliness of the situation hangs heavy over me. Even with Jackson gone, the court order locks me into staying at my mother's house. Still, I have the slightest glimmer of hope. The faintest flicker of a dream.

Chapter 23

Jack

I'm on the phone with Ian the entire drive back to the city. In the background, I hear the noise of voices and men working.

"I'm almost at the end," he says. "Your name pops up in almost every document."

My heart sinks. "I was second chair on the case. I'm probably in everything."

Which means there's no way of proving I didn't know about the hidden evidence, the prescription drugs or the violations.

"I did, however, find one early interview. It's with the driver of the truck—you weren't there."

"They talked to the driver without me?"

"It looks like it was right after the accident occurred. A detective I don't know, two counties over conducted it. Brice was present. I'll send it to you."

My grip tightens on the wheel. I can't wait. "I'll be driving another hour. Tell me what it says."

"The driver keeps saying he's sorry. The detective made some notes that he seemed dazed and jittery, possibly under the influence."

"Brice would have characterized it as shock." It's a go-to defense, especially in the case of traffic fatalities.

The sound of pages turning echoes in my ear. "Driver says he can't lose this job. He's too old to start over... He makes few references to breaks, meals... if you establish a timeline, it's what you're looking for."

"The only problem is proving I didn't know about it."

Ian does a little grunt. "Can't help you there."

My jaw tightens, and I turn the matter over in my mind. Over and over, it's all I've been doing for the past two days.

"Any luck finding Tiffany Rogers for me?"

"You asked me to search two hours ago," Ian laughs. "I haven't had a chance to start."

"I'm sorry." My voice is tight. "Things have become more urgent, that's all."

"Finding people isn't so hard. It's possible I can have something for you by the time you're back at your place."

"I can't thank you enough. Keep me posted."

We sign off, and I focus on the beige concrete in front of me. I'm impatient at how long it's taking to get to my condo. The Beast nearly overheated when I flew back to Oceanside after Ember's call. I'll have to switch to my Audi and give this old guy a rest. It's strange how quickly I've adjusted to a different pace, the country versus the city.

Ember is on my mind. I can still see the heartbreak in her eyes, the confusion. Déjà vu tightens my shoulders. I'm having flashbacks of what happened to us before, only this time Coco is the weapon.

I was a kid when we were broken apart the first time. I'm not a child anymore, and this time the outcome will be different. Determination tightens my stomach.

I've saved us once. I'll do it again.

* * *

True to his word, Ian texts me an address just as I'm pulling The Beast into my parking garage.

Last known whereabouts of Tiffany Rogers. And by last, I mean as of this morning. She's working as a temp at an advertising agency called Radical Bureau. Odd.

I text right back,

But memorable.

I know exactly where she is — less than an hour away. I head up to my condo to shower, grab some food and the keys to the Audi, and I'm back on the road.

My teeth grind as I get on the expressway. Every red light feels like it lasts a half hour. Every block draws out like I'm in the Matrix. At last I'm pulling into a parking garage for a multi-office complex. I take a ticket and make my way to a parking space, thinking about the possibility of her being out, of her coming back and seeing me before I see her and panicking.

For a few moments I waver… perhaps I should wander around and come back closer to five. Maybe with a witness just in case…

I can't wait that long. I don't know what's happening in Oceanside, and Ember can't wait. Coco can't wait.

Hustling to the elevator, I repeatedly press the little white button. Once inside, I pull out my phone, staring at the lock screen photo, a shot I'd taken of

Ember and Coco on the beach that Sunday. How is it possible she already feels like mine?

The door opens with a ding, and I dash through the first floor to the building directory. Radical Bureau is on the second floor. I skip the elevator and take off down the empty hallway to the staircase lining the wall of windows. Holding the shiny steel rail, I pull myself up the stairs, trying to move faster.

The agency is in the center of the second floor. I pause a moment before approaching the glass doors. I'm wearing black jeans and a dark gray, long sleeved sweater with a light blazer on top. My hair has grown longer on the sides, my beard is a little thicker. I run my hands over both, hoping to smooth away any wildness. I want to appear friendly, non-threatening.

With a deep breath, I go to the door. My hand is on it when she looks up from her desk in the center of the reception area and our eyes meet.

Hers widen, and I pull the door open quickly, trotting to catch her as she's out of her seat, making a dash for the side hall.

"Tiffany! Wait—I just need to talk to you!" I catch her hand on the door handle, and she gives a little cry.

The office is pretty empty. I assume most of the employees are at lunch.

"You're not to be within a hundred feet of me, Jack Lockwood! I have a restraining order on you."

I swear, you could dump ice water on my head, and I'd be less shocked. "Tiffany, why? What's going on?" My voice breaks. "Why are you doing this?"

"I'm protecting myself!" She's saying the words, but her eyes don't meet mine. She doesn't even try to pull her hand away.

"Please..." I look around the empty room. "Can we go somewhere and talk? Just for a few minutes? Whatever they told you, I can explain —"

Her blue eyes blink wide. "What can you explain? I went with you thinking you cared then you shoved me in a taxi in the middle of nowhere. You didn't even give me back my shoes! Those were thousand dollar Louboutins!"

"Your shoes?" I step back, trying to remember. "You did this for a pair of shoes?"

"No!" She jerks her hand out of mine. "Brice said you hid a bunch of evidence about that case, the one where the little girl was killed? He said you're trying to blackmail the firm and put everyone out of business."

"He's right about the last part." Holding out my hand, we return slowly to the reception area, allowing the hall door to close. "The first part is a total lie. Brice hid the evidence. I found it. It's why I was so upset that night, why I called the Lyft to take you back to the city. I went to his estate that night and confronted him."

"You should have kept your word," she sniffs. "Anyway, it doesn't matter now. I have enough money to buy twenty pairs of Louboutins. And you have to leave me alone."

A pain pierces my forehead. "Tiffany, tell me what Brice said. What deal did you make with him?"

"I'm not incriminating myself. Wagner and Bancroft are protecting me."

"But it's wrong." I say the words quietly, evenly. "You know it's wrong."

"I know a poor old man who is about to retire could lose his job. He's sorry it happened — he knows he made a mistake. Brice did what he had to do to protect him and keep the company in business."

My throat is tight. My stomach is tight. My shoulders are tight. Everything is right here — Tiffany is the skeleton key to the whole fucking thing. Slipping my hand into the pocket of my blazer, I fumble with my phone as she goes around behind her desk.

"I'm going to give you one minute to leave before I call the cops and have you arrested." She sits, her nose tilted in the air as if she's won a victory.

"Tiffany..." I step to the side, leaning closer over her desk. "Tiffany Rogers."

"That's my name. Don't wear it out."

"If you only knew the truth. I hated cutting that night short. I wanted the same thing as you. I can still see you in the moonlight... you have such a beautiful body."

"What?" Her brow furrows. "I-I'm not sure you're allowed to say that to me."

"Why not? It's true. When you pulled off your dress and threw it over your head? It was pure sex. Remember that?" I grin, and she blinks down.

I don't want her to be nervous. Switching gears, I look up to the ceiling. "What song was playing? It was that A-Ha song, 'Take On Me,' right?"

She leans forward and lowers her voice. "No, it was the Neutron Dance."

"Yes!" I pretend to chuckle. "I hadn't heard that song since I was a kid."

"I'd never heard it before at all." Her eyes dart around the room, blinking quickly.

"You were dancing." I exhale a groan. "I can still see your body moving. Damn, girl." Pulling my lip between my teeth, I raise an eyebrow. "I wanted you so bad that night."

Her eyes darken and she leans closer, pushing out her bottom lip. "You had a shitty way of showing it. I was on my knees when you called that Lyft."

Swallowing the tense knot in my throat, I lean closer. "That was the hardest call I've ever made. I wish we could go back. I dream of that blowjob you almost gave me."

"Dream on," her voice is cocky. "I would have blown your mind."

"Too bad it never happened."

"Too bad for you."

I laugh and give her a wink. "I could kick myself for wasting that opportunity."

She smiles and stands out of her chair, leaning closer to me. "You can make up for it now... just say the word."

"I wish I'd touched you. Do you wish it?" I lean close, turning on full seduction. "Do you wish I'd tasted you, had you screaming my name?"

"Jack... I've always wanted that."

Reaching up, I touch her lip with my thumb. "Why not just ask me?"

"I'm asking now," she gasps.

Stepping back, I exhale loudly. "Perfect. That should do it." Reaching in my pocket, I pull out my phone and speak into the recorder. "Thank you for clarifying, Tiffany Rogers, nothing happened between us that night."

Tiffany's eyes go round. "What?"

"I recorded you admitting you lied — nothing happened between us that night."

"You can't record me without my consent!"

"The law varies from state to state." Looking down, I slide my finger over the face and send the file to Ian for safekeeping. "It's permissible here, and I just sent it to Detective Ian Carney."

"You're a bastard, Jack Lockwood!"

"No, I'm not. I'm also not a sex offender." I lift her purse off the back of her chair. "If you want to save your neck from a filing a false police report, what could be a felony charge, you're coming with me now. You're going to tell Ian the truth about Wagner and Bancroft and clear my name."

"B-but..." She only hesitates a moment.

"Let's go."

Chapter 24

Ember

"Fear and loathing..." Pastor Green's voice is not a shout. It's a thoughtful tone, an observation. "We live in troubled times where the minds of men are unsettled and God's ways seem far from our ways."

My eyes roam the small sanctuary. Tabby is two rows in front of me beside Chad Tucker. His arm is around her shoulder, and she looks content.

Coco sits beside me in the pew coloring in her children's version of the program — Jesus and his disciples surrounded by the mermaids, goldfish, and sea horses she added.

"The story of the Good Samaritan tells us to love our neighbor as ourselves, even when that neighbor is from a tribe or people group we abhor. Who can follow this command? The disciples asked this question..."

First thing Wednesday morning, the judge's order had been rescinded. The woman who'd accused Jackson of sexual assault withdrew her claim.

Jackson had called to tell me from his condo. When I saw his face on the screen, I actually hesitated before answering,

Looking back, I hate that I hesitated...

I hate that my mother got in my head enough to make me hesitate.

"It was all a lie," he'd said, his warm voice causing tears to fill my eyes. "The crazy part was I didn't even know they were doing it. I'd gone home to try and get my head straight, then I found you, and it wasn't until I decided I had to set the record straight that I found out. I'm glad I didn't wait any longer."

"How can they do that without you knowing?" I'd asked, sitting on the swing with my daughter in my lap. "It seems like you'd have to be notified or they'd serve you with papers..."

"They were building a case against me to protect themselves. In case I came back to expose their corrupt practice, which I did." The growl in his voice made me want to hold him, to soothe away the anger with my kisses.

"What now?" I'd asked quietly, hoping he would say he'd be home that night.

He didn't.

"I'm going to finish up here, get with a realtor to sell my condo, take care of one other thing, and I'll be home Sunday. I want you and Coco to go back to the cottage today."

And we did.

Since Wednesday, we've been living in our home, waiting for my man.

"Therefore we live with this dichotomy — we want to help others, but we're afraid of them." Pastor Green catches my attention with those words. "So many people are afraid of so many things all at once. It leads to a poverty of mind... But God said, 'Perfect love casts out all fear.'"

My eyes move to my mother sitting rigid at the end of the pew. I wish her expression would open to the words he's saying, but instead she's closed, irritated.

I'm pretty sure it's because Pastor Green has stopped following her "sermon notes." There's no way in hell my mother would write a sermon about perfect love casting out fear or loving your neighbor, even when it's someone you've been taught to hate.

Sitting in this holy place, I look down at my daughter, then press my eyes closed and pray for strength.

Maybe one day I can do things I simply can't do now. Maybe one day I'll be able to forgive this broken woman for all the misery she inflicted through bitterness and fear. As it is, when I left her house on Wednesday, I vowed never to look back.

It would take a miracle to change how I feel.

Pastor Green says his final words. "And now, let us pray to learn his perfect love."

I bow my head, but I feel a tug on my sleeve. Cracking my eyes open, I see little round brown ones looking right up at me.

"I love Atlantia like it's perfect. That's how Jesus loves." She blinks at me a few times, waiting for my approval.

"That's how Jesus loves you."

Her little brow relaxes and she smiles. I can see the pride in her face, and I'm pretty sure it would be hard for me to love anyone as much as I love Coco. Well, with one exception...

Out on the front lawn, my stomach tightens and a bubble of anticipation grows in my chest. Jackson is coming back today, and I want to see him, I need to see him so badly. I need to say I'm sorry I ever doubted him. I need him to hold me.

A little hand tucks into mine, and I glance down, thinking with a laugh, I need Coco to take a nice long nap.

We slowly make our way from the church. I don't have to wait for my mother anymore, since there's no way in hell I'm going to her house for lunch or anything else. Even that thought can't deflate the happiness in my chest.

Tabby exits through the double wooden doors with her hand clutching Chad's bicep. She finally got over herself and gave him a chance. He looks pretty proud of himself, too.

I'm lost in that thought when a pinch on my elbow makes me jump. "Ow! What?"

Betty Pepper is at my side speaking conspiratorially — like nothing ever happened. "Tabby and Chad make a handsome couple." The old woman smiles, and I'm about to tell her I'm not baking Chad's penis if that's what she's after... But she surprises me. "Saw your store on the internets last night. Tabby told me to look at it."

"Is that so? On the *internets*? What did you think?" I'm not about to tell her I haven't even seen the site yet.

Getting the store's website up and running has been Tabby's pet project since forever, but I didn't know she'd launched it.

"She thinks I should team up with you and add a page for André and his sandwiches. Do a page for the town." Her mouth twitches, and I swear, as long as I live, I'll never know if Betty Pepper likes or dislikes André. "Never knew he'd get to be such a celebrity when he asked if he could sell those poboys out front."

"André's poboys are amazing." I unquestionably think André is pretty great. "It's a smart business move. Tabby is really excited about modernizing the town and helping bring back the tourists."

She tugs on her pale blue blazer and sniffs. "How much are you paying her to do all that?"

"She gets a percentage of the sales she generates, so she basically pays for herself."

A stiff nod. "I'll think about it."

Just then Bucky walks up, and I take a step back. My jaw tightens, and it's the one thing that pricks the bubble in my chest.

"Hi, Ember." He ducks his head and looks up at me through those enormous glasses.

I'm about to turn on my heel and walk away when Betty pinches his arm, causing him to jump. I don't miss the stern look she gives him.

"I'm sorry for acting inappropriately. I'm working on treating women..." his eyes drift to the right, and BP mouths the words. "Right... I'm working on treating women with the dignity and respect they deserve."

Betty turns her face toward me, chin lifted as if she's the proud mother of a first grader. It kind of reminds me of something that happened in church just now... I look down at the little girl holding my hand and waving across the lawn to Polly.

"I accept your apology." My tone is crisp, and I don't even try to mask my annoyance. "I hope you'll keep working until you master the behavior."

His face breaks with that awful grin. He leans forward, and I recoil. "Want to try another date?"

"I'd rather kiss a mangy —"

"Mommy!" Coco jerks my hand. "Mommy, look!"

She's jumping up and down, and my eyes go to where she's pointing. In that moment, everything melts away.

At the street is a sleek black Audi, and leaning against it with his arms crossed, his dark hair moving in the breeze, is Jackson Cane. That panty-melting smile appears, complete with dimple and straight white teeth.

Every nerve ending in my body lights up, and an enormous smile splits my cheeks. Coco tosses my hand aside and takes off running to him. I follow her slowly, my eyes never leaving his.

"Ember?" Bucky calls after me. "What about our date?"

"Not in a million years."

Jackson bends down and sweeps Coco onto his hip, and I continue moving forward, drawn by unstoppable force. He reaches out his hand, and mine quickly goes into it. The crowd on the front lawn of the church stills, and all eyes are on us. I couldn't give a shit. I go straight into his embrace, and he leans down to kiss me, slow and sure, lips parted, tongues caressing. It's possible my leg bends.

"You're kissing Mommy again," Coco grumbles from where she sits on his arm, and our kiss is broken by our laughter.

I pull back so our eyes can meet, and when I see ocean blue, I'm swept away.

"Let's go home."

* * *

Lunch finished, we're on the beach in our secluded cove. Coco sleeps on a quilt spread under the umbrella. I'm on a fluffy white towel leaning my cheek against Jackson's damp, salty shoulder.

"So that's it?" I've been watching the waves gently rolling over themselves while he told me the story of the last week. "Once you found Tiffany, she confirmed you'd been framed because you found that hidden evidence?"

"That's the short version anyway," he says, looking down. Warm lips press against the side of my head, and I smile. "We had to go through a few other formalities, file complaints, make official statements, have Tiffany's original complaint withdrawn... But essentially, yes. Once I'd caught her in the lie, it all fell apart like a house of cards."

As happy as I feel, I can't shake the one thing nagging at me. "I'm sorry I ever doubted you."

"Shh—I've already said not to worry about it." He leans back against the wooden prop, and I cross my arm over his lined abdomen. His warm hands move up and down my back. "You were worried about Coco."

"Still, I should have let you explain. I've known you since we were kids."

"You were appropriately cautious."

My lips press into a frown, and he leans forward to kiss it away. "Think we can walk out into the water while she sleeps?"

The sizzle in his eye heats my bikini bottoms, and I glance at my sleeping daughter. "If she wakes up, she'll come to where we are." His expression changes, and I clarify. "We should have plenty of time to get ourselves together if that happens."

Eyebrows waggle, and I laugh, standing and holding his hand as we walk into the warm water. We continue walking, the water rising slowly up my legs, to my knees, up to my waist. Without realizing it, I shiver, wrapping my arms over my stomach.

Jackson is with me at once. "What's wrong?"

"I don't know," I shake my head. "I've never had this feeling in the ocean, this fear. I've only ever felt it in my dream…"

"Your dream?" Our eyes meet, his full of concern. "Tell me about it."

We're deep enough that I can wrap my legs around his waist. He holds me against his chest, and I lean my head forward, speaking close to his ear.

"It started in middle school. I don't know what triggers it, but some nights, I'll dream I'm being held down in the dark. I'm with my dad and Minnie… I sense they're there, but they don't answer me when I call." Another little shiver and his arms tighten around me. "Water pours in from the window in clear arches. It rises from the floor, higher and higher up my legs." Pausing, I consider what Betty Pepper told me. "I didn't know I was in the car that night. The dreams stopped when we were together, and when they started after you left, I thought it was because I missed you so much."

He's quiet the entire time I'm speaking. When I stop, he slides his hands down to my waist and moves me back so we can face each other. "You don't remember what happened after the crash?"

"I don't remember the crash," I say, shaking my head. "Momma never talked about it. I stayed with Tabby's family for long time after it happened, but I guess I blocked the actual night out of my head."

His hand comes out of the water, and he slides his thumb down the line of my jaw. "I was there."

"I know. You were with your dad. You told me."

"Maybe I need to tell you the rest of the story."

We're quiet a moment, only long enough for me to say, "Please—I want the truth."

"So, I was in the car with my dad, and I saw your car go off the road at the intercostal canal." His eyes move above my head. "I watched my dad jump in after it and swim to the passenger's side... I thought I could help him, so I ran down the bridge to the bank."

"The car was sinking fast," I say, remembering my dream. My body shakes, and he holds me tighter, secure against his chest. "It was like suction pulling it to the bottom, like a dark force."

"Your window had a crack. I slipped my fingers in and pushed it down."

It's all coming back to me—the hands grasping my arms, jerking at my waist, me trying to scream, salt water filling my mouth, drowning my voice.

Jackson is still speaking, "My hands shook, and I almost couldn't get the seatbelt unfastened."

It's in that moment I see the truth shining like the sun, cutting through the green, murky water.

"You pulled me out of the car," I whisper, our eyes locking. "You saved me."

"After that day, I felt this protectiveness." His voice is thick, his eyes grow darker. "You've been mine since I pulled you out of that water, Ember Rose. It was years before you were completely mine." Leaning forward he kisses my lips, my jaw. "Now I want it all. I want everything." Another kiss... "I want your body..." a kiss... "Your heart...

your dreams..." his eyes hold mine. "Your daughter... all of our children."

Emotion trembles low in my belly, and my skin heats. Holding his bearded cheeks, I rise out of the water and press my mouth to his. It opens and our tongues unite, curling and sliding together. His hand slides down my waist, over my hip, fingers slipping into my bikini bottoms, making me moan.

"Please," I beg.

His tongue slides over my neck, his lips close around my skin. A hot pull, a gentle bite, and he plunges deep into my clenching core.

"Ember," he groans against my neck, his rough beard scuffing my sensitive skin.

Rocking in the waves, we move together until we find our release, our souls uniting through the decades.

Chapter 25

Jack

Sitting on the table, I hold the camera above Emberly as she works. In the late afternoon light, a spiral of dark brown hair has slipped from her high ponytail and is touched with gold. She's so beautiful. A month in, and every day we grow closer.

"You're supposed to be filming me work." Dark brown eyes flicker up at me, and she does a sexy little smile.

"If you don't stop looking at me that way, I'll have to carry you upstairs," I tease.

She rolls her eyes and places the glass bowl on the mixer. "Can you get this?"

Changing my location, I take an angle from above. "Ready."

The soft hum surrounds us, and I film the white batter slowly turning a delicate shade of pale beige.

"That's three quarters of a cup of champagne," she says, holding the glass measuring cup in her slim hands.

Emberly said Donna's wedding cake is the most elaborate of her career. It's a three-layer cake with strawberry buttercream filling and champagne buttercream frosting, and Tabby says we have to film it for the website.

So I bought a digital camera and watched the food channel a few days. *Everyday Italian* has the best camera work, and Emberly is so beautiful. I mimic how they shoot it: close-ups of her hands working, pouring, and slicing, combined with shots of her eyes, her smile, a dark curl resting on her soft cleavage...

"The tiers will slowly decrease in size from the fourteen-inch bottom layer to the ten-inch top," Ember says in an even, professional voice. "The entire cake will be covered with edible champagne glitter, and a waterfall of fresh white and yellow Gerber daisies will spiral down the side."

She moves her hands in a waterfall effect as she speaks. We'll edit and add music once it's all finished. André offered to help with the soundtrack.

"Once this is in the oven, I'll start on the cupcakes." She does a little shoulder raise and grin.

I grin right back, looking at her through the viewfinder. "You've got to be the sexiest baker I've ever seen."

"I want a cupcake!" Coco hops up on the stool beside where I sit, and I cut the camera, pulling her onto my lap. "Are they purple monster number four?"

"No, baby." Emberly steps over and kisses her daughter then stretches her chin up. I gladly take her lips with mine, and our eyes meet for a brief, burning moment. "These cupcakes are for little kids. They don't like spicy chocolate."

"They're dumb." Coco crosses her arms in a pout.

"Donna's lucky to get same-day service," Em says. "If I were a bigger bakery, I'd make the sponges ahead of time and freeze them."

"You'll get there."

The bell above the door rings, and Tabby trots into the store. "Five more orders from the website," she calls. "André is killing it with his lunch specials. We're going to have to hire a delivery guy!"

"One of those trick bicycle riders!" Ember says, and I give Tabby a wave. "Come take over the filming."

"Where are you going?" Tabby frowns, taking the camera from me. "You're the cinematographer!"

"Coco and I have some business. See you at the wedding."

"The wedding's at six o'clock!" Ember calls. "Coco's a flower girl. Do you know what she's supposed to wear?"

"I'll drop her off at the church with Donna's cousin. You'd better hurry up," I tease, carrying the squealing preschooler over my shoulder out the door.

I've been carefully planning what happens after the wedding since I got back from the city.

* * *

Before I left, I'd gone to my father's office to tell him everything. He'd sat behind his desk while I described how my senior partner had provided phony driver's logs, lied to investigators, and obstructed justice.

I'd gone back to the firm to return my keys and access card only to find I was locked out. *Assholes.* Brice Wagner had made a point to meet me in the lobby for his final parting shots, and it couldn't have been more perfect. I had to bite back a satisfied grin.

Brice stood there glowering at me. "You've been fired, Jack Lockwood. We stand by our reasons, and now it's your word against mine."

"Actually," I'd said, holding out my things with the noise of approaching police cars growing louder outside. "It's your own words against you. I made a copy of the files, Brice. Tiffany withdrew her police report, and Ian Carney has the original driver's interview. You're going to jail."

Ian had walked through the large double doors with the media right behind him. Amidst cameras flashing, I'd found my redemption. My name was cleared publicly, and Brice was arrested.

As they dragged him out in handcuffs, I saw real fear in his cold blue eyes.

It made me smile.

Retelling the story, my father's brow lowered, and he had the decency to act appalled at how I was treated.

"It's been the top story for the last two days," he said. "I know several law firms clamoring to add you to their rosters. You can take your pick of where you want to go."

Shaking my head, I could only laugh at his refusal to listen. "I'm going back to Oceanside. I'm going to ask Ember to marry me. We'll live in the cottage and start a family—"

Smack! His palm slammed against his desk, cutting me off. "You insist on doing this!" It was just short of a growl. "After all this time, you insist. How can you?"

My back to the windows, I answered him truthfully. "It's what I've always wanted. It's the only thing I want."

His eyes tightened, and he looked at me several long moments. "How can you choose to be with the daughter of the man who destroyed our family? Explain this to me."

My throat tightened. I never expected him to say that. I was glad we were finally clearing the air, but I wished I'd had a moment to prepare. "Ember is innocent. She doesn't even remember that night."

"I will never forget. I will never forgive what they did." He spoke as if to himself. "And she looks just like him."

Taking a moment, I'd stepped back. Never is a long time, and I knew if I handled it right, healing could happen.

Speaking carefully, I tried to explain my heart. "Loving Ember isn't a choice for me. It's been in me since I pulled her out of that water. It grew when we were together in school. It solidified when I made her mine. Now it's..." Looking out the glass at the horizon, I tried to find the words to explain something inexplicable. "She's my other half, Dad. She knows me. We understand each other in a way that's... elemental."

He dismissed me, but when I said goodbye, I could see it in his eyes. The wall had been breached, if only by the smallest crack.

It was a start.

* * *

Donna's beach wedding is nice, I guess. I'm not much of a judge when it comes to weddings, and to be honest, the only thing on my mind is what's coming at the reception.

Ember is glowing. She's always beautiful, but tonight she's wearing a long flower-print dress with a deep V-neck and a high slit up the side. Her hair ripples around her shoulders in the breeze, and when her skirt flutters open, I get a glimpse of her sexy brown legs.

I have to adjust myself.

Since that afternoon in the ocean when I told her the memories she'd forgotten, it's like we already made the most important vow of our lives.

"I hope she likes the cake," Ember whispers without looking up.

Her worry pulls me to the present, and I slide my palm up and down her back. "It's a masterpiece. She'll love it."

I lean down to kiss her ear, and her shoulder rises. She reaches up to scratch her fingers along my cheek, through my beard.

Coco is in the wedding party, and she takes her role as flower girl very seriously. She has another job she's doing for me that she's very serious about as well...

The ceremony ends, Pastor Green announces them husband and wife, and we're all making our way to the canopies where the reception tables are set up. The cake is a gorgeous centerpiece, and Donna searches the crowd for Ember, hugging her close and whispering something in her ear. They both laugh, and Ember covers her mouth, cheeks pink.

It's some secret, and it's sweet and cute... and I'm ready to get on with the show.

The music starts and we all dance. Donna and Liam dance. Donna dances with her father...

Finally we're cutting the cake. It's delicious. Ember feeds a piece to me, but I'm almost too anxious to swallow.

Finally, the DJ announces it's time to throw the bouquet.

Coco runs up and grabs my hand. "Now?" Her brown eyes are round with excitement.

I drop to one knee and place my hand on her small waist. "Now."

She squeals and claps, and I smile.

"Oh!" Running away to where she left her flower-petal basket, she pulls out a small black box and brings it to me.

"Thanks," I whisper, giving her a wink.

When I look up, I see Ember watching us, a little smile-frown on her face.

Donna waves to the crowd. "Before we toss the bouquet, we have one very special announcement." She starts to giggle. "I'm so excited because I consider this person one of my closest friends... And we wanted to do this first because we don't want to jinx it!"

"Come on, Jackson," Donna says through her smile, slanting her eyes at me.

She holds out her hand, and I go to where she's standing.

My throat is tight, and my hands are clammy. It's ridiculous. I'm a fucking lawyer. I've tried cases in front of grumpy judges, hostile witnesses, and impatient juries all the time. This is a room full of (mostly) friends. My eyes choose that moment to land on Marjorie Warren, scowling as usual.

All of this is simply a formality...

"Emberly Rose Warren," I say, clearing my throat and holding out my hand.

Her lips press together, and she's blinking fast. Still, she crosses the room to where I'm standing. I take both her hands in mine.

"Our paths crossed twenty years ago on a night that changed both our lives. Then ten years later, we met and you told me to kiss you."

The crowd titters, and Ember's eyes fill with tears.

I keep going. "It was the best kiss of my life. It changed my life."

Someone in the back hoots loudly, and she covers her watery smile.

"You've owned my heart since that very first night. I hope you'll share your life with me officially."

Dropping to one knee in the sand, I open the box. Her hand is still over her lips, two crystal tears hit her cheeks, and she starts to nod.

"Oh, Jackson, you've owned my heart for so long."

Rising quickly, I slip the ring on her finger and gather her into my arms. "Is that a yes?"

"It's a yes, please," she says, laughing.

Cheers and applause surround us, and I kiss her with all the truth and love and passion of the rest of our lives together.

Lifting my head, I feel a little tug on my pants leg. I don't even hesitate before bending to scoop Coco onto my hip.

"I said it was okay for him to ask you," she says to her mother.

Emberly only laughs more, her eyes shining as she hugs us both. My arms go around my fiancée, and soon friends surround us. It's a group hug with Tabby, Chad, and Donna — even André holds out a fist for me to bump.

It's a moment of optimism and joy. We've found our happily ever after, and before long, our lives will become one...

But I see the hint of sadness in my girl's eyes. She's looking past the support of friends to the lone woman standing at the edge of the crowd. The lone woman with her arms crossed and a frown that almost looks like a grimace. It puts an ache in my stomach. In spite of everything, my girl still wants things to be different.

"I'll be right back," she whispers, and I nod.

The DJ spins another tune, and everyone starts to dance, bouquet-toss momentarily on hold. I trail behind Emberly at a distance, just close enough to hear, enough to intervene if she needs me. I won't let her do this alone.

"Emberly." Her mother's voice is clipped. "I guess best wishes are in order."

"Thank you." Ember's voice is quiet but firm. "I hope you'll be happy for us. I'd like you to be happy for us."

"I'd hoped for more for you, but you've always been willful." I can't see her face, but my fists tighten.

"Jackson completes me, Momma. I wish you could understand that."

"I'll never understand you."

"You believe what you believe, and you force interpretations, even make things up, and that's how you construct your world. Then you find others who like what you say and go along with it, support it, because it gives them a group, a community." Emberly's voice breaks. "That's fine for you—only I don't agree. It's not what I want or what I believe. I focus on God's love, but you only focus on the judgment."

"I don't know what you're talking about." For the first time, I hear emotion in the woman's voice.

"You don't know the pain I've suffered because of that family."

Ember's voice is gentler. "Jackson isn't like that. I wish you wouldn't blame him."

Time passes. I hear a sniff, but I can't tell who is crying, until Ember's clear voice speaks.

"We all start out like Coco—strong and pure. Then we encounter these people, these negative forces. We make mistakes. We hurt people. We're hurt... We're introduced to shame, and we carry this with us. We try to cope with the pain in different ways. Some of us cope better than others."

She pauses for breath, and I'm not staying back any longer. My girl is baring her soul, and my arms long to hold her.

"The best we can hope for is to find love... friends, lovers to help us get through, to ease the pain."

I'm with her now, and I wrap her in my arms. She leans her head against my shoulder, and I pour all my love into her.

"What's the point?" her mother asks, and I hear the break in her voice, I hear a flicker of softening.

"I've found love. Why is it so hard for you to let me have it?"

Marjorie walks slowly to where we're standing, and when she speaks, it's directly to me. "I wouldn't let him take another daughter."

Ember's chin drops and I slide my hand along her back. "What if no one takes?" I ask. "What if we make room for each other, see if it's possible to grow together?" Thinking, I find the words. "I never wanted to be hurt either, but saving Ember was the best thing I ever did."

"You saved her." Marjorie's voice is skeptical.

"He saved me, Momma." Ember pleads. "Would you at least try? If not for me, for Coco?"

The woman exhales deeply and holds up her hands. "I can't make any promises." Tension ripples through my girl, but her mother isn't finished. "Still... I might try. For Colette."

Ember's body melts against me. She starts to laugh. "Oh, Momma..." she groans. "I guess that's something."

I pull her to me, holding her, hugging her. Her mother drifts away, toward the party, but we stay where we are.

Whether her mother succeeds or not, I know our love covers the sins of the past.

When we touch, the hurts are healed. The dream changes from darkness and fear to a story of fantasy and rescue, of pirates finding magical mermaids, of two hearts uniting in an unbreakable bond no ancient bitterness or hurt can break.

When we touch the dream comes true.

Epilogue

Ember

Many months later...

Jackson Cane is salt-water kisses, happy days in the sun, and great sex.

When he paints, his long fingers twist in the back of his hair, right at the base of his neck, and he tugs.

Tugs...

Tugs...

I like to slide my tongue along his jawline and nip the lobe of his ear with my teeth.

Then I'll give his hair a tug.

"You shouldn't look at me like that in front of the children." His low voice ripples to me through the ocean breeze and I laugh.

"How is Mommy looking?" A little brown head pops up, and I lean down to kiss her button nose.

"Like Daddy is a Purple Monster Number Four cupcake."

"Daddy is not a cupcake." Coco snorts and resumes her pose.

It's possible my hormones have me a little more interested in sensual delights these days. We're sitting on the sand with the waves crashing behind us. I'm one with the sea, the sand, and the moon.

Two days ago, Jackson stretched a canvas, only this time the painting is different. This time I hold a sparkling little mermaid in my lap. She rests her soft cheek on my growing stomach. Her palm is flat against my skin, and it's as if she's listening to what's happening inside—the sound of a heartbeat, a song of a little girl, perhaps the call of a brother...

Just like before, his eyes move along the sweep of my neckline. Blue eyes follow the curve of my lips. His gaze is so intense, it's like a touch on my shoulder. It's hot as a firecracker, it melts my insides.

When his eyes trace the curve of his baby in my stomach, we share a secret smile. I've barely started to show, and he wants to add to it, make it bigger. *Artistic license,* he says.

Coco becomes restless. She doesn't like sitting in the same position for so long. She gets cranky, and we pack up to return to the cottage.

We've made it through the darkness. Our lives are officially one, and he's even started the paperwork to adopt Coco. Brandon was more than happy to let that happen.

My mother is trying.

It's the best I can say, but I suppose it's saying a lot.

As time has passed, I've tried to put myself in her shoes and imagine how I would feel if I lost the love of my life and my daughter on the same night, if I also lost my best friend, who was running away and taking them from me. I can at least grasp the concept of that root of bitterness. I can see the need to hide away in status and power and bending everyone to her inexorable control.

I wouldn't do it.

I don't accept it.

Still, I can understand it.

So she's trying, I'm trying, and I don't expect twenty-plus years of behavior to change overnight.

Or in a year.

* * *

The sun is gone, and cicadas *scree* from the trees all around us. Their noise is deafening, but comforting. It's the sound of my favorite season and memories of staying up late and sleeping until noon.

Coco is tucked away in her bed in Atlantia. She's given her orders, and she's sleeping like a princess. We'll have outgrown our cottage in less than nine months, but I can't imagine moving our family away from here.

Jackson steps from the bathroom, his dark hair messy, a dimple in his cheek. The lamplight casts shadows along the lines of his body. Ocean-blue eyes blink to mine, and just like always electricity hums in my veins.

He smiles. I smile, and it isn't long before our lips touch. I climb onto his lap in a straddle as I open my mouth, and his delicious tongue finds mine, heating every part of my body. Large hands cover my stomach, and he bends down to press his mouth against our growing baby.

Our kisses are languid and deep, chasing and tasting.

Salt-water kisses.

Happiness.

Love.

We kiss passionately, deeply, life giving, life saving. We sizzle like fireworks on a hot summer night...

When we touch, it's not only us, it's our family, our future.

Jackson Cane is so much more than my first love. He's more than my teacher, my painter, my passionate lover.

He's my savior.

My dream come true.

The end.

* * *

Start my new contemporary romance series with *The Prince & The Player*, Book #1 of my "Dirty Players" series.

It's a sexy story of two con-artist sisters doing whatever it takes to survive... until they're given an offer they can't refuse, and things get dangerous. (eek!)

Keep turning for an Exclusive Sneak Peek...

See the inspiration board for *When We Touch* on
Pinterest: http://smarturl.it/WWTpin

Check out the Book Trailer on YouTube:
http://smarturl.it/WWTtrlr

* * *

Never miss a new release!

Sign up for my New Release newsletter, and get a
FREE Subscriber-only story bundle!
(http://smarturl.it/TLMnews)

Join **"Tia's Books, Babes & Mermaids"** on Facebook
and chat about the books, post images of your
favorite characters, get EARLY exclusive sneak
peeks, and MORE!
(*www.Facebook.com/groups/TiasBooksandBabes*)

* * *

Get Exclusive Text Alerts and never miss a SALE or
NEW RELEASE by Tia Louise! Text "TiaLouise" to
64600 Now!*
(U.S. only.)

Your opinion counts!

If you enjoyed *When We Touch*, please leave a short, sweet review wherever you purchased your copy.

Reviews help your favorite authors more than you know.

Thank you so much!

* * *

Books by Tia Louise

The Last Guy, 2017
(co-written with Ilsa Madden-Mills)

THE ONE TO HOLD SERIES
One to Hold, 2013
One to Keep, 2014
One to Protect, 2014
One to Love, 2014
One to Leave, 2014
One to Save, 2015
One to Chase, 2015
One to Take, 2016

THE DIRTY PLAYERS SERIES
The Prince & The Player, 2016
A Player for A Princess, 2016
Dirty Dealers, 2017
Dirty Thief, 2017

PARANORMAL ROMANCES
One Immortal, 2015
One Insatiable, 2015

Available on all eBook retailers, in print, and audiobook formats.

Exclusive Sneak Peek

The Prince & The Player
(Dirty Players Duet, #1)
© TLM Productions LLC, 2016

Zelda Wilder

My legs are wet. Thunder rolls low in a steel-grey sky, and the hiss of warm rain grows louder. I lean further sideways into the culvert, closer against my little sister Ava's body, and grit my teeth against the hunger pain twisting my stomach. There's no way in hell I'm sleeping tonight.

Reaching up, I rub my palm against the back of my neck, under the thick curtain of my blonde hair. A shudder moves at my side, and I realize Ava's crying. We're packed tight in this concrete ditch, but I twist my body around to face her.

Clearing my throat, I force my brows to unclench. I force my voice to be soothing instead of angry. "Hey," I whisper softly. "What's the matter, Ava-bug?"

Silence greets me. She's small enough to be somewhat comfortable in our hideout. Her knees are bent, but unlike me, they're not shoved up into her nose. Still, she leans forward to press her eyes against the backs of her hands. Her glossy brown hair is short around her ears and falls onto her cheeks.

Our parents were classic movie buffs, naming her after Ava Gardner and me after Scott Fitzgerald's crazy wife Zelda. We pretty much lived up to our monikers, since my little sister wound up having emerald green cat eyes and wavy dark hair. She's a showstopper whereas I'm pretty average—flat blue eyes and dishwater blonde. So far no signs of schizophrenia (*har har*), but you can bet your ass I can keep up with the boys in everything, which brings us to this lowly state.

"Come on, now," I urge. "It can't be as bad as all that."

Her dark head moves back and forth. "I'm sorry." Her soft whisper finally answers my question. "This is all my fault."

"What?" Reaching for her skinny shoulder, I pull her up. She's the only person I've ever known who looks pretty even when she's crying. "Why would you say something like that?"

"I tried cutting my hair off. I tried not brushing my teeth—"

"Don't be doing shit like that!" I snap, turning to face front. The rain keeps splashing on my side getting me even wetter. "We can't afford a dentist."

"I don't know what to do, Zee."

Pressing my lips together, I clench my fists on top of my knees. "We ain't going back into no foster home. I'll take care of us."

"But how?" Her voice breaks as it goes high in a whisper.

"Hell, I don't know, but I got all night to figure it out." I press my front teeth together and think. We're not that far from being legal. I'm seventeen, but Ava's only fifteen. Looking at the sand on my shoes, I get an idea. "We got one thing going for us."

"What's that?" My little sister sniffs, and I hear the tiniest flicker of hope in her voice. She'll trust whatever I tell her, and I take that responsibility very seriously.

"We live in the greatest state to be homeless. Sunny Florida."

"Okay?" Her slim brows wrinkle, and the tears in her eyes make them look like the ocean.

"We don't have to worry about getting cold or anything. We don't have to worry about snow..." I'm thinking hard, assembling a plan in my mind. "During the day, we fly under the radar—keep your head down, don't attract attention. I'll see what I can find us to eat. At night we can sleep on the beach. Or here, or hell, maybe one of these rich assholes forgets to lock his boathouse. Have you seen how nice some of these boathouses are? They're like regular houses!"

Her eyes go round with surprise. "Why are they like that?"

"Hell, I don't know. Rich people are crazy. Some rich men even get their nails polished, and they aren't even gay!"

Air bursts through her lips, and she starts to laugh. I smile and pull her arm so she can lie down with her face on my bony, empty stomach. "Now get some sleep."

The rain is tapering off, and my little sister is laughing instead of crying. I don't have any idea if anything I just said is possible, but I'm going to find out. I'll be damned if I let another foster asshole touch her. It's what Mom would expect me to do. I'm the biggest. I have to take care of us, and I intend to do it.

* * *

Crown Prince Rowan Westringham Tate

The navy fabric of my father's uniform coat stretches taut across his shoulders. It's the tangible warning sign his anger is rising, and the person addressing him would do well to *shut up*.

"Monagasco has been an independent nation for eight hundred years." His voice is a rolling growl pricking the tension in my chest.

The last time my father started on our nation's history, the offending party was thrown out of the meeting room by the neck. He's getting too old for such violent outbursts. I worry about his heart... and my future. My *freedom*, more specifically.

"I think what Hubert was trying to say—" The Grand Duke, my mother's brother Reginald Winchester, tries to intervene.

"I KNOW what Hubert is trying to say!" My father (a.k.a., The King) cuts him off. "He thinks we should cede our southwestern territory to Totrington! Even though their raiders and bandits have pillaged our farms along the border for *generations*!"

Leaning back in my heavy oak chair, I steeple my fingers before my lips and don't say what I want. As crown prince, I've attended these meetings for three years, since I turned nineteen. I've learned when to speak and when to discuss things in private with my father.

I could say I agree with Reggie, we should consider a trade agreement with our neighboring nation-state, but I'm more concerned about the

King's health. I've never seen him so worked up before.

"Independence at all costs," he continues, his naturally pink cheeks even pinker. "We will not give those savages an open door to the control of Monagasco."

"No one's suggesting —"

"Shut UP, Hubert!" My father shouts, and I glance down to avoid meeting the earl's offended eyes.

Hubert's sniveling voice is like nails on a chalkboard, and I privately enjoy my father chastising him. I've always suspected him of conspiring with Wade Paxton, Totrington's newly elected Prime Minister, from the time when Wade was only a member of their parliament.

"I've had enough of this." My father walks to the window and looks out. "I'd like to speak to Rowan in private. You can all go."

"Of course." Reginald stands at once, smoothing his long hands down the front of his dark coat.

Tall and slender, with greying black hair and a trim mustache, my uncle embodies the Charmant line of our family. I inherited their height and Norman complexion. My father, by contrast, is a Tate through and through. Short, pink, and round.

As soon as the room is cleared, he stalks back to the table, still brooding like a thunderstorm. "Reggie's in league with them as well," he growls.

"Not necessarily." My voice is low and level, and I hope appeasing. "My uncle does have an idea, and of the two, it's the least offensive. Hubert would combine our countries and walk away —"

"Exactly!" Father snaps, turning to face me, blue eyes blazing. "My own cousin, born and reared in our beautiful land. He's been promised a place in the new government, I'll bet you. They'll throw the lot of us out — behead us if they can."

"I'm pretty sure beheading is no longer tolerated in western civilization."

"Harumph." He's still angry, but at least he's calmer. "It would break your mother's heart. The Charmants founded Monagasco. We can't let those Twatringtons in."

His use of the unofficial nickname for our southwest neighbor makes me grin. Rising from my chair, I brace his shoulder in a firm grasp.

"We won't let that happen." Our blue eyes meet. It's the only feature we share. He's a few inches shorter than me, but he makes up for it in stubbornness. "We're flush with reserves, and the economy can change at any time."

His thick hand covers mine. "I'm doing my best to leave you a strong country to rule. The country I inherited."

"We would do well to reduce our dependence on foreign oil reserves." He starts to argue, but I hold up a hand as I head for the door. He's finally calm, and I'm not interested in riling him up again. "In any event, you'll be around long enough to see the tides turn. Now get some rest." I'm at the enormous wooden door of the war room. "We can't solve all our problems in one day."

"Goodnight, son."

The tone in his voice causes me to look back. He's at the window, and a troubled expression mars his profile. A shimmer of concern passes through my stomach, but I dismiss it, quietly stepping into the dim hallway. It's enormous and shrouded with heavy velvet curtains and tapestries.

I grew up playing in these halls, hiding from my mother and chasing my younger brother. I'm tired and ready for bed when the sound of hushed voices stops me in my tracks.

"Pompous ass. He's going to kill himself with these outbursts. We need to be ready to move when that happens." The glee in Hubert's sniveling voice revives the anger in my chest. I step into the shadows to listen.

"By climbing into bed with Wade Paxton?"

I recognize my uncle's voice, and my jaw clenches. *Is Father right? Is Reginald conspiring with that worm against the crown?*

"Wade Paxton would unite the kingdoms and make us both leaders in the new government."

"Wade Paxton is a thug."

"Not very respectful verbiage for the Prime Minister of Totrington, also known as our future partner."

"He's no better than one of those mob bosses on American television. Savage." Reggie's voice is laced with snobbery. "He'd tax the people and change the very nature of Monagasco."

Hubert's tone is undeterred. "Some things might change, but as leaders, you and I can help maintain the best parts, the heart of the nation. Once Philip is out of the way, of course, which could be sooner than we think."

My fists tighten at my sides. I'm ready to step out of the shadows and shake Hubert's traitorous neck until his teeth rattle. The only thing stopping me is my desire to hear the extent of this treachery.

"You're right about one thing," Reggie says. "Philip's health is tenuous. We need to be prepared to act should a crisis arise."

"What about Rowan? If he's not on our side, we could end up in the same position — and with a much younger king to wait out."

"Possibly." My uncle pauses, and I feel the heat rising around my collar.

"Wade has a plan for managing such a contingency. Should Rowan prove... difficult."

"I'm sure he does," Reggie scoffs. "And Cal? Shall we wipe out the entire Tate line?"

Hubert's voice is low and wicked. "Perhaps being in league with a 'thug' as you put it has its advantages."

How dare these bastards! What they're saying is high treason! My body is poised to move when Reggie's words freeze me in place.

"I'm sure Wade's tactics won't prove necessary. When the time comes to do the right thing, we can count on Rowan."

Count on Rowan? Is it possible he thinks I would even consider a merger with Twatrington? Their voices recede down the corridor as my level of disgust and loyalty to my father rises. The king has had a difficult evening. I'll let him rest tonight, but I will present him with this conspiracy first thing tomorrow. Reggie is right. When the time comes, I will do the right thing.

Looking back, I had no idea the time would come in less than twenty-four hours...

* * *

Get *The Prince & The Player* Today!
Also available in print and audiobook formats.

Acknowledgments

After the hardest summer of my life, writing this book was cathartic in so many ways. I thank God for helping me get through the days, and I thank Him for all the amazing people in my life who've supported me along the way.

To my dear friends Aleatha Romig and Ilsa Madden-Mills, who are always so super encouraging—thank you from the bottom of my heart. I'm blessed to know you.

I can't thank my troop of speedy, dedicated beta readers enough—Ilona, Lisa, and Mr. TL, you guys are my rockstars! And HUGE thanks to a new member of the team, my fantastic, hilarious editor Tamara "That's what she said" Mataya. ((hugs))

To all the FAB author-friends who made room for me in your crammed schedules, Tijan Meyer, A.D. Justice, Tara Sivec, A.L. Jackson, Adriana Locke, Willow Winters, Rachel Van Dyken, Bella Love-Wins, Kristen Hope Mazzola, Laurelin Page, Sierra Simone, Rebecca Shea, Melanie Harlow, Lexi Ryan, Katy Regnery, Kennedy Ryan, Nora Flite, Stacie Scott, Ella James Leigh Shen, and Meghan Quinn... Can I say BLESSED? I appreciate YOU so much more than I can say. You have no idea.

Special thanks to Sara Eirew for the beautiful cover image, and to Shannon of Shanoff Formats for the gorgeous cover design and teasers. You brought my vision to life! *To every reader and/or blogger who makes teasers, please know those beautiful little works of art flood my insides with so much joy!

HUGE THANKS to Jenn Watson for her tireless advice and guidance. It's so great to have you on my team! I appreciate you more than I can ever say.

To my MERMAIDS, *Thank You* for giving me a place to relax and be silly. THANKS to ALL the bloggers who have made an art and a science of book loving. Sharing this book with the reading world would be impossible without you. I appreciate your help so much.

To everyone who picks up this book, reads it, loves it, and tells one person about it, you've made my day. I'm so grateful to you all. Without readers, there would be no writers.

So much love,

Stay sexy,

<3 *Tia*

Thank you,

<3 *Tia*

About the Author

Tia Louise is the award-winning, international bestselling author of the ONE TO HOLD and DIRTY PLAYERS series and co-author of the #4 Amazon bestseller *The Last Guy*.

From "Readers' Choice" nominations, to *USA Today* "Happily Ever After" nods, to winning the 2015 "Favorite Erotica Author" and the 2014 "Lady Boner Award" (LOL!), nothing makes her happier than communicating with fans and weaving new tales into the Alexander-Knight world of stories.

A former journalist, Louise lives in the center of the USA with her lovely family and one grumpy cat. There, she dreams up stories she hopes are engaging, hot, and sexy, and that cause readers rethink common public locations...

Keep up with Tia online:
www.AuthorTiaLouise.com

66961132R00192

Made in the USA
Lexington, KY
29 August 2017